BOOK ONE

SilverFin

A JAMES BOND ADVENTURE

CHARLIE HIGSON

Disney · HYPERION BOOKS

New York

SilverFin copyright © 2005 by Ian Fleming Publications Ltd. All rights reserved.
SilverFin is a trademark of Ian Fleming Publications Ltd.
Young Bond is a trademark of Ian Fleming Publications Ltd.

®is a registered trademark of Ian Fleming Publications Ltd.

Published by Disney • Hyperion Books, an imprint of Disney Book Group. No part of this book may be reproduced or transmitted in any form or by any means electronic or mechanical, including photocopying, recording, or by any information storage and retrieval system, without written permission from the publisher.

For information address:
Disney • Hyperion Books
114 Fifth Avenue
New York, New York 10011-5690

New Disney • Hyperion paperback edition, 2009
10 9 8 7 6 5 4 3 2 1
Printed in the United States of America
ISBN 978-1-4231-2262-3
Library of Congress Cataloging-in-Publication Data on file.

Visit www.youngbond.com and
www.hyperionbooksforchildren.com

For Frank
and my own Uncle Max

* * *

*My thanks to Kate Jones for thinking
of me, everyone at Ian Fleming Publications
Ltd. for trusting me, but most of all to
Ian Fleming, without whom none of
this would be here.*

The boy crept up to the fence and looked around. There was the familiar sign:

KEEP OUT!
PRIVATE PROPERTY.
TRESPASSERS WILL BE SHOT.

And hanging next to it, just to make sure that the message was clearly understood, were the bodies of several dead animals. Strung up like criminals, wire twisted around their broken necks.

He knew them so well; they were almost like old friends. There were rabbits with their eyes pecked out, tattered black crows with broken wings, a couple of foxes, a few rats, even a wildcat and a pine marten. In all the days he'd been coming here the boy had watched them slowly rotting away, until some of them were little more than flaps of dirty leather and yellow bones. But there were a couple of fresh ones since yesterday, a squirrel and another fox.

Which meant that someone had been back.

In his thick brown poacher's jacket and heavy green cotton trousers the boy was fairly well camouflaged, but he knew that he had to be on his guard. The signs and the fifteen-foot-high fence twined with rusted barbed wire were enough to keep most people away, but there were the men as well. The estate workers. A couple of times he'd spotted a pair of them walking the perimeter, shotguns cradled in their elbows, and although it had been a few days since he'd seen anyone up here, he knew that they were never far away.

At the moment, however, apart from the sad corpses of the animals, he was alone.

The afternoon light was fading into evening, taking all the detail from the land with it. Here, on this side of the fence, among the thick gorse and juniper and low rowan trees, he was well hidden, but soon . . . soon he was going under the wire, and on the other side the tree cover quickly fell away. He could just see the scrubby grassland dotted with small rocks, which sloped down toward the peaty brown waters of the loch.

Soon he'd be fishing those waters for the first time.

The trek up here had taken nearly an hour. School had finished at four o'clock, and he'd had nothing to eat since lunchtime. He knew that once he was inside the fence there would be no time to eat, so he slipped his knapsack from his shoulders and took out his ham sandwiches and a crisp apple. He quickly ate them, gazing up at the mountain that stood watch over the loch. It looked cold and barren and unfeeling. It had stood here for millions of years, and would stand for millions more. The boy felt small and alone, and when the wind vibrated the wires in the fence, making them moan, he shivered.

Before the new laird had come there had been no fence. The land had been open for miles around. The loch had been a good fishing spot then, and the old laird hadn't been bothered by those few hardy folk who braved the long haul up from the village. What did he care if one or two of his trout went missing each year? There were always plenty more.

But that had all changed when the new fellow had taken over five years ago. Everything had changed. The land was fenced off. The locals were kept away.

But not this evening.

The boy chucked his crusts and apple core into the bushes, then crawled over to the fence and pulled away the pieces of turf that covered the hole he'd dug.

The turf rested on a grid of strong sticks, which he quickly removed. The ground up here was rock hard and full of stones, so it had taken the boy several days to hack this narrow tunnel under the fence, scrabbling in the dirt with his mother's gardening tools. Last night, he'd finally finished the work, but it had been too late to do anything more so he'd reluctantly gone home.

Today, he'd been too excited to concentrate at school; all he could think about was coming up here, ducking through the hole, going down to the loch, and taking some fish from under the new laird's nose.

He smiled as he made his way into the hole and pushed aside the old piece of sacking that he'd used to cover the entrance at the other end. His tackle bag and knapsack he easily pulled through the tunnel behind him, but his father's rod, even when broken down into three sections, was too long to fit through, so he went back, took it out of its case and slotted the pieces one by one through the fence.

Five minutes later, his rod in one hand, his tackle bag in

the other, he was darting between the rocks down toward the water.

Before he'd died, his father had described Loch Silverfin to him many times. He'd often come up here as a lad to fish, and it was his stories that had inspired the boy. His father had loved fishing, but he had been wounded by a shell blast in the Great War of 1914 and the pieces of shrapnel buried in his flesh had slowly ruined his health, so that by the end he could barely walk, let alone hold a fishing rod.

The boy was excited. He was the man of the house now, and he pictured the look on his mother's face when he brought home a fine fresh trout, but there was more to it than that. Fishing is a challenge—and this was the biggest challenge of all.

Loch Silverfin was shaped like a huge fish, long and narrow and fanning out into a rough tail at this end. It was named after a giant salmon from Scottish folktales—It' Airgid. Which in Gaelic meant Silverfin. Silverfin was a fearsome salmon that was bigger and stronger than all the other salmon in Scotland. The giant Cachruadh had tried to catch him, and after an epic battle lasting twenty days, the fish had at last swallowed the giant, and kept him in his belly for a year before spitting him out in Ireland.

Legend had it that Silverfin still lived in the loch, deep in its dark waters. The boy didn't quite believe that, but he did believe that there were some mighty fish here.

The loch looked wilder than he'd imagined it; steep, sheer rocks bordered most of the shore beneath the mountain, and a few stunted rushes were all that grew there. Way down at the other end, partially shrouded in the mist rising off the water, he could just make out the square gray shape of the castle, sitting on the little island that formed the eye of the fish. But it was too far away, and the light was too bad for anyone to see him from there.

He scouted along the shingle for a good place to cast, but it wasn't very encouraging. The shoreline was too exposed. If any of the estate workers came anywhere near, they'd be bound to spot him.

The thought of the estate workers made him glance around uneasily and he realized how scared he was. They weren't local men and they didn't mix with the folk in the village. They lived up here in a group of low, ugly, concrete sheds the laird had built near the gatehouse. He'd turned his castle into a fortress, and these men were his private army. The boy had no desire to bump into any of them this evening.

He was just thinking that he might have to chuck it in and go home when he saw the perfect spot. At the tip of the fish's tail was a fold in the edge of the loch where a stream entered. The water here was almost completely hidden from view by the high cliffs all around. He knew that the trout would wait here for food to wash down the stream.

Twenty feet or so out in the lake stood a single huge granite rock. If he could get out there and shelter behind it, he could easily cast toward the stream without being seen by either man or fish.

He sat in the grass to pull his waterproof waders on. It had been a real slog, lugging them up here, but he needed them now. They slipped over his clothes like a huge pair of trousers attached to a pair of boots, coming right up to his chest, where they were supported by shoulder straps. They smelled of damp and old rubber.

He fastened his reel to his cane rod and quickly threaded the line through the loops. He'd already tied on his fly line, so he took out his favorite fly, a silver doctor, and knotted it to the end.

He skirted the water's edge until he was level with the big rock, and then waded out into the water toward it. It took him a few minutes to pick his way across, feeling with his feet for safe places to step. The bottom of the loch was slippery and uneven, and at one point he had to make a long detour around a particularly deep area, but once he neared the rock it became shallower again and he grew more confident.

He found a good solid place to stand, and from here he had a clear cast over toward the stream. He checked his fly, played out his line, then with a quick backward jerk of his arm, he whipped it up into a big loop behind him, before flicking it forward, so it snaked out across the water and landed expertly at the edge of the loch.

That part had gone very well, but it turned out to be the only part that did. He didn't get a single touch. Try as he might, he couldn't attract any fish onto his hook. He cast and recast, he changed his fly, he tried nearer and farther— nothing.

It was getting darker by the minute, and he would have to head for home soon, so, in desperation, he decided to try a worm. He'd brought a box of them with him just in case. He dug it out of his pocket, chose a nice fat lobworm, and speared it on a hook, where it wriggled enticingly. What fish could resist that?

He had to be more careful casting the worm and he flicked it gently away from him. Then he got his first bite so quickly it took him completely by surprise; the worm had scarcely landed in the water before he felt a strong tug. He tugged back to get a good hold in the fish's mouth, then prepared for a fight.

Whatever it was on the end of his line, it was tough. It pulled this way and that furiously, and he watched his rod bow and dip toward the water. He let the fish run for a few moments to tire it, then slowly reeled it in. Still it zigzagged about in the water in a frantic attempt to get free. The boy grinned from ear to ear—it was a big one and wasn't going to give up easily.

Maybe he'd caught the awesome Silverfin himself!

For some time he played it, gradually reeling in as much line as he dared, praying that the hook wouldn't slip or the line snap. . . . This was a very delicate business; he had to feel the fish, he had to try to predict its wild movements. Then, at last, he had it near; he could see something moving in the water on the end of his line; he took a deep breath, hauled it up, and his heart sank. . . .

It wasn't Silverfin, it was an eel, and, even as he realized it, something brushed against his legs, nearly knocking him off balance. He looked down and saw a second eel darting away through the water.

Well, there was nothing else to do: he had to land the thing to retrieve his hook and line. He hoisted it out of the water and tried to grab hold of it, but it was thrashing about in the air, twisting itself into knots, snarling itself around the line and, as he reached for it, it tangled around his arm. It was a monstrous thing—it must have been at least two feet long, streaked with slime, cold and sleek and brownish gray.

He hated eels.

He tried to pull it off his arm, but it was tremendously powerful and single-minded, like one big writhing muscle, and it simply twisted itself around his other arm. He swore and shook it, nearly losing his footing. He told himself to calm down and he carefully moved closer to the rock; he managed to slap the eel against the rock and pin it down. Still it squirmed and writhed like a mad thing, even though its face showed nothing. It was a cold, dead mask, flattened and wide, with small, dark eyes.

Finally, he managed to hold its head still enough to get a grip on the deeply embedded hook, and he began to twist and wrench it free. It was hard work. He'd used a big hook and the end of it was barbed to stop it from slipping out, once it had stuck into a fish's mouth.

"Come on," he muttered, grunting with the effort, and then—he wasn't sure how it happened, it went too fast—all at the same time, the hook came loose, the eel gave a frantic jerk and, the next thing he knew, the hook was in his thumb.

The pain was awful, like a freezing bolt shooting all the way up his arm. He gasped and clamped his teeth together and managed not to shout. . . . It was a still evening and any sound up here would travel for miles, bouncing off the high rocks and water.

The eel slithered away and plopped back into the water. A wave of sickness passed over the boy and he swayed, nearly fainting. For a long while he couldn't bring himself to look at his hand, but at last he forced his eyes down. The hook had gone in by his palm and right through the fleshy base of his thumb, where it stuck out the other side. There was a horrible gash and flap of skin where the barb had broken through on its way out. Blood was already oozing from the wound and dripping into the icy water.

He was lucky that the point had come out and not stayed sunk deep inside his flesh, but he knew that he couldn't just pull the hook free; it had the curved barb on one end and a ring on the other where the line was attached.

There was only one thing to do.

He rested his rod against the rock and, with his other hand, he reached into his tackle bag and got out his cutters.

He took a deep breath, clamped the cutters on the end of the hook where the line was knotted, pressed them together and—*snak*—the end broke off. Then, quickly, so that he didn't have time to think about it, he pulled the hook out by the barb. A fresh pain hit him and he leaned against the rock to stop his knees from giving way.

He knew he wouldn't do any more fishing today. He started to cry. All that effort for this: a lousy eel and a wounded thumb. It just wasn't fair. Then he pulled himself together. He had to do something about his situation. Blood was flowing freely from the wound. He washed his hand in the loch, the blood turning black and oily in the cold water, then he took a handkerchief from his shirt pocket and wrapped it tightly around his thumb. He was shaking badly now and felt very light-headed. As carefully as he could, he secured all his gear and set off back to the shore, wading through the dark slick in the water that his blood had made.

And then he felt it.

A jolt against his legs.

And then another.

More eels. But what were they doing? Eels never attacked people. They ate scraps and frogs and small fish. . . .

He pressed on; maybe he'd imagined it.

No. There it came again. A definite bump.

He peered down into the water and in the dim light he saw them . . . hundreds of them, a seething mass in the water, balled up and tangled together like the writhing hair of some underwater Medusa. Eels. All around him. Eels of all sizes, from tiny black slivers to huge brutes twice the length of the one he'd caught. The water was alive with them, wriggling, twisting, turning over and over. . . . They surged against his legs and he stumbled. His wounded hand splashed down into the water, and he felt hungry mouths tug the bloodied hand-kerchief from his hand and drag it away into the murky depths.

He panicked, tried to run for the shore but slipped and, as his feet scrabbled to get a hold, he stumbled into the deep part of the loch. For a moment his head went under and he was aware of eels brushing against his face. One wrapped itself around his neck and he pulled it away with his good hand. Then his feet touched the bottom and he pushed himself up to the surface. He gulped in a mouthful of air, but his waders were filled with water now . . . water and eels, he could feel them down his legs, trapped by the rubber.

He knew that if he could get his feet up he might float, but in his terror and panic his body wasn't doing what he wanted it to do.

"Help," he screamed, "help me!" Then he was under again, and this time the water seemed even thicker with eels. The head of one probed his mouth and clamped its jaws onto his lip. He tore it away, and his anger gave him fresh strength. He forced his feet downward, found a solid piece of ground, and then he was up out of the water again. All about him the surface of the loch was seething with frenzied eels.

"Help, help . . . please, somebody, help me . . ." His mouth hurt and blood was dripping from where the eel had bitten his lip. He thrashed at the water, but nothing would scare the beasts away.

And then out of the corner of his eye he saw someone . . . a man running along the far shore. He waved crazily and yelled for help again. He didn't care anymore if it was an estate worker. . . . Anything was better than being trapped here with these terrible fish.

The man ran closer and dived into the loch.

No, the boy wanted to shout. Not in the water. Not in with the eels. But then he saw a head bob to the surface. It was all right. He was going to be rescued.

The man swam toward him with strong, crude strokes. Thank God. Thank God. He was going to be saved. For a while he almost forgot about the eels and just concentrated on the man's steady progress toward him, but then a fresh surge knocked him off balance and he was once more in the snaking embrace of a hundred frenzied coils of cold flesh.

No. No, he would not let them beat him. He whirled his arms, kicked his legs, and he was out again, gasping and spluttering for breath.

But where was the man? He had disappeared.

The boy looked around desperately. Had the eels gotten him?

It was quiet, the movement in the water seemed to have stopped, almost as if none of this had ever happened. . . .

And then he saw him, under the water, a big dark shape among the fish, and suddenly, with a great splash, he rose out of the loch, and the boy screamed.

The last thing he saw before he sank back into the black depths of the water was the man's face; only it wasn't a man's face . . . it was an eel's face, a nightmarish face—chinless, with smooth, gray, utterly hairless skin pulled tight across it, and fat, blubbery lips that stretched almost all the way back to where the ears should be. The front of the face was deformed, pushed forward, so that the nose was hideously flattened, with splayed nostrils and bulging eyes forced so wide apart that they didn't look in any way human.

The ghastly thick lips parted and a wet belching hiss erupted.

Then the waters closed over the boy and he knew nothing more.

PART 1—ETON

CHAPTER 1—THE NEW BOY

The smell and noise and confusion of a hallway full of schoolboys can be quite awful at twenty past seven in the morning. The smell was the worst part—from this great disorderly mass rose the scent of sweat and sour breath and unwashed bodies, mixing with the two-hundred-year-old school odor of carbolic and floor polish.

Boys as a rule don't notice bad smells—they've other things on their minds—but one boy did. He stood alone in the center of all this chaos, while the torrent of excited youth barged past him, and wished he were somewhere else. He wasn't used to these crowds, these numbers, this noise, this smell.

He was a new boy, tall for his age and slim, with pale, gray-blue eyes and black hair that he had tried to brush into a perfect, neat shape but, as usual, failed. One stray lock dropped down over his right eye like a black comma.

A moment ago the hallway had been empty, and the boy had been wondering where everyone was, but now it was alive with shouting pupils who streamed down the stairs and into the dining room.

"You, boy!" barked a voice, and the boy looked around.

A man stood there glaring at him and, despite the fact that he was short, shorter even than some of the boys, he had an air of self-importance about him.

"Yes, sir?"

"What's your name, boy?"

"Bond, James Bond."

"James Bond—*sir*."

"Yes. Sorry, sir."

The man peered at him. He was stick-thin, with pale skin, deep-set, blue-rimmed eyes, wiry gray hair, and a very short, very black beard that covered nearly half his face. He reminded James a little of King George.

"Do you know who I am, Mr. Bond?" he said coldly.

"I'm afraid not, sir. I just arrived."

"I am Mr. Codrose. Your housemaster. I am to be your father, your priest, and your God for the duration of your stay at this school. I should have met you yesterday evening, but some damned fool boy walked into the path of an automobile on Long Walk and I spent half the night in the hospital. I trust you saw the Dame?"

"Yes, sir."

"Good. Now you had best run along or you will be late for early school. I will see you for a chat before supper."

"Yes, sir." James turned to walk away.

"Wait!" Codrose stared at James with his cold fish eyes. "Welcome to Eton, Bond."

James had arrived the day before at nearby Windsor station, peering up through clouds of steam at the great walls and towers of Windsor Castle. He had wondered if the king was in there somewhere—maybe he was even sitting at a window, looking down at the train?

He had followed a group of boys out of the station and into Windsor, where they had crossed over the wide, gray waters of the river Thames, which divided the town in two. On one side was the castle and on the other was Eton College. He was amazed at the size of the school; it took up nearly half the town, spreading out chaotically in all directions. More than a thousand boys studied here, all living in the numerous houses scattered haphazardly about the place.

He had asked for directions and eventually found himself wandering, lost, down a long footpath called Judy's Passage, looking hopelessly at the tall, unmarked buildings on either side.

A slightly overweight Indian boy with a white turban had approached him.

"Are you the new chap, by any chance?" he had asked.

"I suppose I might be," said James.

"You are James Bond?"

"Yes."

The boy smiled and shook his hand.

"Pritpal Nandra," he said. "I have been looking out for you."

He led James into a nearby ramshackle building.

"I have the room next to yours," Pritpal said. "I shall be messing with you."

"Messing?"

"We will cook our tea together," Pritpal explained. "And take turns to eat in each other's rooms. You, me, and a third boy. We were wondering what you'd be like."

"Will I do?"

Pritpal smiled again. "I think so."

James followed Pritpal into the dim interior of the house,

through the hallway, and up three flights of ancient stairs, before arriving at a long, winding corridor.

"Here we are," said the Indian boy as he pushed open a creaky door, thick with layers of dark-blue paint, and James got the first sight of his room.

It was tiny, with a sloping roof reaching almost to the floor in one corner and a great black beam cutting the ceiling in two. James was relieved to see that his trunk had arrived safely. It was a small reminder of his life before school.

"Your new home," said Pritpal. "Not much to look at now, is it? But you can fix it up. There's your burry."

"My what?"

"Your burry." Pritpal pointed to a battered piece of furniture that consisted of a chest of drawers with a desk on top supporting a small bookcase. It was scratched with the names of previous owners, and one enthusiastic boy had even burned his name into it with a hot poker.

James looked around; as well as the burry there was a small table, a washstand, a Windsor chair, and a thin, faded rug that lay on the floor next to the fireplace. James frowned, there was something missing.

"Where will I sleep?" he asked.

Pritpal laughed.

"Your bed's behind here," he said, indicating a curtain that hung over a bulky object on one wall. "Our boys' maid will fold it down for you just before evening prayers. There is quite a lot to get used to here, but you will soon learn. First thing you must do is get some more pieces for your room. You shall need an ottoman, an armchair, boot box, brush box, some pictures from Blundell's . . ."

"Hold on," said James, slumping into the chair. "Not so fast."

"Sorry, old chap," said Pritpal. "But it is important that you make yourself comfortable in here. You will spend half your life in this room."

Half his life? James tried to take that in. This was all so strange for him. For the past couple of years he had been educated at home by an aunt. To be suddenly plunged into this new world with its ancient traditions, its crowds, and its own strange language was quite unsettling.

"Come along," said Pritpal, pulling James up out of his chair. "No shilly-shallying, there is a great deal to be done. Let's go and see who you're up to."

"Up to?"

"Who's going to be teaching you. Follow me, we have to go to School Yard."

Pritpal led James out of Codrose's and back down Judy's Passage to Long Walk, where he stopped, nodding toward an ornate lamppost decorated with elaborate floral ironwork, that stood on an island in the middle of the road.

"That is the Burning Bush," Pritpal said. "It is a famous Eton landmark and a very useful meeting point. Are you getting your bearings all right, old chap?"

Before James could answer Pritpal dragged him across the road and through a large doorway set into the side of a long, square building.

"This is Upper School," said Pritpal, as they passed through the gloom and out into a busy redbrick courtyard on the other side. "The heart of Eton. The statue in the middle is the school founder, King Henry VI. And that's Lupton's

Tower behind him. That clock will rule your life! Now, let us see what your fate is."

They squeezed through the pack of boys crowding around the noticeboards and Pritpal talked James through the complicated tangle of lessons and teachers. James tried to follow it all, but could hardly keep up. All he could gather was that some teachers, or beaks, as Pritpal called them, were good and some bad, and some were demons from the very lowest level of hell.

He did learn, though, that his classical tutor, the man in charge of most of his education, was to be a Mr. Merriot, which was apparently a good thing.

After studying the noticeboards they walked down the High Street to buy some Latin grammar books, though not before Pritpal had explained that as lower boys they must only ever walk on the east side of the road.

"Even if you're coming out of W V Brown's and going to Spottiswoode's, which is only ten yards farther on, you have to cross the street and then recross it when you're opposite Spottiswoode's."

"But why?" asked James.

"Ours is not to reason why, and all that," said Pritpal.

"But there must be a reason. It's ridiculous."

"You will soon learn that there are a lot of traditions here at Eton whose meaning has long since been lost. Nobody knows why we do most of the things we do. We just do."

James hadn't slept well. His room was freezing and the springs in his bed had dug into him through the thin mattress. He had been troubled by dreams about his parents and had woken in the middle of the night not knowing where he was. He had eventually managed to get back to sleep only to be roused again at a quarter to seven by his boys' maid, Janet, a red-faced old woman with swollen ankles. She had clattered a pan of hot water outside his door and shouted for him to be up, even though it seemed as if he'd only just nodded off.

James had crawled out of bed, fetched the water, poured it into the basin on his washstand, and washed his hands and face. Then he took a deep breath and steeled himself for the hardest task of the morning—putting on his school uniform for the first time.

He got into each new item with mounting discomfort: the long, black, itchy trousers; the white shirt with its wide, stiff collar; the waistcoat; the fiddly black tie that was little more than a scrap of stiff paper; the bum-freezer Eton jacket and, most ridiculous of all, the tall top hat. To a boy like James who was used to wearing simple, comfortable clothes, it was torture. He felt awkward and self-conscious, as if he were at some dreadful fancy-dress party. They weren't his clothes and they were one more unreal element in this whole unreal situation. As he tied the laces on his heavy black boots, he cursed. He hated laces.

Once dressed, he had hurried downstairs expecting to find the hallway crowded with boys, but it was empty and the house was deathly silent. He looked nervously at the clock—it was ten past seven. He had been told that early school started at half past seven, so where was everybody?

He checked the dining room—empty. Perhaps they'd been teasing him, playing a trick on the new boy. He had certainly been horrified to learn that he would have his first lesson before breakfast.

He had looked out into the passage; there was nobody else about.

Then he'd gone back inside and watched the long minutes tick by on the clock. Quarter past . . . twenty past . . . He had been just about to go upstairs to look for Pritpal when there had been a noise like an avalanche, and a horde of boys had crashed down the stairs and pushed past him into the dining room, where they had quickly stuffed their faces with stale buns and cocoa before stampeding out of the building.

Now here he was, pushing an unruly lock of hair off his face and trying not to say the wrong thing to Mr. Codrose.

"Didn't you hear me?" said the cold-eyed little man, rubbing his beard with a noise like sandpaper. "Hurry along or you will be late for early school." Codrose strode off and a group of boys parted to let him pass.

"Yes, sir, thank you, sir," James called after him.

The torrent of boys surged outside into the alleyway and James followed, though he had no clear idea of exactly where he was meant to be going. He was trying to keep up, but he felt as if he was in a dream with its own mysterious set of rules. He hurried along, praying that he was heading in the right direction, and with a great feeling of relief he spied Pritpal and ran to catch up with him.

"You have just learned your first lesson at Eton, James," said the Indian boy, panting loudly. "Never get up before a quarter past seven."

James laughed. "Will I ever get the hang of all this?"

"Oh, yes. Don't worry too much. Now, come along, I'll show you to your schoolroom."

"Thanks."

"So, what was your last place like?" Pritpal asked. "A lot smaller than this, I should imagine."

"Yes," said James. "A lot smaller." And he explained about being educated at home by his aunt.

"That sounds like excellent fun."

"It was certainly very different from all this."

Pritpal laughed. "Imagine how it was for me, coming from India," he said. "It's so cold in England and the sun is so dull . . . and the food! My God! You English are a barbarous race. Look out . . . !"

"What?"

But James was too late; as he raced around a corner he collided with a pair of older boys.

"Watch where you're going, you idiot," sneered one of them—a large boy with a big square head, bristly hair, and a gap between his front teeth.

"I'm sorry."

"Sorry's not good enough," said the second boy, who was probably a couple of years senior to James. "You can't go charging into people like a maniac."

"Leave him alone, Sedgepole," said Pritpal. "He said he was sorry, we'll be late for early school."

"Well, you'd better get your skates on, Nandra," said Sedgepole. "You don't want to get into any trouble, do you?"

"No," Pritpal muttered, then looked apologetically at James and ran off. As he went he passed another boy, who let fly a slap at his head that he just managed to dodge.

The third boy walked over to join them.

"What's all this, then?" he asked in a casual drawl.

"It's nothing," said James. "There was an accident, I bumped into someone."

"Did you, now?" said the newcomer, prodding James in the chest. "I don't think I know you." He was a tall, handsome, blond-haired boy of about fifteen, and he spoke with an American accent.

"My name's James Bond, this is my first term . . ."

The three boys laughed at him. "Term?" said the American boy. "Term? What's a term? Do you know what a 'term' is, Sedgepole?"

"I think he means 'half,' " said Sedgepole.

"Yes, I forgot," said James. "You call them 'halves' here, don't you?" He kept his voice even and looked away, not wanting to start a fight on his first day.

"Well, James Bond," said the American boy, "I don't like the idea of you barging into my friends."

"I didn't barge into anyone," said James. "I'm late . . ."

"And you're going to make us late," said the American, "which wouldn't do at all."

James was very aware of the three larger boys huddling around him threateningly, and he began to get scared. Scared of what they might do, scared of what would happen if he were late, scared of the unknown.

"Actually, we *had* better go," said Sedgepole, and the American nodded slowly.

"There's no time to deal with you now, Bond," he said. "We'll see to you later."

The first two boys strolled off, but the American

hung back and stared at James, daring him to stare back.

"You've got a look about you, Bond, that I don't like. I'll remember you. And think on this." He leant closer and James studied him.

He was different from the English boys. He looked healthier—as if he'd been pumped up with vitamins and goodness, with orange juice and milk and fat steaks. He had wide shoulders and clear, suntanned skin. His big, strong jaw was packed with gleaming white teeth and his eyes were so blue they looked unreal. There was something almost too perfect about him, like an illustration of a dashing pilot in a boys' adventure book, but behind it all James sensed a craziness that unnerved him.

He broke his gaze and looked down at his shoes.

"You're not at home now," said the American in a baby voice, sniggering at James. "You can't go running to Mummy . . ."

A hot, wild anger welled up in James. He felt his throat tighten and tears of rage come into his eyes.

"Hey, I hope you're not a crybaby, Bond." The boy laughed.

But James wasn't going to let anyone make him cry. He fought back the anger and took control of himself.

"I'd better go," he said flatly, brushing past the American and walking away. He fully expected the older boy to try to stop him, but all he did was call out, "Crybaby bunting, Daddy's gone a-hunting . . ."

James clenched his teeth; if this was the trouble he got into on his first day, what was the rest of his time at this strange school going to be like?

"**A** dry bob is a boy who plays cricket, and a wet bob is one who chooses rowing."

"Really?"

"Yes, really."

"And what do you call a boy who doesn't do either?"

"A slack bob."

James shook his head and laughed. He was eating tea in his room with the two boys who made up his "mess," Pritpal and Tommy Chong. Tommy was a small, tough boy from Hong Kong who loved to argue and play cards and had the largest vocabulary of swear words that James had ever heard. The three of them were huddled around the fireplace with their plates on their knees, making the most of the warmth from the small fire. They were allowed coal only every other day, and tonight it was a "hot" day for James. On cold days the little rooms were absolutely freezing, and James didn't think he'd ever get used to being chilled to the bone half the time. It was no better in the classrooms: none of them were heated, and many of the boys did their lessons wearing gloves.

Pritpal and Tommy were attempting to explain some of the more unusual terms used at Eton in time for his Colors Test, an examination that all new boys had to take to make sure that they were properly learning their way around the school.

"Mesopotamia?" said Pritpal.

"I know that one," said James. "Isn't that the field where they play cricket?"

"Cricket in the summer, football in the winter," said Pritpal.

Since that first day, James had gotten to know Pritpal quite well. He was the son of a maharajah, a genius at maths and science, and completely uninterested in anything else— except his food.

He was sitting comfortably in a wicker armchair attacking his tea with fierce concentration. The chair was a recent addition. In the few weeks that James had been at the school he had managed to make his room feel more like home. He had put up some pictures: a rather lurid depiction of a naval battle, a portrait of King George, and a painting of a hot and sunny South Sea island. He had also bought a few bits of furniture, the most useful of which was the ottoman on which Pritpal was sitting. It was a long box with a padded seat that contained a hideous jumble of bits and pieces, odd items of clothing and sports equipment as well as sweets and biscuits and other treats, which at Eton were known as "sock."

"What about 'Pop'?" said Tommy Chong.

"That's the prefects, isn't it?" said Bond.

"Yes," said Pritpal. "Properly called the Eton Society."

James had quickly learnt that it was the boys themselves who were mainly responsible for discipline in the school. Older boys in Pop, easily distinguishable in their brightly colored waistcoats, strutted about the place in a rather swanky manner, keeping the younger boys in order. The senior boys in charge of each house were known as the Library, and their powers were quite extensive. They could even beat younger boys if they felt their behavior deserved it. Though, luckily, James had so far avoided this.

"Do you know your tickets?" said Tommy Chong.

"I think so . . ." James concentrated, thinking about the hateful slips of paper that dominated his life at Eton. "There's 'house tickets,' which you need to get signed if you go out of the house after lockup, 'leave tickets' for written permission to be away from school, white tickets if you've done something wrong, and yellow tickets if you've done something very, very, very wrong."

They were eating fried eggs and sausages that they had cooked on the little electric stove out in the passage under the watchful eye of the boys' maid. Everyone bought extra food at the school stores or at Jack's or Rowland's in town; this was absolutely necessary to stop the boys from starving to death, as the meals that Codrose served up were almost completely inedible. The quality of food in the different houses was up to each house tutor, and Codrose had a reputation for being the worst. Today's lunch had consisted of a tough old piece of meat with some watery boiled potatoes and a terrible, slimy pile of grayish beans.

"Calx?" said Pritpal.

"Erm . . . Oh yes, those are the goals in the Wall Game."

"We don't call them goals, we call them shies. There's good calx and bad calx."

"I'm not sure I really understand the rules of the Wall Game," said James. "Will that count against me?"

"Don't worry," said Tommy Chong. "Nobody understands the rules."

James had settled in well; whilst he was never going to win any prizes for his schoolwork, he was a bright boy and very observant. Once he'd gotten the hang of lessons and how things were done at the school, he coped well. In fact, although he'd started one half later in the year than most other boys, he found that he was keeping up fairly easily. Like most boys, he'd never been that keen on learning, but he realized that his aunt must have taught him well. In fact, apart from Latin, which he hated, he found some lessons a little too easy—French lessons were a bit of bore, as he already spoke the language as well as he spoke English. This came from having a Swiss mother and spending half his childhood in Switzerland. He was also fluent in German, but there were no German classes at the school, so he kept his hand in by chatting with a German-Jewish boy called Freddie Meyer who was part of his loose circle of friends.

Despite all this, James still felt as if he didn't really fit in here. He had learned the jargon, he wore the uniform, but he didn't belong. He was used to being his own man and he was constantly aware of the mass of boys he was always surrounded by at Eton.

And the rules.

Endless rules and traditions.

James hated rules.

A great deal of his day was spent studying alone in his room, which suited him, but you couldn't take a step anywhere at Eton without being reminded that thousands of boys before you had taken that step, and you had to do it exactly as they had done.

"Well, I think you are doing all right, James," said Pritpal. "I think you will pass your Colors Test without too much trouble."

"It's hard work, keeping up," said James, buttering a piece of bread. "I don't come from an Eton family. My father went to school at a place called Fettes, in Scotland."

"I have heard of it," said Pritpal. "Very tough."

"You don't talk about your family very much, do you?" said Tommy.

"No," said James flatly.

"Is there some secret we should know?" said Pritpal, smiling mysteriously.

"I'll bet they're criminals, aren't they?" said Tommy. "Your parents are in prison somewhere and you're too ashamed to talk about them."

"No, I know," said Pritpal. "They're secret government agents, working undercover."

"No," said Tommy. "I've got it—they're mad scientists and they've built a space rocket and gone to the moon."

"There's no secret," said James with a friendly smile. "I'm an ordinary boy like you two."

"You are not," said Pritpal. "With all this ghastly running you do. It is not seemly for people to be dashing about the place."

It was true, despite the huge choice of games on offer at Eton, from rugger and soccer to squash and even beagling, the sport that James preferred was running. James wasn't keen on team sports and running suited his solitary nature, even though it set him further apart from the other boys.

"Running is no use," said Pritpal. "You are an excellent sportsman, James. You must join in more . . ."

James was about to reply to this when they heard the sound that all lower boys dreaded, a long shout of "B-o-o-o-o-o-o-o-y!" from upstairs. This was "boy call." The three of them dropped everything and raced out of the room, along the corridor, down one flight of stairs, and up another. James was easily the fastest, and he even passed three more boys on the way up. Pritpal was the slowest, and, as the last to arrive, it fell to him to do whatever needed doing.

"Come on, you inky little fourth-form scugs," said Longstaff, the senior boy who had made the call. "Oh, Nandra," he said, as Pritpal puffed up the last few steps. "You again. I want you to take a message for me. It's for David Clasnet, he's a scholar."

Pritpal took the folded note and began to trudge back down the stairs.

"You see," said James, catching up to him. "There is some benefit to being able to run."

"It's not fair," said Pritpal. "My food will get cold, and I am wasting away with hunger."

"Here," said James. "I'll take it for you."

"No, James . . ."

"It's no trouble. If we didn't have to get in so early for lockup I'd go for a run every night. I've just about finished my tea. Come along. I'll enjoy it."

James snatched the note from Pritpal and jumped down the stairs four at a time. He found Codrose and got him to sign a house ticket, then dashed out into the cool night air.

Judy's Passage was deserted and it felt good to run off the effects of the stodgy food and the hot fire.

He crossed over the road by the Burning Bush and went through the arch into School Yard. As a scholar, David Clasnet would live in College, the original school building built by Henry VI in 1443. The scholars were the academic elite of Eton, with their own separate rules and traditions.

James had never been into College before and he was unsure which entrance to use. He was standing uncertainly in School Yard, peering at the note to see if it held any clues, when he heard voices and turned to see a good-looking, gray-haired man with the white collar of a priest. James had sat through enough of his dramatic sermons in chapel to know that this was the Head Master, the Reverend Dr. Alington, known by some of the boys as Creeping Jesus. He was striding across the cobblestones, deep in excited conversation with two other people, and as they got nearer James groaned.

One of them was a boy—the American boy with whom James had had his run-in on his first day—and the other person could only be the boy's father. The similarity between the two of them was extraordinary. The father was simply a larger, more perfect version of the son. He radiated health and energy. With his golden tan and thick yellow hair, he almost seemed to be glowing. The only major difference was that the father sported a big mustache.

As James watched, the father threw back his head and laughed loudly at something the Head Master had said, and the sound echoed off the walls of the buildings. The Head Master, surely the most important man in the school, was looking at him in awe, like a boy meeting his childhood hero. Everything about the big man said that here was somebody rich and strong, here was somebody who felt he could rule the world. A true Roman emperor. Even his clothes were designed to make him look powerful. His tweed suit was cut wide at the shoulders and narrow at the hips, so that he resembled a wedge and the brogues on his feet were so polished they shone like mirrors. James felt sure that his clothes couldn't possibly hold him, however, and that at any moment he might burst out of his suit and charge, half-naked, through the school like Tarzan, beating his chest and roaring.

James tried to hide in the shadows but the Head Master spotted him and called him over.

"Are you meant to be here?" asked Dr. Alington, and James showed him the note and explained that he was running an errand.

"And what is your name, young man?"

"Bond, sir. James Bond."

"James Bond?" boomed the American giant. "I used to know an Andrew Bond. Any relation?"

"Yes, sir, my father, sir."

"Well, there you go. They say it's a small world. Andrew and I are in the same line of business."

"Selling armaments?" said James.

"That's right. Without weapons our armies can't fight. We were busy men after the war. A lot of countries needed new weapons, as all the old ones had been blown to smithereens." He laughed loudly, and Dr. Alington nodded his head, a weak smile on his lips.

"Is your father still with Vickers?" asked the huge man, wiping his mustache.

"No, sir, he is not," said James.

"He's a good fellow. Sure, we were rivals, but I always liked him. He's a man's man. Pleased to meet you, by the way. I am Lord Randolph Hellebore." He shook James's hand. "Maybe you know my son, George."

James glanced nervously at the boy and nodded. "We have met," he said, and George narrowed his eyes.

"I wonder, are you like him?" said Hellebore, leaning down close to James. "Can you run? Can you swim? Can you wrestle alligators?"

Lord Hellebore laughed into James's face and his hot breath, which smelled sour and sulfurous, blasted him, almost making him choke. James was reminded of one time when he had been to London Zoo and standing too close to a lion's cage; the great beast had roared right at him. The lion's breath had stunk of meat and of something else, something inhuman and frightening. Without the bars between them, that stink would have been the smell of death. But it wasn't only Lord Hellebore's breath that smelled. He was damp with sweat and there was an unpleasant, animal odor seeping from his body like a poisonous gas. James wanted to hold his nose and run, but Hellebore pierced him with his gaze. His pupils were very wide and very black, like two deep, black holes surrounded by thin pale-blue rings. He moved closer and James felt a great heat coming off him, as if he were burning inside, like a volcano ready to erupt.

There was a long, nervous moment as Lord Hellebore stared into James's eyes. James didn't know what to do or what to say, and he was painfully aware of the Head Master, shuffling nervously.

"Do you box, Mr. Bond?" Hellebore asked at last, offering a smile that showed two rows of immaculate, gleaming white teeth.

"A little," said James.

"Come on, then, show me what you're worth." Hellebore put up his fists in a defensive stance, and James felt even less sure just what exactly was expected of him.

"Go on, take a swing at me." Hellebore sounded like a cowboy or a gangster from an American film.

James took one halfhearted swing, which Hellebore easily blocked with the palm of one huge hand.

"Is that the best you've got?" he bellowed, and then he turned to Dr. Alington. "They say your school is full of limp-wristed fops and sissies. They say you don't really take your sport seriously enough. Well, I aim to change all that. Come on, Bond, do your worst."

James took another swing, this time putting all his weight behind it, and as he swung George Hellebore said, "Dad!" in a slightly embarrassed way, as if trying to get his father to stop. Hellebore glanced over at his son and at that moment James's fist connected with his jaw.

It couldn't have hurt him at all, although to James it was like punching a brick wall and sent a jolt of pain all the way up his arm. For an instant, though, Hellebore glared at James with wild fury in his eyes, and James backed away. The moment quickly passed and Hellebore disguised it with a smile, but not before James had had a frightening glimpse behind the big man's gleaming exterior.

"Hey, you caught me off guard, there." Hellebore rubbed his jaw. "Not a bad punch. I need to look out for you, Mr. Bond. You could be trouble."

"Come along, Randolph," said Dr. Alington nervously. "We don't want to be late for supper, and this boy needs to get back to his house."

"Sure," said Lord Hellebore, and he straightened up and turned away, instantly dismissing James. Dr. Alington led him off, and George tagged along behind, but not before giving James one last look full of hate.

Now what had he done? James realized that his heart was beating fast, and he took a couple of deep breaths to calm himself down before going inside.

The scholar, David Clasnet, smiled when James gave him the note.

"I was watching you out of the window," he said. "Good punch. I must say I enjoyed that."

"I'm not sure I did," said James. "This is going to mean big trouble for me."

CHAPTER 3—CROAKER

"**A**re you ready to be put through your paces, Bond?"

"I think so, sir."

"Good lad. I'm going to work you hard today."

"That's nothing new, sir," said James. "You always work us hard."

"You know, Bond, you really shouldn't answer back to the beaks. If I were a stricter master I'd have you running laps for cheek."

"Sorry, sir."

"In fact, I think I will have you running laps. Four times around Dutchman's. Off you go!"

Bond sighed and set off. Not that he really minded. He was never happier than when he was running, feeling his muscles working, his heart pounding, and his lungs straining. It cleared his mind and woke him up and helped to digest the heavy lump of Codrose's food that sat at the pit of his stomach.

When he was running, he really felt alive.

He'd always preferred to run somewhere rather than walk but, until he'd come to Eton, he hadn't realized just how fast a runner he was, and Mr. Merriot had spotted his potential right away.

Mr. Merriot was his classical tutor, the man who would

supervise James's education at Eton, and he was also in charge of athletics.

He was a tall, thin man with gray eyes, untidy hair, and a big, hooked nose sticking out of the front of his face like a fin. His black gown was too small for him, barely hanging down to his waist, and he was rarely seen without a pipe in his mouth, unlit as often as lit.

James liked Merriot. He was friendly and kind and was very fond of saying that he was there for the boys and not the other way around as some beaks seemed to think was the case. He was excited about what he taught and easily distracted into talking about one of his favorite topics rather than what they should have been studying.

And he was absolutely fanatical about athletics.

He was forever telling the boys that he had been a runner for the Royal Navy and had even represented Great Britain at the Olympics in 1924, where he had won a bronze medal in the mile. But a riding accident had put an end to his running career, and he had taken up teaching. Now his enthusiasm and encouragement were slowly making the sport more popular at the school. But he had a long way to go. There was no proper running track at Eton and, apart from the annual steeplechase, most races were run on the roads, and for training the boys had to make use of a piece of land called Dutchman's Farm.

Today the sky was a heavy, dull gray, and a yellow fog hung over the ground, draining it of color. It was easy to feel gloomy on a day like this, but James found that exercise kept his spirits up and when he was running he could let his mind roam free.

When he had finished the laps he stood with his hands on his knees, breathing heavily.

"We need to build up your strength," said Mr. Merriot, coming over and checking his stopwatch. "I have you down as a long-distance runner, Bond."

"Really, sir?"

"Yes. Sprinting's for the show-offs of this world, but the real test is distance. Now, you're a tall lad and that helps, and even though you're only a new boy, a lowly F-blocker, if we build up your stamina I don't think there are many boys in the school who could better you over a long course."

James didn't know what to say, so he said nothing.

"Now, I'm going to let you in on a little secret, Bond," said Merriot, relighting his pipe. "And you have to promise to keep it under your hat."

"Of course, sir."

"'Of course, sir!'" Merriot had a habit of repeating back to you what you had just said. "There's a big event coming up at the end of term," he went on, "part of which involves running, so you'll have to train harder than ever."

"What sort of event, sir?"

"One of our parents is inaugurating a new Eton trophy, strictly for Lower School, so you'll be in with a good shot."

"What sort of a trophy, sir?"

"It's an odd fish, sort of an all-around affair, needing strength, speed, courage, endurance, and marksmanship."

James couldn't think of any sporting activity that needed all those skills, but Mr. Merriot explained.

"It's a triple cup. You'd need to compete in three games in one day—running, swimming, and shooting."

"Swimming, sir? But it's not summer."

"I know, Bond. You'd have to be mad to go in for it. Are you mad?"

James shrugged. "I'll give it a go."

"'I'll give it a go,' he says. Good man. Maybe the Hellebore Cup will be yours."

"Hellebore?" James blurted, before he could stop himself.

"Yes. Do you know that American lad, George Hellebore?"

"Yes," said James, trying to give nothing away. Ever since the incident in School Yard, the American boy had done his best to make his life difficult and Bond had done his best to keep out of his way, but hadn't always been successful. On one occasion Hellebore and his pals had chased James across College Field. James didn't know what they were intending to do with him if they caught him, but he didn't want to find out.

"It's all his father's idea," said Merriot. "Lord Randolph Hellebore. Fabulously wealthy individual. Been very generous with his money, given a great deal of it to scientific and medical research, you know, trying to find cures for some of the terrible diseases that ravage mankind. But still not sure I utterly approve of the man. Made all his money in the war . . . selling weapons, you know. I suppose that's where the shooting thing comes in—guns are in the family, so to speak."

James bit his tongue, not wanting Mr. Merriot to know that his own father had worked for an armaments company. He remembered his conversation with Lord Hellebore that night in School Yard. He must have been at Eton discussing the cup with Dr. Alington. That would explain all the talk about sports and being strong.

Mr. Merriot looked into the distance. "Too many boys and masters from this school were killed in the war," he said. "Eton is changed forever. England is changed forever. Do you think they would have employed a duffer like me to teach you lot if there had been better men to choose from? But those men are lying dead under the mud at the Somme and Ypres. And the boys too—boys of eighteen and nineteen. What a waste. Young men who should have gone on to become great sportsmen, politicians, scientists, writers, artists, musicians . . . gone forever." He lit his pipe and sent up a huge cloud of smoke. "But enough of this." He clapped his hands. "Let's get you running, boy . . ."

The next day Pritpal took James on a tour of the swimming spots. First they went to "Athens," a stretch of the Thames opposite the Royal Windsor Racecourse where a concrete structure had been built for diving.

"That is called the Acropolis," said Pritpal. "Rather a grand name for an ugly pile of concrete, don't you think?"

James peered into the murky water, which was the color of cold tea. He had been horrified to learn that there was no pool at Eton and that all swimming was done in the river.

"What did your Mr. Merriot say to you?" laughed Pritpal as he saw the look of disgust on James's face. "That this was a test of strength and courage? I think you will also need the skin of a rhinoceros."

They went next to a small backwater called Ward's Mead that had been widened and provided with diving boards and steps. And just below Ward's Mead was Cuckoo Weir, where the less experienced swimmers, known as non-nants, could enjoy themselves under the watchful eye of a waterman.

"There is also Romney Weir," said Pritpal as they walked back along the riverbank. "But that is only for the very best swimmers."

"Maybe I should pull out," said James, with a shiver. "I can't say the river looks too inviting."

"Oh, in the summertime I'm sure it's very refreshing," said Pritpal. "But you wouldn't catch me dipping so much as a toe in it at any time of year. This cup of Hellebore's is likely to cause the deaths of many boys."

"It seems a strange mixture of events," James said, kicking a stone into the water. "Swimming, running, and shooting."

"Not really," said Pritpal. "It makes perfect sense."

"In what way?" James was puzzled.

"Well, they are the three sports that George Hellebore is best at."

James laughed. "Really? I knew he was a good swimmer, and Merriot said he's a fast runner, but shooting?"

"Apparently he shoots all the time on his father's estate in Scotland."

"Scotland? But they're Americans, aren't they?"

"They are. But they have a home in Scotland as well." Nandra raised his hands as if aiming an imaginary shotgun. "Bang, bang! No bird is safe when George Hellebore is around. Have you ever shot before?"

"Once," said James. "On a holiday in Italy."

"I shot a tiger once," said Pritpal.

"Really?" said James.

"Yes, it was a pitiful, sick old beast, three steps away from death's door. I'm not sure, but I think they might even have tied one of its feet to the ground. We went into the jungle on elephants, my father said it would make a man of me."

"And did it?"

"No. It just made me never want to kill another living creature as long as I live."

A little farther along they came across the bent figure of an old man who appeared to be fishing. It was Croaker, the oldest and most famous of the men who looked after the boats for the school. At this time of year Croaker and the other men were less busy, which was why he was spending his afternoon here with his fishing line.

Croaker was ancient, and always had been ancient. Boys would tell about how he had been ancient even when their fathers were at the school. He was short and square-shaped, with a huge mustache, tiny little red eyes, a fat, bulb-shaped nose, and an ever-present flat cap on his bald head.

The two boys wandered over to him.

"What are you fishing for, Croaker?" asked Pritpal.

"You'll see," he chuckled. "You'll see."

In a few moments, as he hauled his catch in, they did see.

On the end of his line was what appeared to be a loop of wool, and attached to it, their mouths tangled in the fibers, were several black eels.

James grimaced, but watched the fish with appalled fascination as they twisted and turned and tangled around one another.

"They can't let go of the wool," said Croaker. "I wove a ball of worms into it. It's called naring. Ooh, they'll be good eaters, these fellers."

"So you're telling me," said James, "that not only have I got to swim in this freezing, dirty water, but it's also full of eels?"

"Oh, eels is 'armless," said Croaker, pulling the squirming fish off the wool and dropping them into a bucket. "There's two types of people in this world. Those as 'preciates eels, and those as don't."

"Are you really going to eat them?" asked Pritpal.

"Oh, yes. Stew them up. Lovely. Very sweet meat he has on him, your eel. Come on, I'll show you."

Croaker picked up his bucket and led them to his hut. Once there, he fetched some tools from inside, then picked the fattest eel out of the bucket.

"Here we are," he said, and without any more ceremony, he nailed the eel to the door of his shed through its head. Then he cut it neatly around the neck, took a pair of pliers, grabbed hold of the skin, and yanked it downward in one quick movement that ripped it clean off the body, exposing the silvery-blue flesh beneath.

"Lovely," he said, running a hand gently down the exposed body. "Just lovely."

James and Pritpal were too amazed to be shocked, but they declined Croaker's offer to join him for supper.

"So? Do you still want to go in for the cup?" asked Pritpal.

James swallowed. Nobody was ever going to accuse him of being a coward.

"Why not?" he said. "Tomorrow I'll start practicing in the river."

CHAPTER 4—WARD'S MEAD

James was shivering. His body felt raw, as if he'd had the skin peeled off it, like Croaker's eel. He rubbed his arms to try to get some feeling back into them, and the raised goosebumps made them feel as rough as sandpaper.

If it was this cold out of the water, what was it going to be like in it?

Well, there was only one way to find out.

It was half an hour before afternoon lessons, and he was standing on a low diving board at Ward's Mead, peering at the water, which looked like some of Codrose's less appetizing soup. Cold soup. Freezing-cold soup.

"Come on, then," he said out loud. "Just do it."

He pulled back his arms, took a deep breath, and flung himself forward. When he entered the water it was like being hit by a cricket bat. He was stunned by the cold and for a moment he couldn't move, but then he came alive, clawed his way to the surface, and gasped. All his limbs were aching and his throbbing head felt numb. The only way to stay in the water and stop himself from jumping out was to swim. He thrashed across the mead to the other side and fought the urge to get out and run back to his room. After a moment's hesitation, he forced himself around and swam back to the other side.

Weak sunlight was filtering through the low clouds and

at least it was warmer than yesterday, but these were hardly ideal swimming conditions. Nevertheless, if he was going to stand any chance at the cup, which was only three weeks away, he knew that he would have to get used to it.

After three widths he found that his body was adjusting to the temperature and, while it could never have been described as pleasant, at least he knew that he was not going to die after all.

He swam a few more widths and when he had had just about all that he could stand he swam over to where he'd left his clothes and prepared to pull himself out of the water. But, just as he was getting his knees up, somebody put a shoe into his face and shoved him back into the mead.

He looked up. It was George Hellebore.

"Hey, if it ain't my old pal, Jimmy Bond," he said.

"Hello, Hellebore." James once more tried to scramble out onto the grassy bank.

"Where do you think you're going in such a hurry?" said Hellebore, pushing him back in again.

"To get changed."

"Always in a hurry, aren't you, Bond? Always got to go somewhere fast."

"I'm cold and I want to get out."

"Yeah, I bet you do. Well, I'm in charge of the river today." Hellebore knelt down and gave James a big, sinister smile. "And if you want to get out, first of all you have to pass a little test."

James looked up into George's face. His china-blue eyes were glinting with crazy amusement, and there was an ugly smirk on his lips.

"Look, Hellebore," said James, holding on to the side. "You're not in charge here."

"Hey, if I say I'm in charge, I'm in charge."

There was no point in arguing. Hellebore was backed up by his usual gang of cronies: Wallace, with his big, square head and gap-toothed grin; Sedgepole, who had an extremely small head and sticking-out ears; and Pruitt, who was rather good-looking and elegant. They leered at James, daring him to try his luck.

"What do you want?" said James, trying not to let his teeth rattle together with the cold.

"You fancy yourself as a bit of a swimmer, do you, Bond?" said the American, and Bond shrugged.

"Well, I've not seen anybody in this country of yours who was half as good a swimmer as me. I practically grew up in the water."

"Yes," said Bond, kicking his legs to try to keep warm. "You're supposed to be quite good."

"Quite good?" Hellebore opened his eyes wide in mock amazement. "Quite good? I'm the best, Bond. Care to have a race?"

"Not now, Hellebore."

"But that's the test you have to pass, Bond, old boy. You have to win a swimming race."

"I'm not racing you, Hellebore . . ."

"Who said anything about racing me? You couldn't beat me in a thousand years. No, you're not racing me." Hellebore whistled, and a boy in swimming trunks shuffled reluctantly over from the bushes where he'd been sheltering. It was Leo Butcher, a robust, cheerful, round boy who played in the school brass band. Bond had seen him puffing away at a recent concert given by the Musical Society in School Hall.

"Hello, Bond," he said sheepishly. It was obvious that he had no more desire to be here than James.

"Hello, Butcher," said James.

"The deal is . . ." said Hellebore, "you get to race Butcher."

Bond frowned. Butcher didn't look like much of a swimmer. What was the catch?

"What do you say, Bond?" Hellebore slapped Butcher hard across the shoulders and Bond saw him wince with the pain. "A race against fatty Butcher here. The loser gives me—" Hellebore paused for dramatic effect. "Let's say, their hat."

Bond glanced at Butcher, who was staring at the ground.

"It should be a fun race," said Hellebore. "But I'll warn you, Bond, Butcher's good. He's the best." The older boys laughed.

"If it's all the same to you," said James, "I'd rather not."

Hellebore suddenly grabbed James by the hair and forced his head under the surface. Taken by surprise, James swallowed a mouthful of muddy water. He came up, coughing and retching.

"You race Butcher, Bond. Or me and my good friends are going to play football with your head. Understand?" Hellebore grabbed him and pulled him onto the bank. "So, what's it to be?"

James stood up; George's hands had left red marks on his arms.

"All right," he said quietly.

Hellebore clapped his hands. "Good fellow," he said. "May the best man win."

James and Butcher arranged themselves at the edge of the mead. Butcher was shivering madly and his knees were knocking together. James wondered what threats Hellebore had used to get him to cooperate.

"Are you all set?" Hellebore called out. "Two widths, loser pays out the forfeit."

Try as he might, James couldn't understand what Hellebore was up to. He could beat Butcher easily—the blond American must be planning some kind of trick. But what?

"On your marks, get set . . ." Hellebore stopped suddenly. Butcher was caught off guard and toppled into the water. Hellebore's pals laughed.

"Oh, I forgot, Bond," said Hellebore as Butcher clambered back out again. "One more thing."

James looked over at him. Here it came.

"You have to stay under the water."

"What?"

"You heard me. It's an underwater race. As soon as you come up for air you're out of the running. If you don't make it back, then whoever gets the farthest is the winner."

James looked over at Butcher, who looked away.

He'd known.

Oh, well. It wasn't the end of the world. James still had a chance. Butcher couldn't be that good, and James was pretty confident that he could hold his breath for quite a while.

"Set! Go!" shouted Hellebore quickly, and they dived in.

James was ready for the coldness this time, but it was

worse having to swim underwater. He could see only about three inches in front of him; it was like trying to peer through a particularly vile greenish brown fog. Indefinable scraps and dross floated past in the gloom, and he thought he glimpsed a pale shape far off that could have been Butcher, but it was gone before he could see it clearly. Slimy weeds brushed against his belly, and the thought of the eels waiting below in the mud made him shudder.

He had no idea how far he'd gone, but he knew that it was going to be a struggle reaching the far side, let alone turning around and swimming back again.

He felt awful, as if there were a cold iron cage clamped around his head; all he wanted to do was to get to the surface, stick his head out and be up in the fresh air, warmth and light. But he resisted the urge and swam harder, using a clean, strong, breaststroke, deciding that the quicker he went, the less time he'd need to hold his breath. However, the quicker he went, the more oxygen he used up, and soon his lungs began to burn. He struggled on, the pounding in his head getting worse and worse. A few more strokes and he had to let some air out, then some more, until his lungs were completely empty and the pain was crippling him. Still he battled on, one more stroke, another, then—no, it was too much, his whole body was crying out for oxygen, he couldn't fight it any longer. He bobbed to the surface and gulped in several great mouthfuls of air. Then he trod water, panting and choking. He'd drifted way off course and was nowhere near the other side, but where was Butcher? He must still be down there somewhere. Was he all right? Maybe he'd got tangled in weeds?

No, he saw his feet splashing near the far bank. He'd reached the other side, but still he hadn't come up. James caught sight of him doggedly sculling back toward the start point. Bond forgot all about losing, forgot all about the cold, forgot all about the older boys jeering from the edge of the mead, and marveled at Butcher's capacity for holding his breath. It was only when he was within five or six feet of the edge that he finally floated up and took in more air, although he hardly seemed out of breath at all.

"Well done, Butcher," yelled Hellebore. "You're a champion turtle."

James swam to them. He was looking forward to getting warm and dry, but, as he reached the older boys, Hellebore suddenly grabbed him by the hair again and forced him back under the water. He had had no time to take a breath and was soon struggling, but, try as he might, he couldn't break free of Hellebore's grip and come up again. The last of his air came out in a huge bubble, and he swallowed a gutful of water. He mustn't panic, that would only make things worse. The American wasn't going to drown him . . . he wasn't . . .

Or was he? A few more moments and he'd be breathing in water. . . . He couldn't force himself upward, the boy's arm was too strong. . . . But if he couldn't go upward . . . maybe he could go the other way.

It was drastic, but it was the only solution.

He suddenly grabbed hold of Hellebore's wrist and pulled. Caught off guard, the boy tumbled over and landed in the water with an almighty splash, letting go of James in the process. James quickly squirmed onto the bank and vomited up a stream of mucus and river scum.

Hellebore was furious; he yelled something, and Sedgepole and Pruitt grabbed James. He knew he was in big trouble now, but anything was better than drowning.

Hellebore clumsily scrambled out in his soaking clothes. His eyes were red, his blue lips pulled back from his teeth in a snarl, his hair flattened to his head. All traces of the handsome young boy had gone, to be replaced by the features of a crazed animal.

"You shouldn't have done that, Bond," he rasped.

But before he could do anything, Croaker appeared.

"Oi, you lot," he called out. "You shouldn't be in the water." Then he noticed Hellebore. "What on God's earth has happened here? Why are your togs all wet?"

Hellebore looked at Croaker, his face showing nothing. There was a code in the school, as there was in all schools: you didn't sneak. You didn't go crying to the masters. If you had a problem with another boy, you sorted it out yourselves. And, while Croaker wasn't a beak, he still had authority and could easily report them.

Would Hellebore break the code?

"What's been going on, then, eh?"

"It's my fault, Croaker," said Bond. "I got into trouble, cramp in my legs. . . . Hellebore here came to my rescue and pulled me out."

"Is that right?" Croaker looked from one boy to the other. "Well, you'd best get dry before one of the beaks catches you. Go on with you, now."

Hellebore and his gang skulked off while James and Leo Butcher dried themselves as best they could and wriggled back into their clothes.

"I'm sorry, Bond," said Leo, rubbing his hair with a thin towel. "It wasn't really fair."

"Never mind about that," said James. "How did you do it? How did you hold your breath like that?"

"I play the trumpet," said Butcher, "and the tuba." He stopped as if this explained everything, but James looked confused.

"I have to control my breathing," said Butcher, "for my music. You need big lungs and a lot of puff. I do special exercises."

James was impressed and intrigued.

"My father's a musician," Butcher went on. "He's been teaching me almost since I was born. Hellebore found out how long I could hold my breath when he tried to suffocate me one day for a joke."

"Good joke," said James, awkwardly pulling his shirt on over his damp skin, and Butcher smiled.

As they walked back toward school along the riverbank, James quizzed Butcher some more.

"You're going to have to teach me that breath-control trick," he said. "It's amazing."

"It's not a trick," said Butcher.

"No, I know. But I think it could really help me with my running."

Before they could say any more, Wallace and Pruitt charged up, and Pruitt snatched the hat off James's head.

"Forfeit!" they yelled, and tossed it into the Thames, where it spun away downstream. Then the two boys ran off, laughing.

"You're going to get into trouble for that," Butcher said quietly to James.

"I know," James replied. "But it could have been worse."

The next chance James got, he discussed the idea of breathing exercises with Mr. Merriot after a classics lesson.

"It certainly can't do any harm, Bond," said Merriot, trying to get his pipe lit, "increasing your lung capacity. D'you know what happens when you breathe?"

"Well, I know that our lungs take the oxygen from the air and pass it into our bloodstream," said James. "And then the blood takes it around to all our muscles."

"That's about it, but don't forget that our lungs also take all the carbon dioxide waste from our blood and breathe it out again. Now, if you breathe too quickly you'll get too much oxygen in your blood and feel giddy and faint, too slowly and you'll feel sluggish. As an athlete you have to get it just right; if you can't get enough oxygen to your muscles, you'll really suffer. Now, will I see you at the track tomorrow?"

"Yes, sir. . . . And, sir?"

"What is it?"

"Some of the boys, sir. They're saying that this Hellebore triple cup thing is a bit of a cheat, sir."

"A cheat? How so?"

"Well, they reckon the idea is that George Hellebore is supposed to win it."

Merriot laughed. "So that's what they're saying, is it?"

"Some of the boys, sir."

"But not you?" Merriot gave him an amused look and stuffed his big hands into his trouser pockets.

"Is he that good, sir?"

"Oh, he's a pretty useful runner, all right. Perhaps not quite the legs for a really long race, but this new cross-country course through the park is only about five miles long, so he should be in with a chance. And I hear there's no one can touch him in the water. As for his shooting, I wouldn't know. But, in answer to your question, I'd say that if anyone had a chance of wining the Hellebore Cup, it would be young George Hellebore."

"It doesn't really seem fair," said James.

"Listen to you," Merriot laughed. "You sound like a Communist. Whatever gave you the idea that the world was meant to be fair? It is the privilege of the rich, Bond, to make the rules. And our Lord Hellebore is one of the richest parents at the school."

"But that still doesn't mean . . ."

Merriot interrupted him. "He's making a substantial donation to Eton in return for having the cup in his name, Bond. Putting a lot of money into the Science Schools. I believe the process is known as 'You scratch my back and I'll scratch yours.' And you won't catch me complaining. As a matter of fact, I think this cup is a jolly good idea. It's something I've been badgering the Head Master about—some sort of recognition for games other than cricket and rowing and the like. I'm not sure about the shooting part; I would have thought that sort of thing was better confined to the Corps, but hats off to Lord H, I say. Wants to be thought of as one of us, I suppose. But, of course, he'll always be an American."

"How do you mean, sir?"

"Oh, the Americans are a splendid lot. Friendly, brave,

cheerful, energetic . . . but winning's the most important thing to them. And very good they are at it too."

"So you think George is going to win the cup?"

"As I say, he's got as good a chance as any." They walked out onto the street. "But let's not worry too much about winning the cup, eh?"

"Oh . . ."

"Don't be dispirited, James. All we're interested in is the cross-country."

"I hope I might do quite well, sir."

"Quite well, Bond? No."

James looked disappointed.

"You're going to do better than quite well." Mr. Merriot smiled. "You're going to win that race, boy."

CHAPTER 5—FALSE START

"**I** come from a country where they don't play cricket, and I confess I don't understand the sport." Lord Hellebore paused for dramatic effect with one hand raised, like a hammy actor, then went on, "To tell you the truth—and if any 'dry bobs' among you will forgive me for saying it— the game just isn't fast enough or tough enough for us Americans. . . ." He smiled, showing his great white teeth, and scanned the crowd of waiting boys.

Tommy Chong, who was standing next to James, poked him in the ribs and whispered out of the side of his mouth, "George Hellebore hasn't played cricket since he was hit by a ball in his first match."

James tried not to laugh. They were standing near the rifle range at the Butts, waiting for the competition to begin, but, at the last moment, Lord Hellebore had stood up on a low wall and insisted on giving a speech.

He was thundering on, sending a spray of spittle over the first few rows. "For me, sports are all about taking the boy and making him into a man. Games make you strong and fit. They say the battle of Waterloo was won on the playing fields of Eton. Well, we have to look forward to future battles and future wars. So, we have to be the strongest!" He opened wide his pale blue eyes and raked the audience with them. "It's a terrible world out there, and if you're not pre-pared to fight, you'll die. Yes, die. I saw things in the Great War—men with their guts torn out, their skin turned green by blossoming decay . . ."

James and Tommy looked at each other. What was Hellebore going on about? This hardly seemed an appropriate speech for a school sporting event. But he hadn't finished. . . .

"I saw men blinded," he yelled, "with no arms or legs, and I used dead bodies as stepping-stones to keep out of the mud, and I thought nothing of it! Oh sure, some men lost their minds, but not me."

"That's debatable," James muttered, and Tommy snorted with laughter. Hellebore looked their way and ranted on. . . .

"It woke me up. I saw things clearly for the first time. I saw the world as it was. I understood then that you are alone in this life and if you don't do whatever it takes to claw your way to the top of the pile, then you'll be buried under the excrement of lesser men!"

A stunned silence fell over the waiting crowd. There was a scattering of applause and then Hellebore shouted melo-dramatically, "So, let the games begin!"

The weather had changed in the last few days, the sun shone cheerfully in the sky and the air was noticeably warmer. It was a Saturday near the end of the half and there was a happy, carnival atmosphere. Nobody except Lord Hellebore was taking the event that seriously.

James waited with the other boys for his turn on the range, enjoying the sunshine and chatting. Pritpal and Tommy had come to watch, though neither of them was competing. In fact, none of James's friends were competing and nearly all the other participants were older than he.

After a while Captain Johns, the master in charge of shooting, called out James's name and he went to fetch his rifle, a .22 Browning.

After a nervous start, James found it quite exciting. The kick of the gun against his shoulder as he squeezed the trigger, the sharp crack, the burning smell of cordite, and then waiting to see how he'd done—the excitement when he got it right, and the disappointment when he was way off target.

"Not bad, Bond. Not bad at all," said Captain Johns, as he handed James his target when it was all over. "That's a very respectable score."

James studied the pattern of holes on the small black-and-white paper target and grinned. He hadn't expected to do this well at all.

"You're a pretty good shot, Bond," said Captain Johns.

"Beginner's luck," said James.

"Well, whatever it is, I look forward to teaching you when you join the Corps."

There was noise and excitement coming from the firing range, and James looked back to see that George Hellebore had taken his place. He was lying on the ground with the rifle tucked up against his cheek, squinting down the length of the barrel toward the target. There were shouts of encouragement from his usual gang of friends, and Captain Johns marched back and called for quiet.

James looked at the American boy, lying there like a professional soldier, with his powerful arms and neat hair. He was impressed by the relaxed and confident way he held the gun. Impressed and just a little bit scared. James wondered how many defenseless creatures had met their deaths like this on George's father's estate.

James backed off. He had managed to keep out of Hellebore's way since the incident at Ward's Mead, and he didn't want to risk the boys turning around and seeing him here now.

The snap of the rifle split the air. Hellebore slid the bolt back, ejecting the spent cartridge, then slotted another bullet into the breach and shunted it home, quickly and cleanly. He paused, squinted, then there was another loud bang. Eight shots later and he was finished. He had done it all coolly and calmly, relaxed and in control, and James was impressed.

Captain Johns brought the target back, Hellebore's pals crowded around, then they cheered and slapped him on the back. He had evidently done as well as they had all expected. He walked away from the range, surrounded by his group of toadies, all congratulating him loudly and trying to share in his glow of success.

Although he tried, James couldn't get out of their way and as Hellebore passed by, he glanced at him just for a moment. His eyes locked with James's, and his was the look of someone scraping something nasty from his boot. Then he looked past James and walked over to his father. The big man beamed at his son, took him by the shoulders and shook him happily. Lord Hellebore was one of the judges for the day's events and he appeared to be enjoying himself greatly. In fact, the only person who seemed more pleased than him was George.

"I doubt we'll see any better shooting than that, today," said Captain Johns, collecting a pile of fresh targets from a table next to James. "Hellebore's the best shot in the school. In fact . . ." the captain paused, checking his score sheet. "there's only one more boy to shoot, Andrew Carlton. Bit of an unknown quantity. Not had him on the range for a little while."

Carlton was a quiet, blond-haired boy of Hellebore's age. He was a champion wet bob, a hero of the school rowing team who devoted all of his time to powering up and down the river. He was a healthy, athletic boy and could have been a great all-rounder, but he'd decided to concentrate on one sport. His father had been Captain of the Boats in his day and had gone on to win many races at Cambridge, so nothing less than the best was expected of young Andrew.

"Good luck, Carlton," said James as the older boy walked past.

"Thanks," said Carlton with a friendly smile. "I shall need it. I wasn't going to take part. I entered only at the last minute. I thought it might be a bit of fun. I saw your shooting, by the way. Not bad for an F-blocker."

Carlton collected his gun and took up his position.

As it turned out, Carlton had a keen eye and a steady hand. After his first couple of shots it was clear that he was an excellent marksman.

A hush fell over the watching boys and masters. Someone had obviously alerted George Hellebore, because he came back, pushed his way to the front of the crowd, and stood there with a black look on his face.

Carlton took his last shot and Captain Johns hurried forward to collect the target. He studied it for some time and called over a couple of fellow masters to help him decide. At last, they all nodded in agreement and Captain Johns returned to read out the results.

James hadn't made the top five but had come in a decent seventh place. In fact, as he hadn't picked up a rifle for at least three years, it was a very good showing indeed. But the big surprise was that Hellebore and Carlton had been awarded equal points and joint first position.

As the results were read out, James looked over at Lord Hellebore, but his face showed nothing. His son, however, was less cool.

"I'll get you in the swimming!" he called out to Carlton, trying to make it sound like a joke. But James knew him well enough to know that he was shaken and would be desperate to thrash Carlton in the race.

James watched as Lord Hellebore beckoned his son and led him to a quiet corner, away from the throng. James followed, fascinated, but kept a safe distance. Randolph was talking heatedly to George, who nodded his head over and over. Finally, Randolph took the boy's chin in his hand, tilted his face upward and leaned very close to him, speaking with such an intense expression on his face that George actually looked scared.

James remembered the time when Randolph had breathed on him, he remembered the heat and the smell, and he almost felt sorry for George. Then a strange thing happened. Randolph took a little glass medicine bottle from his pocket, glanced around to make sure that they were unobserved, and tapped some pills out into his palm.

George protested and tried to turn away, but Randolph shook him quickly and thrust the pills into his hand.

Deflated, George swallowed the pills and returned to his friends.

James didn't have time to reflect on this, as they were all soon herded away from the Butts and down through town to the river for the second event—swimming.

On the way James found himself next to Carlton again.

"That was pretty good," said James, and Carlton grinned.

"I went on a camp in the summer," he said. "It was run by the army, and we did a fair bit of shooting, but I must say I never expected to do so well."

"I think you've got Hellebore rattled."

"I don't know about that; he's a very fast swimmer."

Later on, as they got changed in the swimming hut, James looked at Carlton. With his shirt off, he could see just how strong the boy was. All the rowers were good swimmers—you couldn't even go on the river until you'd passed a swimming test—but exactly how good Carlton was nobody knew.

Several floating rafts had been anchored in a quiet stretch of the river to make an even platform for starting the races. The swimmers had to dive in, swim downstream, around a marker post, then head back upstream against the flow of the river. It was a tough course and one or two competitors dropped out as soon as they saw it.

Just how tough it was James didn't find out until his first race. The water was a tiny bit warmer than it had been, but it still took his breath away when he dived in. Swimming down current to the marker was easy enough, but swimming back against the current was murder; at times it felt as if he wasn't moving at all, and when competitors finally reached the rafts they were all exhausted and fighting for breath.

Carlton was in the first heat, which he won by a good ten feet, but in the second heat Hellebore was nearly twice that distance ahead of the boy behind him, and he remained the overall favorite. James got off to a good start and came in third in his heat, but he couldn't keep up with the older boys in his second heat and managed only fourth place.

There were eight boys in the final race, with four clear favorites: Hellebore, Carlton, Gellward, and Forster. Gellward was a stocky, broad-shouldered lad and Forster was the oldest boy in the tournament. The oldest and also the largest. He was a huge, loud boy with ghostly white skin and a tangle of thick black hair who was always either laughing or furious, but nowhere in between.

They lined up on the rafts and Croaker stood ready with his starting whistle. There was a large turnout of rowdy boys on the bank, ready to shout and cheer. Croaker called for quiet, but he was largely ignored. As the day had gone on, the festival atmosphere had grown.

James, his shirt sticking to his wet back and his hair still damp, joined Pritpal, Tommy, Leo Butcher, and Freddie Meyer, who were sitting on a bench.

"Bad luck," said Pritpal.

"It doesn't matter," said James. "I didn't expect to be in with a chance of winning the cup. Just so long as I do well in the cross-country."

They were interrupted by a shout of "On your marks" from Croaker, quickly followed by "Get set . . ." But before he could shout "Go!" a joker in the crowd let out a loud whistle and three of the racers dived in. There was much laughter and jeering from the boys and dark looks from most of the beaks, although James noticed that a couple of them, Mr. Merriot included, were trying to hide smiles.

Lord Hellebore was furious. "That's enough of that," he roared. "You need to take this more seriously."

One of the three embarrassed boys climbing out of the river was George. He was shaking his head and laughing, but even though it had been a practical joke, it still counted as a false start. So there was a slightly nervous mood among the swimmers now. James looked at Carlton and Hellebore. Carlton was standing, relaxed, taking the same casual approach to this race as he had done to the shooting. He was doing it for the fun of it and didn't really expect to win. Hellebore, however, had quickly stopped laughing and was now crouched in a dramatic starting position of his own, every muscle tensed, staring grimly at the slate-gray river.

He had lost all his coolness and poise from before; now he looked jittery and kept clamping his jaw. James wondered just what had been in those pills.

"On your marks . . . get set . . ."

A gasp went up. Hellebore had made another false start. He'd been so anxious to get ahead, he'd jumped the whistle for real this time. After a few moments the boys began to snigger again, but Hellebore got out of the water with such an angry look on his face that they soon stopped. James looked over at Randolph Hellebore, who was with the other judges on the rafts. His glow seemed to have dimmed a little; he was sitting tight-lipped but otherwise showing no emotions.

"Come along now, boys," said Mr. Merriot. "Concentrate. One more false start, Hellebore, and you'll be disqualified."

Hellebore threw him a very dirty look. He didn't want to be reminded.

The tension was now felt by all. James's heart was beating faster. The pressure on Hellebore must be terrible.

"On your marks, get set . . ."

James couldn't believe it: Gellward dived in before the whistle and, in his panic, Hellebore followed him. When Hellebore surfaced, he thrashed the water with his fists and cursed silently. Despite everything, James felt sorry for him. He had wanted to win so much, it had cost him the race.

Randolph had looked away, but he turned back as Croaker waddled over to the judges and they had an animated head-to-head. Mr. Merriot tried to take charge, but the furious lord was having none of it. In the end he slapped his hand down on the bench and the discussion was obviously over. Mr. Merriot stood up to make an announcement, shouting over the noise of the river and the crowd.

"We have reached an agreement. Although, technically speaking, Hellebore has had three false starts and should be excluded from the race, the judges have decided that as the first one was caused by an as-yet-unidentified boy, it cannot count as the swimmer's fault. However, it cannot be ignored, so, although Hellebore will be allowed to race, he will have a ten-second handicap. On the first whistle, the other swimmers will start, and Hellebore will start on the second whistle."

There was a rumble and a murmur of voices from the

assembled boys and much discussion, some for and some against the decision, until Merriot once more called for quiet and Croaker prepared to start the race for, surely, the last time.

In fact, if anything, the boys were so scared of having another false start that they held back, and on the first whistle they all got off a little late. Hellebore, too, waited till the second blast was well and truly sounded before he hurled himself into the water and set off at great speed after the others.

He really was a great swimmer, and his powerful front crawl soon took him past first one swimmer and then another, so that, by the time he rounded the halfway post, he'd caught up with the leaders and it looked as if it was going to be a close finish. There was no doubt that if he hadn't had the handicap, Hellebore would have won the race easily, but now it was between him, Carlton, and the big, curly-haired boy, Forster, all three pulling desperately against the flow of the mighty Thames.

"Go on, Hellebore! Come on, Carlton! Forster! Forster!" The roar from the spectators was deafening, and James added his own voice, calling for Carlton. But Carlton was tiring and slipping back, Hellebore edged level with him and was now right behind Forster. Forster must have sensed this and he managed to put on a final burst of speed, so that his hand touched the raft just a fraction of a second before the other two.

So, Forster had won, but who had come second? A hush descended on the watching boys.

One of the judges, Mr. Warburton, had been kneeling at

the edge of the raft to catch the finish. He stood up, his face ashen, then smoothed his trousers and walked nervously over to the judges where Lord Hellebore sat waiting like a giant bronze statue.

Mr. Warburton said a few words and Lord Hellebore's eyes grew wide for a moment, then he stood up.

"In first place," he growled, "Lawrence Forster. In second place . . ." He looked around the expectant racers. "Andrew Carlton . . ."

The rest of his words were drowned out as the place erupted. Nobody could have anticipated that it would be such a tremendous race and that Carlton would be a new school hero.

The talk at Codrose's that lunchtime was of little else, as the boys went over the events of the morning: Carlton's surprise result in the shooting, Hellebore's false starts, Forster's winning the swimming. Then, of course, there was excited speculation as to what would happen in the cross-country.

Pritpal had been studying the score sheets. After each event there had been much learned discussion among the boys as to how things lay and who had the best chance of winning the cup; but to make sure that there was an outright winner and that no two boys could end with the same number of points, there was a fiendishly complicated scoring system. Pritpal was one of the few boys who fully understood it.

"As we all know," he said, pushing his plate to one side, "even though Forster won the swimming, it's still between Hellebore and Carlton. But it is very close. Hellebore's upset in the river has cost him dearly."

"So, whichever of them beats the other in the cross-country wins the cup?" said Tommy.

"Not exactly," said Pritpal. "If Carlton beats Hellebore, then he wins outright. But for Hellebore it is a little more tricky."

"How d'you mean?" asked James.

"Provided Carlton finishes somewhere in the first three, then Hellebore must win the race to win the cup."

"So, in other words—unless Hellebore comes first then he hasn't got a chance?"

"Exactly. But I think he can probably beat Carlton, so that leaves only you. Can you do it, James?"

"I don't know," said James. He shoveled in a mouthful of food and thought it over while he chewed the tasteless mush. He was trying to eat as much as he could to give him energy for the race, but the food was as foul as ever: chicken pie with stringy chicken and rubbery, gray pastry with a portion of ancient, bulletlike peas and watery boiled potatoes.

He decided that he no longer felt sorry for Hellebore. After the swimming race, surrounded by his usual gang, he had behaved as badly as ever, storming about the school, complaining loudly, threatening people, and generally acting like a spoiled bully. So, perhaps, this was a way to settle everything between the two them.

"I don't know if I can beat him or not," James said at last. "But I'm going to try. Hellebore and I have some unfinished business."

CHAPTER 6—THE RACE

The forty or so boys who had entered for the cup were in a loose group, ready for the cross-country. It was a warm afternoon and James hoped that the heavy food in his stomach wouldn't make him sluggish. He jogged on the spot for a while to get his circulation going and to wake up his muscles. He was eager to get started. He knew how George Hellebore must have felt, standing ready for the swimming race, too tense to think straight.

Hellebore. How must he be feeling now? He would have counted on winning the shooting and swimming and only needing to be placed in the running. As it was, he now had to win the cross-country or he would lose the cup.

James could bear the waiting no longer; he decided to stretch his legs but, as he turned to clear himself from the crowd of boys, he almost ran straight into Lord Hellebore.

"Not so fast, young man," he said. "A little eager, aren't we?"

"Sorry," said James, and he looked up into the big man's tanned face with its glistening skin and wide mustache. Once again he was aware of the strange animal smell and the heat coming off him.

Lord Hellebore studied him, like a snake watching his prey, ready to strike. "I know you, don't I?" he said.

"I'm James Bond . . . Andrew Bond's son."

"Ah yes." Randolph's face brightened and then almost immediately clouded as he remembered.

"You're the fellow who hit me."

"Yes . . ."

Randolph swung at James as if he were going to hit him full in the teeth but pulled the punch at the last moment and grinned, though not before James once again saw a madness behind his eyes, a madness that his son had not yet learnt to control or conceal. It was well hidden in Randolph, but James caught a glimmer of it raging deep down inside him, and James wondered just what it would take to let it loose, to release the fire that was burning him up.

"Take your place and get ready for the race, boy," he said, and James gratefully hurried off into the center of the pack, where he found Carlton.

"Have you heard the news?" Carlton asked.

"What news?" said James, breathing in deeply, trying to get the wet-dog stink of Lord Hellebore out of his nostrils.

"There have been some changes over lunch, with the marshals."

The marshals were boys who were spread out around the route of the race at strategic points to keep an eye on things. It was their job to watch the runners and make sure that they didn't get lost or stray from the track.

"What sort of changes?" said James.

"A group of them have been replaced by friends of Hellebore's."

"Really?" For a moment James forgot all about running

the race as he considered what this meant. "How many?"

"Quite a few of them," said Carlton, "including Sedgepole, Wallace, and Pruitt."

"I don't like the sound of that," said James. "But surely Hellebore wouldn't consider cheating?"

"I wouldn't put it past him," said Carlton. "He's more scared of his father than of anything else. Imagine what would happen if he lost. . . ."

James glanced back at the huge figure of Lord Hellebore and remembered the madness behind his eyes. He thought about his own father: a quiet, serious, and distant man. When he was younger, James had been a little scared of him, but he couldn't imagine what it must be like to have a character like Randolph Hellebore as a father.

Mr. Merriot was wandering around among the boys, offering encouragement. He came up to James.

"All set, Bond?"

"Yes, sir. As set as I'll ever be."

"Just do your best. . . ." He smiled. "Good luck. And remember to pace yourself, it's a long race."

"I know, sir."

"I know you do."

Merriot went on his way, chatting to some of the other boys.

This was the first time a cross-country race had been run here in Windsor Great Park. A large, rowdy bunch of spectators was lined up, ready to cheer the runners on, but James knew that once the race was under way they would soon be out of sight. It was a five-mile course, beginning and ending out here in open parkland, but the heart of the race would take place up and down a series of low wooded hills.

Lord Hellebore was to start the race, and he couldn't resist making another speech.

"Sport is what makes a man of a boy. It is what prepares him for his life. Now you go out there and you run, you run as hard and as fast as you can. You may feel at times that your feet can't carry you any farther, but that's when you have to say to yourself, 'I can do it! I can go on. I will be a winner.' Although, of course, there can be only one ultimate winner."

James wasn't sure if anyone else noticed it but, as Lord Hellebore said this, he glanced very briefly at his son, whose lips twitched into a sly smile.

"Take your positions, please," Lord Hellebore bellowed, and a quietness settled over the massed runners.

"On your marks, get set . . ."

Bang!

He fired his starting pistol and the boys set off in a great unruly mob, jostling for position. The spectators yelled and whistled, but the sound of them quickly died away as they were left behind.

James held back and made his way to the side of the pack where there was more room. It was a long race and he'd practiced a great deal over this distance. He knew not to tire himself early on, but there was a big difference between practicing for a race and actually running it. There were all sorts of extra factors to consider in a real race: nerves, tension, excitement, the other runners, the weather, the condition of the ground. . . . James would have preferred a cooler day, but the weather was the same for all of them and it wouldn't give any runner a particular advantage. It had rained a lot during the last few weeks, so the ground was soft, which could cause difficulties, but at least it felt light and springy underfoot.

After a few minutes the field opened out, the weaker runners falling behind and a small pack forming at the front. James increased his speed, passing several laggers, until he was comfortably settled in at the rear of the leading group. He spotted Carlton and Hellebore pounding away at the front, as well as Gellward and Forster and several other of the older boys, some of whom were already growing tired and beginning to pant and wheeze a little.

James checked his own body, almost as a detached observer, and he was pleased to report that he felt fine, coasting along comfortably, with plenty held in reserve. So far the race was going according to plan.

As they hit the first major hill, two or three of the leaders slowed down and dropped back, which encouraged James. He dug his feet into the soft ground and almost flew up the slope. As they sped down the far side, the gaps between the runners widened, so that the leading group was getting very strung out. James measured his steps, keeping them even, working his body just as much as felt safe. In the weeks since the underwater swimming race with Butcher, the chubby horn-player had been working with him every day on his breathing. He pictured his lungs expanding and contracting like a mechanical pump, smooth and regular, filling slowly with air, extracting the precious oxygen, then releasing the spent gas in a long, even flow, but the signs of stress were beginning to show: there was a rawness in his throat and his heart was hammering away in his chest like a blacksmith at the forge, forcing the blood to his hungry, aching leg-muscles—but in a way the pain felt good. He was on his own, running against himself as much as against the other boys.

They came to the second hill, which passed without incident, then the third and biggest of them all, Parson's Hill, where there was a hard climb up a winding track through the trees, which got steeper as it rose. James had to shorten his steps, and for the first time he could feel his body really straining. No matter, it was a strain he could deal with. He could certainly cope better than Gellward, whom he had been running behind and using as a pacemaker; halfway up, the stocky boy stopped and bent over, clutching his side and gasping for air. James passed him and even put on a bit of speed, so he was soon behind the next runner.

There was a short flat section at the top of the hill before the even steeper descent, where two marshals stood counting the runners. James glanced from side to side—they were Sedgepole and Pruitt, but he thought nothing of it as he was concentrating fully on his running.

The top of Parson's Hill marked the halfway point and, as they came down the other side, the going got very tough. The track was made up of loose dirt and shingle, plus some larger stones that the lead runners had already kicked to life. James had to be very careful not to lose his footing, and all he could do was focus on his feet directly in front of him. He lost track of most of the other boys but, in the mad scramble down the slope, he saw another runner fall and go skidding and sliding off into bushes. James slowed down; it would be terrible to go out of the race through a silly and careless accident, but he got down without mishap and joined the tail of the leading group.

He looked around. There was Carlton, and Forster, but where was Hellebore? What had happened to him in the scramble down the hill? James glanced behind him. Gellward was leading a second, smaller pack of runners. Hellebore might be one of them; they were too far back for him to see clearly. . . . Or was it possible that he had gotten in front? What if, even now, he was streaking ahead by himself? James knew that the hardest part of the course was behind them, so he could risk pulling forward and setting the pace for a while. He urged his body on and steadily moved through the pack of puffing boys until he was level with the leader, Carlton, who turned and made a face at him that said, "This is tough, isn't it?"

"Have you seen Hellebore?" James panted.

Carlton shook his head.

"Is there anyone ahead of us?" James asked.

"Not sure . . ." Carlton grunted. "Don't think so."

There was only one way to find out. James increased his speed still more and left the others behind. Now he was truly alone, out ahead by himself and running faster than he had wanted to at this stage. He must save some strength for the final long, straight haul up to the finishing line. But where was Hellebore? James cursed himself for not paying more attention as he came down Parson's Hill.

He pounded up the next, mercifully smaller, hill, took a great wide turn and was suddenly aware of something moving off to his right, through the bushes. He glanced up; it had been a streak of white but now it was gone. There was a long, high ridge running alongside the track that would have extended all the way from the top of Parson's Hill. Could it have been a boy? Another runner? Surely not. He must have imagined it.

He accelerated and tore around a tight corner between steep banks, and there, just ahead of him, was Hellebore! But it was not possible that James could have caught up with him so quickly. If George had been on the track ahead, James would definitely have seen him before now.

There was only one explanation.

Hellebore must have cheated and taken a shortcut; instead of coming down the hill he had nipped off to the side, knowing that the other runners would have been too busy trying not to fall over to notice him. James crackled through a pile of twigs and fallen wood and Hellebore heard him. He glanced back and looked very surprised to see James catching up with him fast.

James spotted a course marshal ahead of them. If Hellebore had taken a shortcut, this boy would surely have seen, but as they drew nearer James saw with disappointment that it was Wallace, standing there scratching his big square head, a self-satisfied smirk plastered across his lips.

Suddenly Hellebore staggered to a halt and clutched his chest.

James slowed down.

"Are you all right?" he said.

"Stitch," said Hellebore bluntly. "I'll be fine. . . ."

James ran on. Well, if he had been cheating, it had gotten him nowhere. James grinned, but his happiness was short-lived. He'd used up a lot of energy scouting ahead, and now he felt utterly worn out. His body, which had seemed so light before, now felt like a dead weight. Never mind, he was confident that he was in the lead, so he could afford to slow down slightly, since the main pack must still be some way behind, and Hellebore appeared to have stopped altogether.

He took long, easy strides and as he broke free of the thick overhead branches of oak and beech and entered a small clearing he felt the sun warm on his back. The leaves of the trees were lit up, bright yellow and gold, and the sky above was a beautiful clear blue. He turned his face up and breathed in the soft air—and then he saw it again: a streak of white off to one side. He stopped and peered down through the trees. It was Hellebore. He'd taken another shortcut. The track here followed a wide sweep around the side of a hill, but Hellebore had gone crashing through the undergrowth straight down the side, cutting off the whole corner. That was why he'd pretended to have a stitch, so that James wouldn't see him leave the track.

The only person who would have known was Wallace.

What to do now? The code of honor of the school meant that he couldn't accuse Hellebore of cheating, particularly as the only witness was Wallace, who could deny everything.

Damn him. This wasn't fair.

James turned and ran back up the track. He had to tell Carlton and the others. Soon he saw Carlton running alone and he waited for him to catch up. Carlton slowed to a grateful stop and rested his hands on his knees. "What's the matter?" he said, his voice broken and husky.

"It's Hellebore," said James. "He's cheating. I saw him take a shortcut down the hill."

"Typical." Carlton straightened up and peered into the trees. "He wants to win so much, he doesn't care how he does it. Well, that's that, then," he spat. "We can't catch him."

"I could," said James. "If I followed him, I might catch up. . . . But then, I'd be cheating too."

"Not really," said Carlton, smiling. "You had this race in the bag, Bond. I could never have caught you if you hadn't come back." Carlton smiled. "Go after him. He deserves it, the dirty cheat."

"Are you sure?"

"Go on . . . I'll square it with the others. See you at the finishing line."

James took a deep breath and leapt over the side of the path down into bushes, all his pain and tiredness forgotten.

There was no track here, so he had to pick his way through boulders and shrubs and fallen logs in a crazy headlong rush down the slope. At one point he tripped and went spinning, head over heels, through a patch of nettles, badly stinging his face and arms, but he barely felt it; all he was thinking about was catching up with Hellebore.

In a minute he came back onto the track. He'd missed out a long stretch, but where was the other boy?

There! A couple of hundred yards or so ahead, lumbering down the path toward the edge of the forest and the open parkland and the finishing line beyond.

For a moment James felt desperately weak and tired. George had missed out two sections of the track, so he hadn't run nearly as far as James, who had also been forced to run back a fair distance to meet Carlton, burning up both energy and time.

Well, this was a real test, then. Could he catch up with George?

He wasn't going to give up now. He was at least going to try.

James forced his feet to run faster, his lungs to breathe deeper, his heart pushed the blood around his aching system quicker. He could barely feel his legs, they were like jelly, separate from the rest of his body. He worried that they might just pack up and collapse under him.

This was the hardest thing he had ever done. None of his training could have prepared him for this. His body was telling him to stop, telling him that it couldn't go on, that he had used up every last drop of strength; but his mind was telling him to keep going. He wasn't going to be told what to do by his stupid body.

He could do it.

Up ahead, Hellebore was nearly at the edge of the trees now, but he was tired too; he had slowed right down and was struggling to keep going.

The ground took one last dip downward. James growled through his clenched teeth and found another pocket of strength from somewhere. It was like breaking through an invisible barrier—suddenly he was racing forward, his feet gliding over the ground.

He was going to do it. He was going to get past Hellebore.

Hellebore finally became aware—too late—that there was someone behind him. He looked back and his red face twisted with fear and anger. Still James raced on. Nothing could stop him. He was level, and now he was pulling ahead.

In his anger and frustration, Hellebore tried to trip James up, lashing out with a leg, but James's senses were on full alert and he simply hopped higher as Hellebore's foot passed harmlessly beneath him. In the process, however, the American tripped himself up and went tumbling off the path into a boggy patch of mud and rotten logs. James heard a splash behind him but didn't risk looking back. He hadn't won the race yet.

Then he was out into the light and he could see the spectators way up ahead and hear their faint shouts. His vision was blurring, everything swimming in and out of focus, his blood whistling in his ears with the sound of a waterfall. He was covered in sweat, which was thick and oily on his skin. It stung his eyes, it dripped into his gaping mouth, it filled his running shoes.

He tried to keep his pace up, but faltered. It was too much, he'd pushed himself too far. He slowed down, closed his eyes and a wave of blackness crashed over him. He was asleep on his feet.

But then a tiny voice spoke up at the back of his mind. "Come on, Bond," it said. "Keep going . . ."

No, wait a minute, he recognized that voice. He opened his eyes and looked to one side; and there was his little group of friends—Pritpal, Tommy Chong, Butcher . . . and there was Mr. Merriot; it was *his* voice that James had heard.

"Come on, Bond . . . keep moving!"

"Go on, James," yelled Pritpal. "There's no one can catch you!"

James glanced back; there was no sign of Hellebore. It was a clear run home. That cheered him up. He was able to summon one final burst of energy . . . and he was home, staggering across the finishing line, the tape wrapped around his chest. He wobbled on for a few steps, then fell to the ground, surrounded by a group of cheering boys. He closed his eyes once again, and for a moment he was bobbing in the waves crashing on a sunny beach somewhere a million miles away . . . but then all the pain he'd been holding back flooded in, from his ruined muscles, the stings on his face and arms, his scalded throat, his tattered lungs. He groaned and someone helped him to his feet.

It was Mr. Merriot.

"Don't lie there, Bond, you'll seize up."

"Sorry, sir."

"Don't apologize, boy. You've won. I knew you could do it."

"Who . . . who came second, sir?"

"They're only just coming in now." Mr. Merriot pointed and James looked back to see Carlton, plodding doggedly along, an expression of mingled pain and concentration on his face, and, behind him, covered in green mud and limping badly, was Hellebore.

The boys cheered them in. Carlton was lifted into the air by his supporters, who knew that the cup was his, and Hellebore fell to his knees, his face in his hands. He was alone. All his friends were out on the track and only his father was here.

Lord Hellebore took one look at his son, in third place, the loser, and turned away, disgusted.

It was an awful thing to see.

George Hellebore raised his face toward his father and

James saw that he was crying. Tears had made little tracks through the mud plastered to his cheeks.

"I did my best, Dad. . . ."

But his father wasn't listening.

George suddenly turned and glared at James. "You," he said, getting to his feet.

"Forget it," said James. "It's all over."

George limped over to him. "You could never have caught up with me, Bond," he said. "Unless . . ."

"Unless what?" said James as boys began to gather around them, sensing a fight. "Unless I'd cheated? Is that what you were going to say, Hellebore?" James stared into the boy's red eyes. "Are you accusing me of being a cheat?"

George looked around at the other boys, then down at his feet.

"No," he muttered. Then he turned and pushed his way through the crowd. Someone started to laugh, then someone else did, until all of them were laughing, and George Hellebore hunched his back and appeared to shrink.

But James couldn't join in the laughter. A bitter taste had come into his mouth.

This wasn't the end. From now on, things could only get worse.

Dearest James,

*I am afraid that your poor Uncle Max is not getting any
better and I do not feel that I can leave him just at the moment.
I therefore think that it would be for the best if you made the
journey up to Scotland and spent your Easter holidays with us
here in Keithly. I am sure that it would do your uncle the power
of good to have a young person about the place and I must
confess that I have missed you terribly. I am enclosing your ticket
and some extra money for food. I can't tell you how much I am
looking forward to seeing you again.*

Your loving aunt,
Charmian

James was on the train to London, rereading the letter
from his aunt. The last two weeks of the half had passed
without incident as life at the school returned to normal.
Despite his fears, James kept his head down and managed to
keep out of George Hellebore's way altogether.

Before the cup, he had been concentrating so hard on his
running that he had almost forgotten about his studies, and
his brief moment of fame as the winner of the cross-country
race soon faded. It was back to the reality of the daily slog—

early school, breakfast, chapel, then classes in the various odd buildings scattered around town: New Schools, Queen's, Warre, Caxton, Drill Hall, and all the others that he had had to memorize. He still got lost at least twice a day.

At twelve he would lug his books to pupil-room and work away on Latin grammar and writing Latin verses and countless other deathly dull exercises under the amused eye of Mr. Merriot, with only Codrose's awful lunch to look forward to. After lunch he would wander in the town or play sports or work alone in his room, and on two days a week there would be more lessons: Latin, mathematics, history, French, English . . . one after the other in dreary succession. And the rules: never roll your umbrella, never be seen chewing in the street, never turn down the collar of your coat. . . . It was a relief to be getting away from it all.

And it was a relief to be back in his own clothes. He hated the stifling school uniform with its itchy trousers, stiff collar, and awkward little tie. He hated the ridiculous top hat and the waistcoat. He was wearing a plain-blue, short-sleeved cotton shirt and gray flannel trousers and he felt like he was himself again, not someone pretending to be a smart schoolboy.

He was sharing his compartment with three other boys, including Butcher the horn-player, and they were all chatting excitedly about their plans for the short holiday.

"I expect I shall have a pretty quiet time of it," said James. "Stuck up in the wilds of Scotland with only grown-ups for company."

"Oh, I should think I shall have an equally boring time in London," said Butcher. "My eldest brother's away in the navy, so I'll be all on my own with my mother and father. Although, they have promised to take me to a concert on Saturday at Royal Albert Hall."

James smiled but said nothing. Butcher didn't know how lucky he was, to be returning home to his old familiar house and the love of his parents. That was something that James would never be able to do again.

James folded his letter away. It was best not to dwell on these things.

At Paddington Station he said good-bye to his traveling companions and dragged his suitcase down the escalator to the Underground station, from where he was to travel across London to meet his connection at King's Cross.

The train was packed and uncomfortable and filled with the thick, choking smoke from a hundred cigarettes and pipes which turned the air yellow. James couldn't find a seat and stood up as best he could, rattled and jolted from side to side as the rickety carriage trundled beneath the streets of London. It was a huge relief to finally arrive and come up out of the smoky depths into the wide-open spaces of King's Cross station with its great roof of iron and glass.

He had nearly an hour to wait before his next train, so once he'd checked the platform number he bought himself a cup of coffee and a bun in the station café, where he spent some time sitting in the warm, steamy fug, surrounded by noisy chatter and entertained by the various comings and goings of the other travelers.

James liked to watch people, to try to work out everything he could about them from how they looked and the way they walked and talked. He invented whole lives for them. The man over there, huddling in the corner behind a suitcase, was a master criminal, plotting a robbery; the woman over there in the fur coat and cheap pearls had murdered her husband and was waiting to meet her lover so that they could run away together; the man over there with all the luggage was a famous explorer off to the Arctic. . . .

Just after seven o'clock James heard a distorted echoing voice booming out of the tannoy system. . . .

"The seven thirty-nine London and North Eastern Railway sleeping car express to Fort William via Edinburgh is ready for boarding on platform six. . . ."

James got up and lugged his suitcase out of the café and along to where a line of people was filing past the ticket collector at the platform entrance. As he got nearer, he noticed a skinny, red-haired boy of about sixteen hanging around the edges of the crowd, trying hard to act casual and to blend in with the other passengers.

James joined the end of the queue and the boy sidled up to him.

"'Ere," he said in an unmistakable Cockney accent, scratching his untidy red hair. "You couldn't do us a favor, could you, mate?"

"What sort of a favor?" asked James.

"Nothing much, it's just I've gone and lost me ticket and I need to get past the bloke. You couldn't, like, keep him busy for me, couldya?"

James wasn't sure he believed the boy, but there was something appealing about him. He was half smiling, as if he knew that James didn't believe his story for one minute but might think it was a good game anyway. Although a few years older than James, he was wasn't much bigger and he had a scrunched-up, wiry body and quick, clever eyes.

"I'll see what I can do," said James.

"Ta," said the boy and he winked.

When it came to James's turn to hand over his ticket, he pretended that he'd lost it and fumbled for it in all his pockets. When he eventually found it, he began to ask the man at the gate a series of complicated questions about the train. At first the railwayman answered them quite happily, but then he grew more and more impatient as the queue of people built up behind James, who finally dropped his suitcase onto the poor man's foot. In the confusion, the red-haired boy slipped past them and strolled off toward the train, chatting with an elderly couple who obviously had never seen him before in their lives.

"Sorry," said James as the ticket collector rubbed his foot and tried not to lose his temper.

"Never mind that," he said. "Run along and get on the bleeding train, or we'll be here all night."

James smiled to himself as he made his way along the platform. Up ahead the huge steam engine hissed and grumbled, waiting to be off. It panted softly and slowly, sending great clouds of steam wafting back down the platform.

James soon found his carriage. It was just behind the dining car that divided the rear part of the train from the first-class carriages at the front. He opened the door and climbed aboard, then made his way along the narrow corridor until he found the right compartment. He turned the handle and went in. Inside, was a tiny washbasin and two narrow bunks. The top bunk was folded away just now so that the lower one made a bench seat. James sat down and settled himself in for the long journey to Scotland.

He got his book out of his suitcase; the latest Bulldog Drummond adventure story. He read a few lines but found he couldn't concentrate and fell to staring out the window and watching the last few passengers hurrying to catch the train. He was amused to see two porters wheeling trolleys loaded with all manner of bags and suitcases, and he wondered to which pampered aristocrat they belonged. But, as it turned out, the bags didn't belong to any grand duke or duchess, but to a boy, and not just any boy, but to George Hellebore, who was striding along behind the porters shouting orders at them.

James sighed. "Oh, no." What luck, to have to share a train with his worst enemy. He tried to relax. After all, Hellebore would be in one of the first-class carriages, so there was no reason the two of them need ever bump into each other on the long journey.

He picked up his book again just as the guard outside shouted, "All aboard!" and blew his whistle. There was an answering whistle from the mighty engine and the train gave a great lurch forward. He felt the carriages jolt and shunt into one another, and then they were off. The engine puffed and wheezed like a fat man climbing the stairs and then the distinctive *di-dum di-dum* of the wheels bumping over the joins in the rails began, gradually picking up speed and mingling with the accelerating coughs of the engine.

The familiar comforting music and gentle rocking movement of the train lulled James and he began to feel pleasantly sleepy. Even though it was still early, he yawned and closed his eyes for a moment, but then a knock at the door made him look up.

"Come in," he said, and the door was opened by the red-haired boy who had sneaked onto the train.

"There you are," he said, and grinned at James, showing a set of sharp, yellow teeth. "I've been looking all over for you. I just wanted to say thanks and all that."

"It's all right," said James. "Don't mention it."

"No, it was a stand-up thing to do, mate." The boy stuck out his hand. "Me name's Kelly. 'Red' Kelly, on behalf of me hair. And 'cause it sounds a bit like Ned Kelly, the Aussie outlaw with the bucket on his head."

James shook his hand. "James Bond," he said simply.

"Pleased to meet you, Jimmy. You don't mind if I sit here for a minute, do you?"

"No, that's all right," said James.

"You going all the way to Scotland, are you, then?" Kelly sat down.

"Yes. Fort William."

"Never been up that way, myself. You been before?"

"My father was from Scotland. I've been a couple of times on holiday."

"Nice, is it?"

"Yes," said James. "I suppose so. It can be quite cold and wet, and in the summer the midges eat you alive, but I like it."

"To tell you the truth," said Kelly, looking out the window at the houses whizzing by, "this is the farthest I've ever been from home. I stay pretty much in London. Summertime we go down to Kent for the hop-picking, and I've been down Margate a couple of times, but this is all new to me, sleeping on a train and that."

"Why are you going to Scotland?" asked James. "Have you got family there?"

"I got family everywhere, mate. Irish originally, come over last century to work on the railways. This line was probably half built by my lot. They went where the work was, spread out all over. I've an aunt up in a place called Keithly."

"Really?" said James. "Me, too. Well, an uncle, but my aunt's up there with him at the moment."

"Nah, you're having me on."

"No. Honestly."

"Small world."

James thought about Hellebore, sitting up at the front of the train somewhere. "It certainly is," he said.

"Reason I'm going up," said Kelly, sniffing, "I've got a cousin, see? Alfie. I've met him only the once, when he come down to London to meet the folks. Nice kid. Only he's gone missing."

"Missing?"

"Yeah, nobody knows for sure what's happened. He was fishing somewhere, they reckon, 'cause his gear was all gone from the house. But he never told his mum where he was going, so they're not really sure. She's right upset, she is, and nobody seems to be doing sod all about it. So I've thought I'll go and have a butcher's, see what's what. We have to look out for ourselves, us Kellys—the coppers don't like us, the judges don't like us, the toffee-nosed posh nobs in their big houses don't like us, sometimes I don't think nobody likes us." Kelly sniffed again.

"So what do you think might have happened to him?"

"I don't know, maybe he fell in a river and drowned hisself, but I aim to find out—just so long as I can get there."

"Well, anything I can do to help."

"There is one thing." Kelly leaned in closer and spoke quietly to James. "Do you think you could hide me?"

"Hide you?"

"When the ticket collector comes around."

James looked at Kelly. What was he getting himself into? Kelly was a wild card, but James found it hard not to like him—there was so much humor in his face, and he had a great fighting spirit about him. James thought that in different circumstances, born into a different family, it could so easily be him sitting there instead of Kelly. But he very much didn't want to risk being thrown off the train or worse, getting into trouble with the police.

"Don't worry," said Kelly, slapping him on the knee. "Anything happens, I'll cover for you, say I made you do it at gunpoint or something."

"Gunpoint?"

"Well, all right, say I threatened to smack you about the head. . . . Don't worry, I'm not going to."

James laughed. "Come on," he said. "There must be somewhere we can hide you."

So it was that twenty minutes later, when the collector stuck his head around the door and asked to see his ticket, James found himself sitting on the bench seat with Kelly folded into the bunk above him, his scrawny body squashed flat against the wall.

"Is it just me in here tonight?" James asked the man, who checked his list.

"Aye, you're all right, son," he said in a broad Glasgow accent. "It's a quiet night. You've got the place to yourself."

James smiled innocently—little did the man know.

When the coast was clear, James rescued Kelly from his hiding place. He was red-faced, sweating, and gasping for air, but they'd gotten away with it.

Later on, using the money his Aunt Charmian had sent him, James ate in the dining car, all the while keeping an eye open for George Hellebore. There was no sign of him, but James wolfed down his food as quickly as he could and stuffed his pockets with bread rolls, fruit, and a couple of sausages wrapped in a napkin for the stowaway in his compartment.

When he got back, Kelly was very grateful for the provisions and greedily stuffed his face.

"Where d'you think we are now?" he said, his mouth full of bread.

"We've been through Grantham," said James. "The next stop is York. . . ." How dull those names sounded. James pictured all those gray English towns whizzing past with their rows of little houses. How much more exciting it would be to be traveling through Europe, how much more romantic those names would sound: Paris, Venice, Budapest, Istanbul. . . .

He stood up. "I'm going to go to the lav before I turn in," he said.

"Good idea," said Kelly. "I'll need the bog myself in a minute."

James left the compartment and wobbled down the corridor, swaying with the movement of the train, but when he got to the toilet he found that it was engaged. He slid the corridor window down for a blast of cold, fresh air and gazed out into the darkness, trying to picture the scenery.

He heard the toilet flush and turned as the door clicked open.

George Hellebore came out. He must have been having a late supper in the dining car. James almost laughed at the expression on the boy's face, which made him look as if he'd just seen the Loch Ness monster.

"Hello," said James. "Fancy us both being on the same train."

Hellebore grabbed him and slammed him back against the door.

"What are you doing here?" he said.

James laughed. "What do you think I'm doing?" he said. "I'm going to Scotland. Same as you."

"I ought to open this door and throw you off the train," said Hellebore.

"Sorry," said James. "I didn't realize there was a law against sharing a train with you."

"I've been dreaming about ways to kill you ever since that damned race."

"Don't you think you're overdoing it?" said James. "It was only a running race. You tried to cheat, and it didn't work."

Without warning, Hellebore suddenly punched James in the stomach, forcing all the air out of his lungs and making him double up in pain. Then, as he was bent over, Hellebore slapped him viciously across the back of the head with both hands. James lost his temper at this and lashed out with his shoe, catching Hellebore on the shin.

Hellebore yelled and staggered back.

"Just for that," he snarled, "I *am* going to kill you."

Hellebore grabbed hold of him and wrestled him back over to the door and, before James could stop him, he had stuck his head and shoulders out the open window.

James was battered by a freezing blast of wind in his face. It stung his eyes and blinded him with tears. There was a deafening roar and the *swish-swish-swish* of trackside posts just inches from his head. The air was thick with the smell of smoke and steam and coal and the engine whistle let out a long scream as it warned of an approaching tunnel.

"Stop it, Hellebore," James yelled, his voice barely audible. "Stop it, you idiot!"

At last George pulled him back in. He was laughing crazily.

"Scared, huh?"

"Of course I was scared. You could have knocked my head off. That was a bloody stupid thing to do."

"But I told you, Bond, I'm going to kill you."

A familiar voice broke in. "No you're not."

James looked around to see Kelly standing there. He stared at Hellebore with such a look of scorn that James was glad he was on his side.

"It's two against one," Kelly went on, "and I think I'd better warn you, I fight dirty."

Hellebore looked confused. He obviously didn't know what to make of Kelly. There was something in the way the flame-haired boy stood and held his stare that warned him not to push it any further. Hellebore huffed and then barged past Kelly, returning to the dining car.

Kelly raised an eyebrow. "Can't leave you alone for a minute, can I, Jimmy-boy?"

Later on, lying in their bunks in the half-light of the sleeping compartment, Kelly asked James what was going on.

"Nothing," said James. "He was just a boy from school. We don't exactly get on."

"I can see that. Where'd you go to school, anyway?"

"Eton," said James.

"Ooh, lah-di-dah," said Kelly, leaning over the edge of the bunk and pushing his nose up with one finger to make a snooty face. "I wouldn't have had you down as one of them toffs. But you're all right, mate. I like you. Come on." He grinned. "Let's get some shut-eye, I'll see you in Scotland."

James lay there, rocked gently from side to side, and tried to sleep, but he found that he was wide awake. A procession of confused thoughts marched through his brain: thoughts about Eton, about the strange boy in the bunk above, about Hellebore and Scotland, and about his mother and father.

He never talked about his parents to anyone. He kept them to himself and he liked it that way. But there was a lot going on in his life, confusing things and he wished his parents were there to help make sense of it all.

He missed them. He missed them terribly.

Every child thinks that their own life is normal, as it is all they have ever known and they have nothing to compare it to. James Bond was no exception, even though his childhood had been far from normal.

His father, Andrew Bond, was originally from Glencoe in the west of Scotland but, after leaving home at the age of twelve to go to boarding school, he had never returned. From school he had gone straight on to study chemistry at the University of St. Andrews, but his education was interrupted by the Great War of 1914 when the whole of Europe, and eventually the world, was thrown into bloody turmoil.

Andrew hadn't thought twice about it; he had joined the Royal Navy at the first opportunity and, having survived numerous sea-battles, a sinking, and a last-minute rescue from the icy waters of the north Atlantic, he had ended the war as Captain of his own battleship, HMS *Faithful*. He lost many friends in the war, and it hardened him and left him with a restless spirit and a will to experience all that life had to offer.

After the war he was offered a job at Vickers, a firm that made and sold weapons. He traveled around Europe, talking to governments, generals, and politicians, trying to convince them that they should buy arms made by his company. For two years he lived in hotels, but on one trip he met a beautiful young woman, Monique Delacroix, the daughter of a wealthy Swiss industrialist, and soon afterward asked her to marry him. They tried to settle down and lead an ordinary life, but Andrew was constantly on the move. James was born in Zurich, and by the age of six had lived in Switzerland, Italy, France, and London. But as James got older, Monique put her foot down. She would live the life of a gypsy no longer. Andrew could travel as much as he wished, but Monique wanted a permanent home for herself and her young son.

For the next few years, James and his mother lived half of the time in a flat in Chelsea, and the other half in a large house in the countryside outside Basle, Switzerland. James went to school in Basle and became fluent in English, French, and German, although at the time he didn't think that there was anything unusual in this.

James was an only child and, because the family was constantly on the move, he had to make friends quickly and be prepared to lose them equally fast. Although he was a popular boy and found the business of forming friendships easy, he quickly learnt to entertain himself, and for much of the time was content with his own company.

His father still worked hard, which meant that he was often away from home for long periods, and when he wasn't working, he liked to lose himself in tough physical activity. Andrew's idea of a holiday was to go skiing, climbing, horseback riding, or sailing. Although James would occasionally be allowed to go with his parents, most of the time it was considered too dangerous for a young boy. But he had had one memorable holiday in Jamaica, where he had learnt to swim, and there was that happy summer in northern Italy, when he had been taught to ride a horse and fire a gun. For the most part, however, he was left behind.

After being alone with his mother for many months, it was always a wrench when she left him to go off on one of her adventures with his father. How well he remembered those partings, as his mother would clutch him tightly and whisper in his ear, "I don't want to go, James. I always miss you so, but what am I to do? I love you both. I want to be with you and I want to be with your father. . . . You have me for most of the year, now it is your father's turn. Don't worry, I'll be back before you know it."

He would feel her tears wet his cheek and would smile bravely and tell her that it didn't matter, that he didn't mind so much. She tried her best to make him comfortable, but in truth he hated her leaving, and over the years he had made a succession of nursemaids and nannies miserable. He didn't like to be told what to do, and they were no substitute for his real mother.

Often when his parents were away he would stay with one of his mother's numerous relatives. She came from a large family and seemed to have aunts, uncles, sisters, brothers, and cousins dotted all around Europe. There was even a branch of the family that had emigrated to Australia.

His father's family was smaller, and consisted of his younger brother, Max, whom James barely knew, and his sister, Charmian.

Aunt Charmian was James's favorite relative and he always enjoyed staying with her. She had a small house southeast of London, near Canterbury, in a tiny village called Pett Bottom, a name that always made James smile. Charmian had no children of her own and she treated James like an adult, letting him get on with things without constantly interfering.

Charmian was an anthropologist; she had studied many different peoples and cultures around the world, and her house was stuffed with paintings and books and odd objects that she'd collected on her travels. She was very well read and could talk to James about almost anything and, what's more, make it interesting. There was always music playing on her gramophone or the radio and exotic food bubbling on the stove.

James felt completely at home in Pett Bottom, where he'd spend his days exploring the local countryside, building dens, getting lost in the fields, and constructing elaborate dams in the little stream that ran behind the house.

James had no reason to think that moving from country to country, staying with odd relatives for long periods of time, speaking several languages, and rarely seeing his father was in any way unusual. So he was surprised when his aunt Charmian said to him one day, "You're a strange boy, James. I would have thought most boys in your position would be rather unhappy."

James was eleven at the time, and it was summer. His mother and father were on a climbing holiday in Aiguilles Rouges, above the skiing resort of Chamonix in France. They would be gone for three weeks, and James had been packed off to England again to spend the time with his aunt. He'd said good-bye to his parents at the station in Basle at the start of his long voyage by train and boat. His mother had kissed him twice in the European fashion, and his father had shaken his hand once in the Scottish fashion. As the train pulled away, James had looked back and seen them standing there, waving, his father tall and serious-looking, his mother elegant and pretty in a fashionable outfit. But before they were out of sight his father had turned and led his mother away, and they had disappeared into a cloud of steam.

James had frowned across the table at his aunt and wondered at her question. Charmian Bond was tall and thin like his father, and although James didn't know a great deal about these matters, he felt that she was beautiful. She had jet-black hair, gray eyes, and she seemed neither young nor old. Maybe that was because she had no children of her own.

"Why should I be unhappy?" James had asked.

"Oh, I'm not saying that you should be. I'm happy that you're not, but you're forever being shunted around Europe like a piece of lost luggage, and now, here you are once again, having to spend the summer with a dry, old stick like me."

"I like you, Aunt Charmian," James said bluntly. "I like it here in Pett Bottom. I like your house. I like your cooking."

"Ah, you're a charmer, James. You know the way to a woman's heart, and you'll no doubt break a few when you get the chance."

James blushed.

"But I do feel that life here can't be very exciting for a young lad," Charmian added.

James shrugged. He didn't know what to say. He'd never really thought about it before, he usually just got on with things.

Charmian stood up and began to tidy away the dirty dishes. "How about tomorrow we drive into Canterbury and visit the picture-house?"

"That would be fun," said James, who liked going to the cinema.

"They're showing an old Douglas Fairbanks film, *The Iron Mask*. Have you seen it? I think he plays D'Artagnan, rescuing the true king of France from scheming villains."

"I've not seen it," said James. "But I liked *The Three Musketeers*."

"I should imagine there'll be plenty of swinging on chandeliers, jumping off high walls, and engaging in all sorts of wild swordplay." Charmian picked up a carving knife and brandished it at James, and he fought back with his spoon.

After supper, James had gone outside to enjoy the rest of the day. It was a perfect summer's evening, and the setting sun sent a golden glow over the fields. Inspired by thoughts of Douglas Fairbanks, James left the back garden by a little gate in the wall and went into the small orchard behind the house to finish building a rope swing that he'd hung above the stream from a thick branch. He'd just tried it for the first time and was about to shorten the rope when he saw his aunt coming through the gate, followed by two uncomfortable-looking policemen.

"James," she said, trying to hide the catch in her voice. "I'm afraid something's happened."

The policemen looked so funny and awkward that James almost laughed. He tried to think if he'd done anything wrong. . . . He'd scrumped some pears from an orchard down the road, he'd thrown some stones at an abandoned greenhouse at the back of the Williams's Farm, but surely that wasn't serious enough to warrant a visit from the local police.

He climbed down out of the tree and went over to them.

"It concerns your mother and father. . . ." said Charmian and, as he got nearer, James saw that there were tears in her eyes.

"What's happened?" said James, who suddenly felt very cold and strange.

"It's all right, Miss Bond," said one of the policemen. "The lad doesn't need to know all the details."

"Yes he does," his aunt snapped angrily. "He has to know. He's old enough. We have always treated him as an adult and never kept anything from him. They'd want him to know. . . ."

She paused, too upset to carry on, and looked away briefly, before pulling her shoulders back and turning to face the policeman.

"It's all right, you may go," she said to the visibly relieved men, and wiped her eyes. "I can deal with this."

"Very well, madam," said the more senior of the two policemen and, after one last confused glance at James, they had left.

"Come and sit with me, James," his aunt said, settling on an ancient wooden bench covered with whorls of colored lichen.

James joined her and for a moment they sat in silence, looking out past the stream and over the cornfields to where a flock of crows flapped about noisily.

"There's been an accident," said Charmian. "Nobody

knows yet exactly what happened, but your mother and father, they . . ." she sniffed. "Sorry. They won't be coming home, James."

"What do you mean?" said James, who knew what she meant but didn't want to believe what he was hearing.

"There's no pretty word for it," said Charmian, "and no easy way to say it, so I will be blunt. They are both dead. They were climbing. There was a fall. Their bodies were found at the foot of the mountain. . . ."

The rest of what she said passed in a blur, the words tumbling toward him, not making any sense, and James not wanting them to make sense, hoping it was all a joke. . . . And all the time, that one simple but terrible word kept repeating in his head.

"Dead."

He hadn't realized at the time how final that word was. How two people so familiar to him, who he'd taken so much for granted, who he'd thought would always be there, simply weren't there anymore, and would never be there again.

Because they were dead.

Two years had passed since then. Sometimes he could hardly remember what his parents had looked like. He'd picture them standing on the platform waving to him, but their faces were unclear, and before he could make them out they would turn and disappear once more into the steam. Then sometimes he would dream about them and they would be very clear to him and very much alive, and he'd wonder why he had ever thought that they were dead. He would get desperately upset and hug his mother and apologize to her, but always, before she spoke, he would wake up and be left feeling angry and cheated.

The dreams were less frequent now. He could cope with them better, but nothing could ever make up for his loss.

Of course, he'd had arguments with his mother and taken her for granted. But he'd always known that if he cut his knee or felt unwell, she would be there to pick him up and hold him and tell him that everything was going to be all right.

And he wished that he had known his father better, but he'd so often been away. Whenever he came back, however, he'd never forget to bring James some small gift—chocolate or a toy soldier or a book. James smiled as he remembered waiting at the top of the stairs in his pajamas for the sound of his father's key in the lock, then he'd run down and wait impatiently for his father to produce the little wrapped packet, while he teased James all the while—"Now where did I put it? Oh, I think I may have forgotten it. . . ."—and then produced it like a magician. "Aha, here it is!"

But the house was sold, and his mother would never again hold him, and his father would never again be coming home. James was alone in the world now and he would have to make it on his own. Sure, it made him tough, but at times like this he would have traded in all his toughness for five more minutes with his mother and father.

In *his* sleeping berth at the front of the train, George Hellebore lay on his bunk and shivered. He couldn't stop it— his whole body was shaking. He hadn't spoken to his father since the race, and he dreaded meeting him. He hoped that the train would never arrive, that he could just rattle on into the endless night on a journey to nowhere.

But he knew that couldn't be. . . . With every moment the train was taking him nearer to home. Nearer to everything he hated and feared.

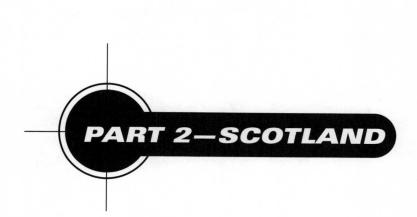

PART 2—SCOTLAND

The powerful engine pulled the long train through the night, up the edge of England along the east coast route, from York to Newcastle, then plowing on north to Edinburgh and Perth, and on in to Fort William in the northwest of Scotland.

James slept well and woke at half past nine, with sunlight streaming in through the window and Kelly swinging his skinny legs down over the edge of the top bunk.

"Wakey, wakey," Kelly said, jumping down. "Och aye the noo and all that. Here we are in the land of the jocks, the old sweaty socks." He peered out of the window. "You know," he said, turning down his mouth, "it looks a lot like England. Fields, trees, houses, roads, clouds . . . miserable-looking people."

"What were you expecting?" said James, looking out. "Men in kilts playing the bagpipes and Bonnie Prince Charlie riding past with Rob Roy?"

"I don't know," said Kelly. "I never been in a foreign country before, I thought it would just look, you know, more foreign."

They had stopped outside the station and could hear the train engine idling. "Look properly," said James. "Look beyond the houses. Look at the hills, and look over there."

"What is it?"

"That's Ben Nevis. The tallest mountain in Britain."

Kelly peered out. "Can't see much," he said gloomily as the train started forward again.

"You never can," said James. "It's nearly always in cloud, but if you're lucky you might get a glimpse of it."

"I'll take your word for it."

James's aunt Charmian was waiting for him on the platform. He held out his hand for her to shake, but she brushed it aside and gave him a big hug.

"You're so formal, James. Sometimes a lady wants more than just a handshake."

Aunt Charmian was wearing olive-colored trousers tucked into high riding boots and a matching jacket with a simple white silk shirt and scarf. You didn't often see a woman in trousers, but Charmian carried herself so confidently that nobody would have dared to criticize her.

"Let me look at you," she said, holding him at arm's length. "See what that dreaded school has done to you."

James smiled at her and tried not to blush under her scrutiny.

"You'll do," she decided. "Though they've obviously not been feeding you. You're skinny as a rake."

"The food's awful," he said.

"Most English food's awful, dear; you'd be lucky to get better in a top-class hotel. You've been spoiled by my cooking, you know."

Charmian had traveled all around the world and had brought back recipes and ingredients from the many countries she had visited. As a result, James had eaten pasta dishes from Italy, curries from India, couscous from North Africa, noodles from Singapore, and he had once even tried chicken cooked in chocolate from Mexico, but that had not been a great success. It was no wonder that the dull, stodgy cooking at Eton didn't exactly set his taste buds dancing.

"You got the packages I sent? The cakes and biscuits."

"Yes, thanks, they certainly helped."

Outside the station, a jostling crowd of passengers was climbing aboard their various modes of transport. One group was piling onto a bus, a couple of gentlemen were putting their luggage into taxicabs, some local people were being met by family or friends with cars and, down at the other end, James saw George Hellebore being helped into a fine black Rolls-Royce by a uniformed chauffeur.

"All right, Jimmy?"

James turned to see Red Kelly striding toward them. "This your aunt?" he said.

"Yes . . ."

Before James could say anything else, Red vigorously shook Charmian's hand.

"Pleased to meet you, Aunty," he said, and winked. "Your Jimmy's a good lad, look after him, now."

"Yes, I will," said Charmian, a little taken aback.

"I'd best get me skates on, the bus'll be off in a minute . . . Maybe see you around, Jimmy, eh?"

And with that, Kelly was gone.

"Who on earth was that?" asked Charmian with a smile.

"Oh, just someone I met on the train. He was good company."

Aunt Charmian had her own car there, a heavy, four-and-a-half liter, four-cylinder supercharged Bentley four-seater sports car. James loved it and had decided that if he ever owned a car, it would be this model. He slung his bag in the back and squeezed in next to his aunt on the hard leather seat. Charmian drove well but fast and had little patience for other motorists, which wasn't a problem on these roads, as there was very little traffic and sighting another car was something of an event.

"We still have a fair old drive," Charmian shouted over the roar of the engine. "And I expect you're famished. We'll stop somewhere for breakfast. There's a little café in Kinlocheil that does a half-decent breakfast. So, are you looking forward to your hols?"

"Yes."

"I thought we might go to the circus tonight. They've pitched their tent in Kilcraymore. It shouldn't be a total bore."

"That sounds fun," said James, who hadn't been to a circus in years and wondered if it would still appeal to him.

"We'll try to make this a holiday to remember, eh?"

They drove around the end of Loch Linnhe and then took the Road to the Isles along the north shore of Loch Eil until they came to Kinlocheil at the far end. There they parked the car and were soon sitting at a little square table in a cafe with views out across the water.

"Best meal of the day, breakfast," said Charmian once she'd ordered scrambled eggs, bacon, toast, and marmalade. "Sets you up for the day."

The waitress came over and asked if they would like a pot of tea and Charmian exploded.

"Tea? Good God, no. It's mud. How the British ever built an empire drinking the filthy stuff is beyond me. And if we carry on drinking it, I've no doubt that the empire won't last much longer. No, a civilized person drinks coffee."

James smiled to himself. How many times had he heard Aunt Charmian's speech about tea drinking? But the thing was, her views had slowly seeped into him. He no longer drank tea and had managed to acquire a taste for coffee, even though he'd found it very bitter and hard to swallow at first.

After breakfast, feeling full and contented, they wandered back to the Bentley and set off toward Mallaig.

"How is Uncle Max?" James asked.

"Not good, I'm afraid, James. You haven't seen him for a while, have you?"

"Not since before Mother and Father died."

"Well, you'd best prepare yourself for a bit of a shock. He's grown dreadfully thin of late, and he has a quite alarming cough."

"How serious is it?" asked James.

"As serious as it can be. The doctor said it's a miracle he's lasted this long, but your uncle's a fighter, tough as old boots. It's unfair, really, to think of all he's been through, all he's survived, only to be felled by a common or garden disease. But then—life is unfair. It's his own body, really, killing him, creating more and more cancerous cells in his lungs, slowly choking him. It's a ghastly business, cancer. But enough of this gloominess—he's very much looking forward to seeing you. I think your visit will really lift his spirits."

A mile or two before Glenfinnan they turned north off the main road and onto the winding route that led to the little West Highland village of Keithly. Keithly was built of low, solid, gray stone houses, huddled and crouching in the shelter of low hills, ready for anything the fierce winters up here could throw at it.

Max's cottage, however, was not in the town itself, and they drove through the narrow high street, past the pub and the post office, before pulling onto a rutted dirt track that followed the course of a small river deep into a pine forest.

"I don't know what it's doing to the suspension, driving up and down here all day," said Charmian as she wrestled with the wheel to negotiate a particularly tight bend, "but they're pretty well built, these Bentleys, thank God." She turned to James and smiled. "It may seem isolated at first, but there're plenty of people in and out. There's a nice couple who have been looking after your uncle: May Davidson and her husband, Alec. May's been cooking for him and cleaning and generally keeping house for years, and Alec's taken over the garden, now that Max is too weak. Then the doctor's up here most days, and an old gillie called Gordon who helps Max with his fishing. . . ."

"Does he fish a lot?"

"Oh, goodness, yes. Didn't you know? It's his whole life. That's why he bought the cottage in the first place—because it's slap-bang on the river and has full fishing rights. He's never without a rod in his hand. I think he wants to be buried with it."

They rounded the final bend, and there was the cottage, nestled in a small clearing, so overgrown with clematis, honeysuckle, and rambling roses you could barely make out the building beneath. James reckoned that when all the plants were in flower the cottage must disappear completely.

And there was Uncle Max.

James was glad that Charmian had warned him in advance, because Max looked very unwell indeed. His sagging skin was a pale yellowish color, and he'd lost so much weight his clothes hung loosely on his body. He was using a walking stick. He had always had a limp, caused by a wound he had suffered in the war, and James thought it was very exciting, but now he was clearly finding it hard to walk. He was desperate to make the effort, however, and he strode over to meet the car as briskly as he could, so that James was reminded for a moment of the dashing, handsome man he had once been.

James's earliest memory of his uncle was when he had taken him to the British Empire Exhibition at Wembley in 1925. Uncle Max had been an impossibly glamorous figure then: tall and lean, with the proud, strong build of a soldier. James remembered getting off the train at Wembley Park Station and holding tightly to his uncle's hand as Max forced his way through the crowd. He remembered seeing the huge wooden structure of the roller coaster towering above them, and he remembered how safe and protected he had felt with Max.

But the man standing before him now, stooped and feeble, seemed like a different person.

"James," he wheezed, clasping his nephew by the upper arms. "Marvelous to see you, lad. Welcome to my little kingdom. . . ."

He sounded dreadfully short of breath, and the effort of

speaking sent him into a barrage of wet coughs that came from deep down inside his chest.

James waited for them to die down, and Max wiped his mouth with a handkerchief. "Sorry," he said. "I'm afraid you'll have to get used to my barking. Here, let me grab your bag."

"Nonsense," snapped Aunt Charmian. "You'll do nothing of the sort."

"You don't have to treat me like a baby, sis," said Max with a touch of humor.

"If you behave like a baby, I'll treat you like a baby," said Charmian, opening the boot of the car and hauling the suitcase out herself. "I'll take the bag. You go on in and show James the lie of the land."

The cottage was actually quite a lot larger than it appeared at first sight. It had originally been two cottages and a cow shed, but Max had knocked down some walls and turned the whole building into a single house. James's room had been the hayloft, and it was tucked up under the rafters of the old cowshed.

"Careful how you go, or you'll be forever bumping your head," said Max, slapping one of the heavy wooden beams that formed the sloping roof.

"I'm used to it," said James. "My room at Eton's half this size."

He looked around. The walls were covered in wallpaper patterned with roses very much like the ones growing outside. There was a neat little iron-frame bed, bare wooden floorboards with a colorful woven rug, and near the bright-blue door stood a chest of drawers with a vase of fresh wild flowers and an oil lamp on it.

"I'm afraid there're rather a lot of my old things in here," said Max, showing James a shelf of tattered books. James spotted a few familiar titles: *Treasure Island*, *The Adventures of Sherlock Holmes*, *The Jungle Book*, *King Solomon's Mines*. A second shelf held a row of painted plaster figurines—two dogs, a cat, a monkey, and a dragon.

"Shooting prizes," said Max. "From the fair. I must have been about your age when I won those, and look here . . ." He showed James a small painting of a stag. "All my own work!"

"You painted it?" said James, smiling.

"Fancied myself an artist once. Studied in Germany for a while before the war. . . . Nothing ever came of it."

James went over to check the view from the window. He could see the wide, shallow river and the trees beyond.

"Fancy a cast or two?" said Max, joining him. "See if we can't catch us a couple of finnock for our lunch."

"Finnock?"

"Sea trout. Fresh from the Atlantic. There's a lovely spring run on at the moment. The river's starting to come alive with fish. Had a good lot of rain a couple of days ago so she's in spate, but the water's clearing nicely."

"I don't really know much about fishing," James apologized. "You might as well be speaking Japanese."

"Don't worry, we'll make a fisherman of you, lad. Isn't she a lovely river?"

"Yes . . . I suppose so."

"You know, James, you can look at a river, you can walk by a river, you can paint it, you can throw stones into it, but if you want to be a part of the river, then you need to fish it. When you stand in a river, fishing with a fly, you're part of nature, you're a heron, you're a kingfisher, you get to know the river like an old friend. Sometimes you'll get lost in it; standing there, you'll forget what you're doing, and then, bang, you've a fish, the line goes heavy, it moves in your hands, like a dog shaking its head, and then it's you versus the fish. . . ."

For the next couple of hours Max showed James the rudiments of fly-fishing, how to thread the rod, how to tie the hooks, and how to cast, flicking the line back over your shoulder, then snapping it forward in a movement like knocking a nail into a wall with a hammer, so that the line whips out over the water and drops the fly exactly where you want it.

James enjoyed learning how to cast, but he got frustrated waiting for a fish to bite. He felt a tug at one point but lost it. Max didn't even get a tickle.

"That's the thing with fishing," he said, sitting down on the bank and taking out a packet of cigarettes from his pocket. "You never know what's going to happen. I think if you were guaranteed to catch a fish every time, you'd soon grow bored with it."

James wasn't so sure about that. It was too much of a disappointment not to actually catch anything. He watched as Max put a cigarette into his mouth and lit it, greedily inhaling the smoke. Max had one brief look of pleasure, before he was convulsed with a series of body-wrenching coughs that were painful to watch. James thought they'd never stop, but at last Max recovered. His eyes watering, he wiped his lips again with his handkerchief and studied the gold-banded cigarette. "I don't suppose these things are doing my poor old lungs much good," he said hoarsely.

"So why don't you stop?" said James as Max painfully cleared his throat.

"Why indeed? Well, for one thing it's too late, the damage is done. I'm going to die sooner rather than later." With that, Max launched into another horrible storm of coughing. "So I may as well"—cough—"enjoy myself"—cough—"while I can . . ."

"I don't think I will ever smoke," said James.

"Good for you . . ." Max managed to gasp. "Here's to the certainties of youth. You know, James, I was certain of a lot of things when I was a boy, but sadly, as you grow older, your certainties crumble. Life has a habit of sneaking up on you and playing you dirty tricks. I started smoking during the war. We all did; we couldn't have cared less, even if we'd known that the cigarettes would kill us, because we had only one certainty—that we were going to die in those filthy trenches. Death was the only thing we could be sure of."

James was thankful that he had missed the war. He couldn't imagine what it must be like to fight, to have to kill another man or risk being killed yourself.

"My father never talked about the war," he said.

"None of us do, it's best to forget. But for me the war was a little more complicated. I was not allowed to talk about it at all." Max raised his eyebrows at James.

"How do you mean?" asked James.

"A lot of what I did in the war was secret."

"My father hinted at things," said James. "But that was all."

"I suppose there's no harm in telling you now. Though I've had to keep things under my hat all these years. I was what you might call a spy."

"Really?" said James. "A spy. How exciting."

"You think so? If constant, belly-rotting fear is exciting. It certainly didn't feel so at the time. At the time it just meant that I was terrified, morning, noon, and night. They recruited me in France. I'd been wounded, nothing serious, caught a bullet in the leg. . . . Here."

Max rolled up his trouser leg and showed James a small puckered dent just above his knee. "Went clean through, but I couldn't walk for a bit. Met a chap in the hospital, got talking. They were looking for a fluent German-speaker and, as I'd been out that way before the war, I was pretty proficient at it."

Max was off in a world of his own now, not looking at James, staring away down the river, talking almost to himself. James realized that most of what he was saying he had never told anyone else before; it was as if he were trying to unload all his memories while there was still time. He told James of the briefings; his promotion to the new rank of Captain; his training in codes and passwords, poisons and unarmed combat; his forged papers; the network of other spies who would help him. And he told how he was smuggled by a boat far behind enemy lines, where he had to pose as Herr Grumann, a railway engineer, and keep a detailed record of train movements. Then he described the long days and weeks pretending to be someone else, praying he wouldn't be discovered, and giving his weekly reports to his contact to smuggle back to France.

And then he stopped and just sat, staring silently into the water.

"What happened?" asked James after a long while. "Were you ever captured?"

Max turned to look at him. He seemed slightly surprised, as if he'd forgotten that James was there.

"That's another story," said Max, "for another day. Come along, we'd best be getting back. Charmian will be wondering where we've got to."

Charmian had roasted a chicken for lunch and they ate it with steamed carrots, potatoes, and spring greens, freshly picked, firm and brightly colored. James savored every single mouthful. After the muck at Eton, it was like eating the food of the gods.

"Do you know anything about a boy called Alfie Kelly?" James asked as Aunt Charmian brought a big apple pie to the table.

"Dreadful business," said his aunt, cutting into the pie and releasing a delicious cloud of steam that smelled of apples and sugar and cinnamon.

"What's that?" asked Max, who looked very tired and on the verge of falling asleep at the table.

"You remember, Annie Kelly's boy. I told you about him, young lad about James's age who's gone missing."

"Ah, yes," said Max, and his whole face came alive. He sat up straighter in his chair. "I did a bit of asking around myself. He was very keen on fishing, you see. Always keep a lookout for fellow anglers, James. Popular opinion is that he fell in some river somewhere trying to catch a fish, which is preposterous. He'd know these rivers, know the dangers. And where's his gear? No sign of it. Gordon says he thinks he might have gone up to Loch Silverfin. Says he saw him a couple of times heading off in that direction just before he disappeared, although nobody from Keithly goes up that way now. If I were in better shape, I'd hike up there and take a look myself."

"But nobody's allowed to fish on Loch Silverfin," said Charmian, serving James a plate of pie.

"Precisely," said Max. "That would have been a challenge for the lad. My God, what I wouldn't give to have another cast at those waters. The fishing used to be some of the best around. But I don't like that place. They're an odd bunch up there. If you ask me, that Lord Hellebore's up to something."

"I beg your pardon," said James, nearly choking on his mouthful of pie. "Did you say Lord Hellebore?"

"Lord Randolph Hellebore," Max explained. "Owns the castle and most of the land around here."

"His son is at Eton," said James.

"That's right. I heard that. Do you know him?"

"He's a couple of years older than me," said James, not wanting to give anything away.

"Yes," said Max. "Interesting business. When the old laird died, a few years back, without an heir, Randolph and his brother, Algar, inherited the place, although his brother died soon afterward in some kind of accident, I gather. The castle was pretty much falling down, the family was heavily in debt and nobody expected Randolph to move back over here, they thought he'd just sell it all off, but he turned up and set to work with his American can-do attitude. Managed to save the place, and how."

"He's very rich, isn't he?" said James.

"Rich as Croesus. I met him once, a year or so ago. Seemed friendly enough, if rather loud. Popular with the locals, though. He's built a new school and a village hall. They're forever having dances there. Wants to be accepted. Wants very much to become a proper British lord. But I don't trust him. He's very secretive, got men all about the place with guns."

"Why?"

"Claims it's for security. He's a got a small arms factory there, but he's definitely up to something."

"What?" said James. "What do you think he could be up to?"

"Ah," said Max, putting down his spoon. "What do I think? I don't know, James. All we have to go on is rumor, and my training taught me one thing; information is the most important weapon in your arsenal. The more you know, the better equipped you are. As I say, if I wasn't such a blasted ruin of a man, I'd go up there and find out what I could. Rumor and gossip are no good to any man, though they keep the womenfolk happy."

"That's enough of that," said Charmian. "I've heard you and your cronies down at the pub gossiping like a bunch of old hens."

Max grinned at James. "Doesn't do to tease your Aunty C., eh, James?"

"It certainly does not," said Charmian. "I can hold my own with any man."

"Now, don't be modest, sis, you could thrash any man I know."

Max started to laugh, and the laugh turned into a cough. Charmian caught James's eye and gave him a reassuring smile, then poured a glass of water and passed it over to her brother. After a minute or so, he managed to stop coughing and gratefully drank the water down.

"I think you'd better take it easy this afternoon," said Charmian quietly.

"The lad won't be here forever, Charmian—let the boys have some fun, eh?"

"Will you be back on the river?"

Max grinned at James. "I'm not sure that James quite shares my enthusiasm," he said. "But I do know something he'll be interested in. . . ."

"There she is," said Uncle Max, swinging the big barn door back on its rusted hinges. "Isn't she a pretty thing?"

It took a few moments for James's eyes to become adjusted to the darkness, but then, as the sun came out from behind a cloud, it sent a shaft of light down through a high, dirty window, lighting up a car that was sitting on the stone floor like a patient beast.

"She's a one-point-five liter Bamford and Martin Sidevalve, Short Chassis Tourer," said Max proudly, stepping up to the car and wiping dust off the bonnet with a clean cloth.

James didn't know a great deal about cars, so most of what his uncle said meant nothing to him, but at that moment, as he set eyes on the small, sleek, powerful-looking machine, he knew that he wanted to find out.

Max switched on a light and James got a proper look at it. It was a two-seater, built for speed, with a long, high bonnet like the snout of a dog and a rounded rear end like a boat. It was white, with black running boards that swept up over the narrow front wheels. Two big, gleaming head lamps, like crabs' eyes on stalks, jutted up above the front bumper and, behind the low, square windscreen, a large steering wheel waited for someone to take hold of it and race away.

"A little dusty, but she still runs all right," said Max as he folded the roof back behind the seats. "She's built for the road, really, but I raced her a couple of times at Brooklands, you know, before I got ill. Just for fun. Never won. Too hotheaded. Always tried to go too fast and lost it on the bends. One time I even took on the great Tim Birkin."

"Really?" said James, wide-eyed. "The racing driver?"

"That's your man," Max chuckled. "Showed me a thing or two, I can tell you. Couldn't see him for dust, except for the occasional glimpse of his famous blue-and-white polka-dot scarf. Come on, let's take her for a spin."

Max folded one side of the bonnet up and fiddled with the engine, then he slammed the flap back down decisively and got into the driver's seat.

"Electric starter," he said, and pressed a button. There was a brief whine, then the engine rasped, ticked rapidly, and roared into life, creating a deafening din in the garage.

"Climb aboard!" Max yelled and the Aston Martin rocked on its springs as James got in.

"I haven't taken her out for a good blast in months," said Max. "But she starts every time without any complaint."

The car felt light and anxious to tear away. Max slipped her into gear, released the brake, and they were off, bouncing out of the garage into the courtyard, where they cornered sharply and shot past the house and away down the bumpy road.

James had never driven this fast before, and at first he was terrified; the wind whipped into his face and within a minute the windscreen was plastered with dead insects. The car jolted and shook, the scream of its engine reflected back off the trees. James felt sure that they would crash but, despite what his uncle had said about losing control on the racetrack at Brooklands, he realized that Max knew exactly what he was doing and was an expert behind the wheel. James slowly grew in confidence, and by the time they pulled out onto the main road he was enjoying himself hugely. Max turned to him and grinned. "They've just scrapped the twenty-mile-an-hour speed limit," he shouted over the noise of the car and the rushing wind. "But I don't suppose I'm going to be around long enough to fully appreciate it. Not that I ever really worried too much about it. I nearly got her up to a hundred one time on the Barnet bypass."

Max's laughter was lost on the wind as they howled through Keithly and out onto the open road across the moors toward Kilcraymore. By now James was thoroughly enjoying himself, and Max seemed to have come alive. Behind the wheel, all his frailty and weakness were gone—he was a young man again, happy and carefree.

They stopped at a petrol station in Kilcraymore, where Max filled the tank and then opened the bonnet to show James what was underneath.

"It's a marvelous thing, the internal combustion engine," he said, gazing lovingly at the oily block of metal. "It's going to change the world."

James peered at the hugely complicated workings.

"So, if you're going to keep up," said Max briskly, "you'd better learn how it works. What can you tell me about it?"

"Not very much, I'm afraid," said James. "I know you have to put petrol in, but that's about it."

"All right. That's a start. So what can you tell me about petrol?"

"It catches light very easily," said James.

"That's it," said Max. "That's exactly it. This engine is powered by exploding petrol."

"Really?"

"Yes." Max ran his hand lovingly over the engine. "Hidden in the middle of all this ironwork are four cylinders, each with a piston inside of it, and it's those pistons that drive the engine. You can't see the cylinders because they're encased in a metal jacket through which water circulates to keep it cool. Then the water passes out through this pipe, to the radiator here."

Max tapped the grille at the front of the car. "The water's cooled by this fan, and here's the fan belt that drives it. Are you keeping up?"

"I think so. But all I can think about is explosions."

"Yes, sorry, old son, I got sidetracked there. That's the beauty of the petrol engine, there are so many parts, all working together in harmony. Now, this is a four-stroke engine, which means that each piston runs through a cycle of four strokes inside the cylinder." Max pumped his hand up and down in the air. "Up, down, up, down. . . . Do you follow me?"

"I think so."

"Good. My starter sets the whole thing in motion, and as the piston pumps down it creates a vacuum above it that sucks in a fine spray of petrol from the carburetor, here. As the petrol mixes with air, it turns into a highly flammable gas. That's the first stroke—the induction stroke. Next, you have the compression stroke, as the piston is forced back up, squashing the gas; then, as it comes back down for the third stroke, it triggers a spark of electricity from these fellows here, the sparking plugs."

Max indicated a row of shiny knobs along the top of the engine and then grinned at James. "Now what do you suppose that little spark does to all that compressed gas?"

"It ignites it," said James.

"Exactly. And there's your explosion. It kicks the piston down with enormous energy. That energy turns the crank shaft and the flywheel and the movements of all the other pistons, and finally forces our piston back up, pushing all the waste fumes from the explosion out of the cylinder and into the exhaust pipe, through the silencer and out here."

Max ran a hand over the engine.

"The noise you hear of an engine roaring," he said, "that's countless small explosions going off, all four cylinders working together, turning that crankshaft."

He slammed the bonnet, straightened up, and gripped James by the shoulder. "How would you like to drive her?" he said.

James looked to see whether he was teasing him, but his smile seemed genuine.

"I'd like that very much," he said. "But are you sure you'd let me?"

"We can give it a go," said Max. "And if it turns out you're a complete duffer, I can always wrestle the wheel back out of your hands and we can concentrate on fishing instead. Deal?"

It was James's turn to smile now. "It was interesting this morning," he said, "but I think learning to drive will be a lot more exciting."

"Excitement," snapped Max. "That's all modern youth is interested in—speed, thrills, noise, and drama! Can't say as I blame you, though. I learnt in the war that you've got to take life by the scruff of the neck, you don't get a second shot at it. What was it the man said? 'I shall not waste my days in trying to prolong them. I shall use my time.'" With that, he wiped his hand on a rag, paid the garage mechanic, and they set off to Keithly.

When they pulled onto the rough track that led to the house, Max slowed down and stopped.

"This is as good a place as any to start," he said. "There are no other cars around and it's private land, so we can do as we please. The surface isn't as flat and firm as it could be but what the hell! If you can learn to handle a car on this, you should find it a breeze when you get out on a proper road."

"But what if I lose control and crash into a tree or something?" said James.

"I shan't be needing the old girl much longer," said Max, staring off down the road. "And I've no one to leave it to when I die. I don't suppose May would have much use for it and sister Charmian already has her beloved Bentley. So . . . if you prang her, then that's life. But, tell you what, if you can look after her, she's yours. That should be incentive enough not to steer toward the nearest mighty oak."

"Really?" said James, beaming. "Do you mean it?"

"Come along," said Max, opening the little door and getting out, so that they could swap seats. "Let's see how you get on."

James slid across into the driver's seat and gripped the steering wheel. Max had made driving look effortless but, sitting here in control, it suddenly didn't look so easy.

"What exactly are all these switches and dials and pedals and levers for?" James said.

Max ran through them all for him. "Well, you've got switches for lights, magneto and electric starter, then there's the radiator thermometer, the clock—I assume you know what that's for."

"Telling the time?"

"Give the man a prize. What else have we got? Electric dashboard light, speedometer, oil pressure gauge, electric meter to show charging of accumulator, and finally, the carburetor flooder. Don't worry about them now; with time you'll know what they all do and they won't scare you one bit."

"And the levers?"

"That's your hand brake and your gear lever. And those pedals there are your foot brake, accelerator, and clutch. Can you reach all right?"

"I think so."

James pushed the accelerator down with his foot; it was hard work, and his leg was only just long enough, but the engine woke up and howled like an angry lion. James grinned, but his heart was racing scarily. He took his foot off the pedal, and the engine died down to a steady purr.

"Right," said Max. "Be gentler next time, because we're going to try and drive her forward. Starting from scratch and moving off is probably the hardest part. For *you* and the car. Picture yourself walking up a steep mountain. To start off, you have to take small, quick, powerful steps; it's a hell of a strain, but coming down the other side, you can take long, slow, easy strides. That's what it's like for a car. To get her moving takes terrific power, but once she's up and running it's much easier. Understand?"

"I think so."

"Good. That's where your gears come in. Ah, where would we be without gears? Wheels within wheels. In first gear the engine turns a tiny wheel that spins round, turning a larger wheel very slowly, then you change to second, and a larger wheel comes into play, then up through the gears until the engine is directly driving the car wheels with no gears in between. Once she's up and running all you really have to do is steer her."

"You make it sound easy," said James nervously.

"Oh. It'll take you a while to get the hang of the gears," said Max. "But soon you won't even think about it. That's when the car becomes a part of you, and you can handle her as easily as your own four limbs."

Max showed James the pattern of the gears on the gear stick, and they practiced without the engine running.

"The theory is simple," Max explained. "You use the clutch pedal to free the engine and ease down on the accelerator to set it turning. Then you select first gear, release the clutch to engage the engine, release the brake, and there you are."

James pumped the pedals up and down.

"Not so rough," said Max. "You have to feel the pedals, get just the right balance between the accelerator and the clutch. Too little power, and she won't cope. She'll stall. Too much power, and she'll leap away from you. Think you're ready to have a go?"

"As ready as I'll ever be."

James's first few efforts at starting were pretty disastrous, but he slowly got the hang of it, and eventually his concentration overcame his nervousness, so that on the seventh attempt the car lurched forward and began to trundle slowly down the track.

"There you go," yelled Max. "You're driving—into a ditch! Look out!"

Max reached over, grabbed the wheel, and steered James away from the danger, then he jammed his foot down onto the brake pedal, crushing James's foot, so that the car lurched to a halt. The engine complained briefly, then gave up and cut out.

Max shook his head and laughed. "Tell you what," he said, "let's try somewhere with fewer hazards."

They relocated to the paddock behind the house which was fairly flat and firm, and a small flock of sheep kept the grass down to a good, tight thatch. James soon got over his embarrassment and was eager to try again. This time he managed to move off after only three attempts and they bounced over the grass with confidence. He couldn't stop a huge grin from spreading across his face as he steered the car around the field, slowly gaining more speed until the engine was whining noisily.

"That means it's time to change gears," Max shouted. "It's exactly the same principle as starting: Free the engine with the clutch pedal, then slip her into second and reengage."

James did as he was told and, more by accident and good luck than anything else, he made a smooth transition into second gear.

"Good lad," said Max. "You're really getting the hang of this."

With that, James stalled the car and they came to a bumpy halt in the middle of the field, where a solitary sheep stood and stared at them, chewing thoughtfully.

They heard a shout and turned to see Charmian striding across the grass toward them.

"Don't get the boy killed, will you?" she said.

"He's a natural," said Max, getting stiffly out of the car.

"How are you feeling?" Charmian asked.

"Never better."

"Feel up to a walk before turning in?"

"That's an excellent idea," said Max, stretching his back. "I'm as stiff as a board."

"Come on, then."

They made their way through the woods and up the hill behind the house, taking it slowly so as not to tire Max. Just as the sun was setting they broke free from the trees and saw open countryside for miles around.

A buzzard soared on the breeze high above them, its broad, rounded wings spread like the wings of an airplane. It let out a piercing and rather sad cry and wheeled away in search of food.

They stood there and looked out over the moors, patterned with heather and gorse and bracken, toward the purple mountains in the distance. There was no sign of any human activity apart from a thin column of smoke rising from a distant copse.

"It seems preposterous that somebody could actually own all that, doesn't it, James?" said Max. "But your Lord Hellebore does."

"Which direction is the castle in?" asked James.

"See where those big hills are?" said Max, pointing with his stick.

"Yes."

"Well, there's a lake behind them, Loch Silverfin, and the castle's on the lake, on a small spit of land, almost like an island. There's one road goes up from the village, but they're pretty much cut off from us mere mortals; they've near as dammit built a small town of their own up there."

James wondered about George Hellebore. It was as if their two fates were somehow bound together.

"We'd best be getting back," said Charmian. "We've got a busy evening ahead of us. It's the circus tonight, and it'll be dark soon."

"And cold," said Max.

James took one last look back up toward the far-off hills and made a decision.

He was going to go and take a look at the Hellebores' castle as soon as he could.

CHAPTER 11—WE DON'T LIKE THE ENGLISH ROUND HERE

Max wasn't up to going to the circus and after a quick supper of rabbit stew that he barely touched, he turned in for the night. James watched him struggle painfully up the stairs to his bedroom, all the life gone out of him. With his hunched shoulders and shuffling walk, he looked very frail, like a ninety-year-old man.

Later, in the Bentley, driving along the road to Kilcraymore, Charmian asked James if he was enjoying himself.

"Yes," said James "very much so. I had a fantastic time in the car this afternoon."

"Good. I was worried you'd be bored, with only adults for company." Charmian didn't take her eyes off the twisting, uneven road. "And Max seems to be having a whale of a time. I haven't seen him so full of beans since I've been up here. Your arrival has really perked him up. I'm a bit of a disappointment to him, I think—I've never been able to quite share his enthusiasm for fishing."

They chatted some more about Max and fishing while they drove down the deserted country lanes, the twin lights of the Bentley carving a path ahead of them through the darkness. All they could hear was the gentle roar of the twin exhausts. James marveled at Charmian's driving; now that he knew how much went into controlling a car, he realized just how expert she was.

The drive seemed to pass in no time, and soon James saw the big striped circus tent, strung with lights, rising up out of the night like a huge birthday cake dropped to earth by some clumsy giant.

Charmian parked in a muddy field, and they joined the throng of excited locals making their way toward the tent. There were so many people that James thought the entire surrounding countryside must have been emptied. There were all types, from tiny babies being carried by their mothers to bent old men with long white beards, all happily chatting and milling around on the trampled grass.

They bought two tickets at a kiosk and joined the queue to get in. Nearby a noisy and smelly steam-powered generator was chuntering away and an organ was playing "Sweet Molly Malone." There was a row of attractions here: a coconut shy, a shooting range, a hall of mirrors, and a fortune-teller, as well as stalls selling sweets and toffee apples. James had wondered if he was too old for all this, but now that he was here he was caught up in the excitement, and he asked his aunt if he could have a proper look around later.

Inside, the tent was dimly lit with colored bulbs, and there was a powerful smell of animals and sawdust. James took his place on a wooden bench as a small, raggedy band struck up a wobbly tune that James recognized as "March of the Gladiators" and then a fat, sweaty ringmaster led in the parade. There were acrobats, jugglers, clowns, horses, a tired old elephant, and a troupe of performing monkeys.

James had seen better circuses before, but he enjoyed himself nevertheless. Sitting there in the dark among the crowd of laughing and clapping people, with the music and the lights, there was a magical, other-worldly atmosphere.

The first highlight was the equestrian act. Two sturdy, white ponies ran around the ring while three girls in sparkly silver outfits balanced on the ponies' backs and jumped from one horse to the other and even turned somersaults.

At one point, the light changed in such a way that it picked out just one face in the crowd: a girl with long, blond hair tied back into a ponytail. The reflections from the acrobats' sequins sent starry lights dancing across her pale skin, and her eyes seemed to shine. They were the most vivid emerald color that James had ever seen. He thought it must be a trick of the light. She was sitting right at the front, almost directly opposite James, and she was absolutely hypnotized by the horses; James had never seen anyone staring with such intense, happy concentration before.

When the horses left the ring, the lights changed and the girl disappeared back into the gloom, so that James didn't see her again. Instead, another section of the crowd was lit up, and sitting right in the middle of the pool of light was a large gentleman with a big, drooping mustache, a flat cap, and a brand-new tweed jacket and tartan trousers. He looked like he had come in fancy dress—as a Scotsman—and was so out of place here among the solid local farmers in their drab earthy colors that James couldn't help smiling. The man was trying so hard to look Scottish that he didn't look Scottish at all.

But then James was distracted by the trapeze artistes,

swinging through space, high above the ring, almost missing their handholds, and always managing to grab on just in time.

James couldn't decide whether they were his favorites or the strongman. He was called the Mighty Donovan and he lifted weights with his teeth and finished his act by picking up four pretty young girls from the audience at the same time, while they squealed and he grinned triumphantly.

When it was finished, they made their way back out into the cold night air and James spotted Red Kelly with a skinny, exhausted-looking woman who gave the impression that she'd rather be anywhere else than at the circus.

"There's my friend from the train," said James, and Charmian looked over.

"Is that Annie Kelly with him?" she said, and they pushed through the noisy crowd toward them.

"Hey there, Jimmy," said Kelly when he spotted James. "How do?"

"Hello," said James. "I didn't see you in there."

"I saw you," said Red. "I waved, but you never spotted me. This is me Aunt Annie, by the way."

"Hello, Annie," said Charmian, who obviously knew her. "Any news about Alfie?"

"No," said the tired-looking woman. "I'm afraid not."

Charmian gave James a handful of coins and told him to go off and enjoy himself while she talked to Annie.

"How are you getting on?" James asked, as he and Kelly wandered over to the fair. "Found anything out, yet?"

"Give us a chance, mate. I'm still finding me feet."

James tried his hand at the shooting, firing at playing

cards with a battered air rifle. He soon worked out that the barrel was crooked and the sights bent but, by adjusting his shots accordingly, he managed to get on target and win a prize.

"I'll get something for my uncle Max," he said. "He'll be pleased." He chose a little plaster model of a guardsman in a bright-red jacket and black busby, and put it in his pocket.

They moved on to the sweet stall and while they were studying the piles of treats on offer James spotted George Hellebore coming out of the palm reader's tent.

"Look," he said. "There's the boy from my school, the one who was on the train."

"The big bully?"

"Turns out he lives near here," said James. "In a castle, up on the Hellebore estate. Have you heard of it?"

"Oh, that's him, is it?"

They looked at George. He had spotted them and was talking to two big farm boys. James saw him slip one of them some money, but thought nothing of it.

They bought a bag of hard toffees and found a low grass bank in the darkness behind the tents to eat them in private.

"My uncle thinks it's possible that Alfie may have gone up there, to the castle, fishing," said James, chewing thoughtfully. "There's a big lake up in the hills, Loch Silverfin. Do you think it's worth investigating?"

"Might be worth a nose around, yeah," said Kelly, prising a piece of stuck toffee off one of his sharp yellow teeth with a dirty finger. "How about tomorrow? You doing anything?"

"No. Tomorrow would be fine," said James.

Just then they were interrupted by a shout.

"There they are!"

James looked up to see the two burly farm boys saunter-
ing toward them. They were big, raw-looking lads with wiry
hair and freckled skin that was tanned and cracked from
being outdoors in the wind and the rain all day. They had on
heavy boots and their hands looked like shovels.

"All right, lads?" said Kelly with a friendly smile as he
carefully put down the bag of sweets.

"Don't you 'All right, lads?' us," said the larger of the two
boys, who had huge ears and a nose to match. "We don't like
the English round here."

James was going to point out that with a Swiss mother
and a Scottish father he was no more English than they were,
but decided that it wasn't worth the effort. These boys
intended to cause trouble whatever the excuse.

Kelly jumped up, still smiling, and took a step toward the
boy who'd spoken.

"If it's all the same to you, mate," he said, "we don't want
a fight."

The boy jostled him while his friend advanced on James,
his red-knuckled fists raised. James stood up.

"You no want a fight, eh?" said the boy in a weasel, high-
pitched voice.

"Typical English cowards." He sneered and shoved James
backward. James stumbled and fell on his backside, and the
boy laughed.

James quickly jumped up again. His attacker was shaking
his head mockingly and shuffling toward him. James held his
ground, looking the boy in the eye, and suddenly realized
that the boy was about to take a swing at him. He ducked the

blow and, without thinking, hit back. It was a lucky punch, and James got him in the stomach before he had a chance to react. The boy was more shocked than hurt and was about to come back at James when he glanced around to see how his friend was getting on.

James had no idea what Kelly had done to the big-eared boy, but he was down on the floor, curled up in a ball, gasping for breath and clutching his belly, his nose bleeding. The smaller boy looked scared now. He helped his friend to his feet.

"Are you all right, Angus?" he said, his voice jittery.

"Aye." Angus looked warily at Kelly, who was standing casually, as if nothing had happened.

Kelly held out his hand. "No hard feelings, eh, mate?" he said, and after a moment's thought Angus shook his hand.

"Come on," said Kelly. "Let's get back and find the girls."

James laughed as they left the stunned farm boys behind, and Kelly joined in with him. The two of them excitedly reviewed the brief fight and when James asked Kelly exactly what he had done, he slyly tapped his nose. "Aha," he said. "I'll tell you one day."

"Will you teach me to fight like you?"

"You seemed to look after yourself all right."

"I was lucky. He was pretty tough—it was like hitting a sack of flour. If he hadn't got scared off, he might have really hurt me."

"Well, that's the trick, you see," said Kelly. "Always try to scare them off before they can get the measure of you."

They eventually found the two aunts, talking by the car. Charmian explained that she had offered to drive Annie back into Keithly and as they all squeezed into the Bentley, James asked if it would be all right if he went off with Red tomorrow for the day. Charmian said it was fine with her, as long as he was back in time for supper and kept out of any mischief.

That night, as James lay in his cozy bed up in the rafters, he looked at the little plaster soldier he'd won at the fair and thought about George Hellebore. It was as if every step he'd taken since meeting him in Judy's Passage had been leading in one direction, toward the big castle up on the moors, and James pictured George somewhere inside that castle, lying in his own bed.

James put the soldier on his bedside table next to his water jug and turned on his side. The moonlight streaming in through his window created a silver patch of light on the floor that danced and shimmered. He slowly felt himself drifting into sleep.

Suddenly, from outside, there came the horrible shriek of a fox, like a child in pain. James shuddered. He was glad he had heard foxes before at his aunt's house in Kent, though the sound always made him feel uneasy even now. But there was something else making him feel this way, a tightness in his chest . . . a restlessness. He sat up and took a sip of water.

He was excited.

Excited and slightly scared.

Tomorrow he would be going to the Hellebores' castle.

CHAPTER 12—THE BLACK MIRE

Max was already up when James came down for breakfast. He was sitting at the kitchen table poking at an uneaten bowl of porridge with his spoon, while a severe-looking woman with scraped-back hair bustled about the place, cleaning around him.

James gave him the plaster guardsman, and Max set it proudly in the middle of the table to keep watch over the salt cellar.

"So," he said brightly, clapping his hands, "all set for another driving lesson? And then I thought we'd give the fishing another try. I feel very optimistic this morning. I'm sure we'll catch us a whole shoal of fish!"

James didn't know how to say it, so he came straight out with it. "Actually, Uncle Max," he said, "I have other plans for today. I'm going off with a friend I met on the train."

He was sure he saw a faint look of disappointment pass across Max's tired face, but it was soon gone.

"Of course," said his uncle, and he forced a smile. "You're a boy. You don't want to be stuck with an old duffer like me the whole time, and you did rather wear me out yesterday. Day of rest will do me good."

James felt terrible about letting his uncle down, but Max

didn't want him to worry. With a cheerful whistle he got up and cleared away his bowl.

"This is May, by the way," he said, putting an arm around the housekeeper. "An absolute treasure. I don't know what I'd do without her."

May nodded briefly.

"Hello," said James, and he introduced himself.

"Pleased to meet ye," said May, and carried on cleaning. Over the coming days James was to learn that May wasn't as gruff and fierce as she seemed at first, she was just a little shy. She didn't like to chatter and was wary of strangers, but once she got to know you she was very kindhearted and she was obviously devoted to Max.

James ate a quick breakfast, and at ten o'clock he was standing outside the pub in Keithly waiting for Red Kelly. Presently he spotted him strolling up the road, whistling, his hands stuffed into his pockets, his cap on the back of his head.

"Wotcha mate!" he called out when he saw James. "All set?"

"I suppose so," said James, holding up the knapsack that contained his lunch, plus a map and compass that his uncle had given him. Kelly had his own food in a small brown-paper bag and didn't really look equipped for a long hike over the moors. He was wearing a thin, collarless shirt, a pair of tatty black trousers held up with braces, and a huge pair of heavy town boots. "So, which way do we go, then?" he said, looking up and down the street and sniffing.

"I've got this," said James, taking a map out of his knapsack.

"Gissa look," said Kelly, and James unfolded it onto a low wall.

"Bloody hell," said Kelly, squinting at it. "Makes you think, don't it? You see a map of London and it's all roads and houses." He jabbed the map with a grubby finger. "There's nothing here, is there? It's all just empty, white space."

Indeed, there were only a few thin traces of roads across the map, which consisted mostly of hills, woods, rivers, and great blank stretches of nothing.

"Here's where we are," said James, pointing to the little cluster of black squares that made up Keithly. "And this is the road to the castle."

He followed the line of the road as it wormed its way across the map.

"It's not very straight, is it?" said Red.

"No, it avoids these boggy areas; see, the little symbols that look like tufts of grass? And it has to connect all these scattered houses and farms, then cross the river at this bridge here. . . ."

"That's a river, is it?" said Kelly, squinting at the map.

"Yes, An Abhainn Dhubh, 'the Black River,' it runs past my uncle's house. He told me that the peat up on the moors seeps into the water and turns it dark brown."

"That's going to take ages, tramping all the way up there," moaned Kelly.

"No. We won't go by road," James explained. "We'll cut across country. It'll be much more direct, but we'll have to be careful, these bogs can be dangerous. We'll try to avoid the worst parts around here, Am Boglach Dubh, 'the Black

Mire.' I think the best route would be to cross the river here, at this ford, then go up the glen, toward this ruined monastery, here." James pointed out a monument symbol next to a ruin symbol on the map. "Then we'll keep to higher ground, along this ridge, skirting the worst of the bogs. The ground should be drier from here on and we should easily get up to the pass at Am Bealach Geal and through to Loch Silverfin."

"Why's there a picture of a fish there?" said Kelly, frowning. "What does that mean?"

"That's not actually a fish—that's the loch. Loch Silverfin. It's named after a giant fish from Scottish folk tales. It's where Alfie may have gone fishing. And this here, that looks like the fish's eye, that's Castle Hellebore."

Kelly peered at the map.

"They've spelled 'castle' wrong," he said. "It says 'Caisteal.'"

"That's the Scottish spelling. This is an old map. Look, they've even got the Gaelic spelling of Silverfin—It' Airgid. . . ."

But James could see that Kelly had already lost interest and was kicking a stone around like a ball. "You're in charge of map-reading," he said.

"All right," said James, folding the map away. "Let's go, then."

They walked out of the village and up a winding track, through a copse of scrappy, twisted birch and hazel trees, toward the moors. They were soon out in the open and faced with a huge expanse of tough, wiry grass which rose steadily away from them.

"Can you see that tower, way over there?" said James, pointing. "It's all that remains of the old monastery. We'll take fresh bearings once we get there."

"You're the boss, Jimmy-boy," said Kelly, whipping at the grass with a stick he'd picked up.

The ground soon became soggy and Kelly complained that his boots were filling with water. Then, when they got to the river, which was wide and shallow at this point, soaking away at the edges into an ill-defined bog, they had to pick their way across it using stepping stones. Kelly slipped in twice and warmed the chilly air with red-hot curses. They plodded along after that, ankle-deep in wet mud.

James was wearing plimsolls that would have been useless on harder rocky ground, but were ideal for this kind of terrain. With each step, though, the soft ground released his foot with a sucking squelch.

Am Boglach Dubh, the Black Mire, was well named. The water was a murky dark brown and sluggish black bugs buzzed around over the surface. James picked a handful of bog myrtle and crushed its grayish green leaves in his hands, releasing the strong scent of resin.

"Here," he said to the disgruntled Kelly, "rub some of this on you. It's a little early in the year for midges, but they'll still be a pest. This'll help keep them away."

Kelly looked at the plants and sniffed.

"No thanks," he said, "if it's all the same to you." And he pushed past James, muttering under his breath, his boots squelching.

Forty minutes later, they began the climb up the side of the low hill where the monastery had once stood. The air was cool, but Kelly was sweating. Halfway up he stopped, swore, and spat on the ground.

"Gordon Bennett!" he said. "This walking business is a bit much, isn't it? I never walked this far in me life before. How much farther is it?"

"We're probably about halfway," said James. "But it should get a little easier once we're up into the hills."

"I thought we was in the bleeding hills," whined Kelly. "What's this, then, if it's not a hill?"

"Yes, but it gets steeper from here on in."

"Steeper? How can it get steeper? I've had enough of this, mate."

"Maybe if you didn't moan so much, you'd have more energy for walking," said James.

"I'm fed up with walking, and I'm fed up with the countryside," Kelly grumbled. "It just seems to go on forever—the same—what's the bloody point of it? There's no shops, no houses, nothing to look at, just miles and miles of bloody grass and rocks and hills and—what's that bloody prickly stuff keeps scratching me legs called again?"

"Gorse."

"Gorse! I don't care if I never see another gorse bush as long as I live. And these bleeding insects!" He slapped the back of his hand. "The countryside is all right in pictures, but in real life it's a dump. I'm knackered. Maybe I'll just wait here and you can pick me up on the way back," he said, sitting down.

James shook his head. He wasn't tired at all. This was nothing compared to the cross-country run at Eton. In fact, he was enjoying being out and getting some exercise. It was glorious up here: you could see for miles, back behind them to the south were the river and the woods and the houses of Keithly, and ahead of them, beyond the rocky hills, were the mountains, shrouded in heavy, gray clouds. Way off to the west, the ground fell away toward the coast, and James was sure he could see just a glint of light off the sea.

He took in a long, deep breath of cool air and let it out slowly. Here they were, in the middle of nowhere, free and alone. What could be better? But even as he had this thought he heard a sound, carried from far away on the strong wind, a sound like drumming. He tried to see where it was coming from and finally spotted, far off in the distance, a dark shape moving toward them.

"Look," he said, turning to Kelly and pointing.

Kelly looked. There was a horse and rider, galloping toward them.

"Looks like a girl," said Kelly, squinting into the sun and shielding his eyes from the wind. "A pretty one at that."

"You've got sharp eyes," said James as he eventually made out the girl, her hair streaming behind her.

"I can spot a pretty girl from a hundred miles, mate."

In a couple of minutes the horse had arrived, and with a slight jolt of surprise James recognized the rider. It was the girl from the circus, the one with the long blond hair and the strange green eyes.

When she drew level, she stopped at the last moment and dismounted, all in one clean, swift movement, like an acrobat.

James was impressed.

"Hi there," said the girl. "Out for a walk, are you?"

"Yes," said Kelly in a mock-posh voice. "Taking the morning air, don't you know."

"Where've you come from?" she asked, patting her horse's neck. The great black beast stood there, steaming and snorting, pacing the ground, eager to be off again. "I dinnae recognize you."

"We're staying in Keithly," said James. "I'm Max Bond's nephew, James."

"Ah, yes. I heard he had a lad staying."

"And I'm his mate," said Kelly. "You can call me Red."

"I'm very pleased to meet you," said the girl. "I'm Wilder Lawless." She stroked her horse's mane. "And this is Martini. Where're you headed?"

"Oh, we're just walking," said James.

"It's grand up here. I often ride this way, you feel like you're queen of the world. I don't usually see another soul, that's why I came over when I saw you. I suppose I'm just naturally nosy."

"Do you never see anyone?" asked Kelly.

"Och, now and then. A crofter out looking for sheep, sometimes a group of hikers."

"D'you know about Alfie Kelly?" said Red. "The boy who's missing?"

"That I do," said the girl. "Everyone around here knows about him."

"He's me cousin," said Kelly, rubbing her horse's nose.

"It's a bad business," said Wilder. "I'm sorry."

"You ever see him up this way?" asked Kelly.

"I don't know. A few days before he disappeared, I was riding up here and I did see a lad with a bag on his back, but

I was too far away to see much more and I didn't think anything of it at the time, because it was before he went missing."

"Did you ever tell anyone?" asked Kelly.

"I mentioned it to the laird."

"To Lord Hellebore?" said James.

"Aye. Because a week or so later I was up this way and I saw Hellebore out with some of his men. They were looking for something. I rode over and spoke to them. It seems they were helping in the search, so I told Lord Randolph what I'd seen and he said he'd make sure the police knew."

"And did he tell them?" asked James.

"Och, I don't know," said Wilder with a shrug. "I'm sure it was nothing. I'd better be off. You enjoy your walk, now." She smiled at James. "Your friend Red looks like he could do with some fresh air."

She put one foot into a stirrup, pulled herself back up onto the saddle, gave a brief wave, dug her heels into her horse's flanks, and thundered away from them, her blond hair flying out in the wind behind her. Kelly watched her go with a smile.

"She's a bit of all right," he said, and whistled.

"What do you mean?" asked James.

"She's a looker. A pretty girl. What d'you think? D'you think she liked me?"

"How am I supposed to know?" said James.

"I reckon she did. I reckon she was giving me the eye."

"And I reckon you're mad," said James. "Come on, let's get on."

But Kelly was still staring after the girl on her horse.

"Come on!" James shouted, and at last Kelly reluctantly turned and followed him, but now, instead of moaning about the walk and the countryside and dragging his feet, Kelly was a bundle of energy, almost skipping over the ground and chatting incessantly about Wilder.

"Did you see her smile? Lovely smile. A girl that smiles a lot is all right in my book . . . and her eyes, did you ever see eyes like that before? Green. Like a witch . . ."

And so it went for the next twenty minutes as they climbed up to the ring of hills that surrounded the loch, then through the gap at Am Bealach Geal, where they got their first view of Loch Silverfin and Caisteal Hellebore at the far end.

James knew that Scottish castles didn't often look like the familiar castles you see in picture books. They tended not to have battlements and barbicans and round towers; instead they looked more like large fortified houses, tall and square. Caisteal Hellebore was no different. It was built of dark-gray granite and consisted of two interconnected square blocks, several stories high. The taller of the two blocks had smaller turrets sticking out at the top of each corner and a very high, sloping roof. The walls were plain and grim, with only a few narrow windows cut into them. In all, it looked cold and mean and unwelcoming.

It had been built on a small island, connected to the mainland by a narrow causeway. At the start of the causeway stood a group of ugly new buildings and a huge, diseased-looking black Scots pine that leant out over the water as if about to fall in.

From here, the two boys also had a good view of

Hellebore's fence, which encircled the lake and the buildings at the far end.

They set off toward the water, and with each step James grew more uneasy. The sun had passed behind a great bank of thick gray cloud and the day had become chilly and dark. The hills seemed to close in round them now, and he had the strange feeling that he was being watched. Kelly sensed it too, and they became more and more cautious, although they had as much right to be there as anyone.

When they reached the fence, they realized that it was taller than it had first looked.

Kelly gazed up at the vicious barbed wire that topped it and whistled. "I wouldn't fancy trying to climb over that," he said. "I can't imagine Alfie bothering to come all this way and get past this bloody thing just to go fishing."

"They're a funny lot, fishermen," said James. "They're not like you and me."

"Yeah, but still . . ."

"Come on," said James. "Maybe there's a gap in the wire or something. Let's scout around it and see if there's anywhere we can get through."

So they began to circle the fence clockwise until they came to where several dead animals had been strung up on the wire.

"Nice," said Kelly. "Which one do you fancy for your lunch?"

"No thanks," said James. "I think I'll stick to my sandwiches."

Kelly read the sign: "'Keep Out. Private Property. Trespassers Will Be Shot.'" He chuckled. "Well, they certainly don't want anyone nosing around, do they? Maybe we should get back home, eh? This place gives me the willies."

"Look through here," said James, who had gone into the bushes nearby.

"What?" Kelly followed him in.

"Fresh earth," said James, studying the ground. "And on the other side of the fence too."

"So?"

"So—it could be that someone dug under the fence, and someone else filled it in."

"Yeah, or it could be that a fox done it . . . and, let's face it, they don't like animals much around here."

"Maybe," said James.

"Hold up!" Kelly suddenly hissed and pulled James down to the ground. "There's someone coming."

They peered through the shrubbery and saw a large man lumbering around the fence from the other direction.

"Keep absolutely still," Kelly whispered. "And don't make a sound."

James lay on the cold, damp ground and peered out through the dark-green spikes of a gorse bush. At first he couldn't see anything, but after a few seconds he saw a man's legs. Had he been following them? Was he one of Lord Hellebore's estate workers? But then, as he saw more clearly what the man was wearing, James realized that he couldn't be. It was the man from the circus, the one with the overly Scottish tartan trousers.

James watched as he wiped his big walrus mustache with the back of his hand, let out a loud puff of air, and looked around. He was definitely searching for something, but was he searching for them?

James wasn't scared. In fact, he had to stop himself from laughing—if the man had looked out of place among the dull farmers at the circus, he looked even more out of place up here on the high moors. This man was from the city, not the countryside. James tried to picture him strutting along Park Lane in London, or past the smart shops in Regent Street, but even there he'd look wrong. Then James realized what it was—he couldn't be British. He was Irish, maybe . . . or perhaps American?

Yes, that was it. He was the sort of character you saw in American films. James could imagine him getting into a fight with Laurel and Hardy, or even shooting it out with gangsters. Yes. He belonged in a shady waterfront dive, not in the Scottish Highlands.

He watched as the burly man squatted down and inspected something on the ground. Then he straightened up, pushed back his cap, and scratched the top of his bald head, before making a big show of yawning and patting his big belly. Finally he sauntered over to inspect the sign, reading it slowly and deliberately.

No, he definitely wasn't an estate worker. But who was he then, and what was he doing here?

The man yawned again and glanced briefly toward the bushes where James and Kelly were hiding, then he turned back to the sign.

"Okay, come on out," he said quietly. "I know you're there."

"Come and get us!" Kelly shouted back, and the man laughed.

"Ah now," he said casually. "I don't mean no harm." His harsh, tough accent was definitely American.

"I've got a knife," said Kelly, drawing a large penknife out of his pocket.

"And I've got a dog named General Grant," said the man. "But that's neither here nor there."

"What you talking about?" said Kelly.

"Just making conversation," the man growled. "You won't be needing a knife." He took a cigar out of his pocket, bit the end off it, stuck it between his fat lips, and lit it with a safety match. James smelled the tobacco smoke drifting past.

"It's all right," he whispered to Kelly. "Let's talk to him."

Kelly sighed and nodded, then the two of them crawled out of the bushes, dusted the dirt and leaves off their clothes, and went over to where the big man had sat down on a rock.

"I *thought* you was kids," he said as they drew near. "I saw you from the top of the hill. Didn't mean to alarm you. I'm just naturally cautious by nature." He stuck out a large square hand and James shook it.

Up close, James took the opportunity to study the man more carefully. He'd certainly lived a bit. He had a flattened, fleshy nose, which made his breathing noisy, his left ear was thick with scars, and one of his eyes was red with broken blood vessels. This was a man who'd been in one too many fights. His purple, blotchy skin also suggested that he'd had one too many strong drinks. James could smell whiskey on his breath. He was sweating heavily and had to wipe his face every few minutes with a large, spotted hand-kerchief.

"The name's Mike Moran," he said out of the side of his mouth, which still held the smoldering cigar. "Better known as Meatpacker Moran."

James and Kelly introduced themselves.

"Pleased to meet you, I'm sure," said Meatpacker, and he spat out a flake of tobacco. "Been keeping an eye on you two," he said, tapping his bloodshot eye. "Wondering what you was up to. Then I come down here, and you've disappeared. Well, nothing escapes the sharp eye of old Meatpacker. You left a trail, see?" And with that, Meatpacker led them over to a patch of earth where he proudly pointed out the footprint of a boy.

"Exhibit A," he said with a broad smile that exposed a row of stubby, broken, yellow teeth. "You should be more careful in future."

James stared at the print. He was no expert, but he felt that there was something wrong, and then he realized what it was. The print was dry, baked into the mud, which meant that it couldn't have been made today. In fact, it must have been made some time ago—when the ground was still soft and damp before the recent sunny spring weather. He looked more closely. No, it definitely wasn't the print of his own plimsoll, or one of Kelly's battered old boots.

Meatpacker strolled back over to the fence and peered through it toward the loch.

"Lonely spot up here. What are you two fellers up to?"

"Just out for a walk," said James, and he signaled to Kelly to look at the print. Kelly squinted at it, but it meant nothing to him and he shrugged.

Meatpacker wandered into the bushes. "What was so interesting in these bushes, I wonder," he said.

"Look properly," James hissed to Kelly, pointing at the print. "It's not one of ours."

Kelly looked and tried to fit his boot into it. It was too big. "I think you could be right," he whispered, just as Meatpacker came crashing out of the undergrowth in a cloud of reeking cigar smoke.

"Eh?" he said. "Why were you skulking in the shrubbery?"

"We saw you coming and thought we'd better hide," said James.

"And just why did you think you might need to do that,

eh?" said Meatpacker, coming very close and glaring into James's face with his good eye.

"They're not too keen on strangers up here," said James. "You've seen the fence and the sign."

"I sure have. Now why d'you think they'd need a fence like that? Right up here, miles from anywhere. Don't seem natural to me."

"No," said James.

Meatpacker laughed and slapped James on the back so hard, he nearly knocked him over. "Now, I expect you're wondering just who I am, huh?" he roared. "Poking around up here myself."

"It did cross my mind," said Kelly. " I mean, you're not Scotch, are you?"

"Nope," said Meatpacker, puffing out his chest. "I'm a New York man. Bronx born and bred, one of the fighting Irish."

"There you go," said Kelly, grinning. "My family's from Galway."

Meatpacker startled Kelly by giving him a big bear hug. "Ah," he said, "it's always nice to meet one of your own. Me granddaddy was from Shannon."

"So, now we're friends, are you going to tell us what you're doing up here?" said Kelly.

"Well, I can't say too much, but as you're one of me own, I'll tell you a little. I don't see as it can do any harm. I'm a detective. From the Pinkerton Detective Agency in America."

"'We Never Sleep!'" said James.

"Huh?"

"That's your motto, isn't it? 'We Never Sleep.' I've read about Pinkerton's."

"That's right," said Meatpacker. "'We Never Sleep.'"

"And are you on a case right now?"

"Now, you'll keep this between yourselves, won't you? As it happens, I'm investigating the nabob who owns this fence and everything behind it."

"Lord Hellebore?" said James.

"That's your man. I expect you know he used to live in the United States."

"Yes."

"Had a brother, Algar, good-looking feller by all accounts, your original man-about-town. He was the golden boy, set to inherit the earth, but then one day old Algar disappears. Now the reason we know this is because Randolph's wife, Maude, comes to us. Seems that at one time she had been keen on both brothers, and couldn't choose between the two of them. Algar was her favorite, but Randolph was more persistent, and he wears her down and wears her down until she agrees to marry him and forget about the brother. But she's always been sweet on Algar, and now he's disappeared. She asks a lot of questions, but is given the brush-off by Randolph. In fact, Randolph dumps her altogether. Cooks up some story about her seeing another man and gets a divorce.

"Maude's not the quitting type, though. She wants to know what happened to Algar, so she comes to us and we starts nosing around, but it's tough. The guy runs a very tight ship. All very secret. Nobody really knows exactly what he's up to." Meatpacker dropped his voice to a conspiratorial whisper. "Except me . . ."

"What?" James leant in closer.

Meatpacker tapped his rubbery nose and winked his bleary, red eye. "I'll tell you what he's up to . . . he's up to no good!" He tilted back his great fat head and roared with laughter.

Once he'd gotten over his joke he carried on with his story. "Soon afterward, Randolph ups stakes and steams across the ocean blue to bonnie Scotland. Now, why do you suppose he did that?"

"He inherited this estate," said James.

"Sure. But he was running a very successful operation in America. Why'd he leave it all behind? What was he running from, d'you suppose? And what happened to his brother?"

"Do you know?" asked James.

"Maybe Hellebore's wife and his brother, Algar, were closer than she let on, or maybe Hellebore just bumped him off, so he could keep the whole shooting match for himself. Or maybe some experiment went wrong."

"Experiment?" asked James. "But I thought he made weapons."

"Oh, that he does. But he's always looking for ways to make new ones. So's he can sell the latest, most deadliest weapons on the market. So I guess he has to do a certain amount of research to stay one step ahead of the competition."

Kelly whistled appreciatively. "So, he's making some new sort of bomb?"

"Dunno," said Meatpacker. "A new bomb? Maybe a new type of gun that shoots around corners? A faster tank? A bigger submarine? Who knows? Maybe even a fancy kinda invisible airplane, or something." He chuckled. "But you can be sure, whatever it is, it's some new way of killing more people more efficiently."

James's mind was turning over this information. "Do you think," he said thoughtfully, "that Lord Hellebore would be prepared to kill someone to stop him from finding out too much?"

Meatpacker sucked his bushy mustache. "Good question," he said after a long pause. "And the simple answer is, I don't know. If he's already killed his brother, who's to say he wouldn't kill again? And there have been accidents, other people have gone missing, guys who worked for him. The wife even claimed that he'd tried to have her done in, make it look like an accident, but there's no hard evidence that he's a killer. . . ."

"Have you heard about a boy called Alfie Kelly?" said James, and he quickly explained to Meatpacker exactly why he and Kelly were there.

Afterward the detective stood up and stretched, the buttons straining on his tartan waistcoat. "So that's what you're up to, is it? Doing some sleuthing of your own."

"We've already found this," said James, and he showed Meatpacker the freshly turned earth behind the bushes.

"Well, now, lads," said Meatpacker, taking a drink from a silver hip flask, "this sort of thing is best left to the professionals. You'll only go getting yourselves into a whole lot of trouble. If this all adds up, it adds up to one thing—that our Lord Hellebore is a very dangerous man. Now, me . . . I'm prepared. . . ."

With a flourish like a cheap magician, Meatpacker rolled

up a trouser leg and displayed a small, pearl-handled revolver strapped to his shin in a leather holster.

"Is that a Derringer?" asked Kelly.

"It sure is."

Kelly laughed. "I thought that was a lady's gun."

"Well, now, and aren't I a lady's man?" said Meatpacker, and he laughed his great booming laugh again. "It may not look much, lads, but it's got me out of many a scrape. Now then, I've work to do. You fellers can tag along with me for a while if you keep your heads down and don't step on my toes. But when it gets serious, I'll have to send you on your way."

Meatpacker did a thorough search of the area, all the while regaling the boys with hair-raising stories about his exploits as a Pinkerton man. He told of stakeouts and shoot-outs and fistfights in back alleys. He told of bloodstained corpses and the bright flash of explosions in the night. It sounded daring and exciting and James asked him question after question. It was obvious that Meatpacker was glad of the company and had been feeling lost and lonely up here on the moors. He was a garrulous chap and used to company.

Once he was satisfied he'd found out all he could here, he led the boys around the fence toward the castle, keeping in the cover of the hills. They soon came to where the water ran off the loch down a small river that eventually fed into An Abhainn Dhubh, the Black River, farther down the glen. It was too wide to ford, but they found a small bridge near the fence.

Meatpacker stopped halfway across and stroked his mustache. "What do you make of that?" he said, nodding toward a complicated structure of cement blocks, wooden runways, and netting that had been constructed where the river flowed under the wire.

"Looks like a dam of some sort," said Kelly.

"Could be," said Meatpacker. "But it don't seem to be stopping the flow of the water none."

"Maybe it's something to do with fish?" said James.

"Yeah," said Kelly. "To keep fish out."

"Or to keep them in," said Meatpacker. Then he spat into the water and walked on. "No matter," he said. "This case ain't about fish."

They pressed on, and after a quarter of an hour they arrived at a sheltered spot with clear views over to the castle. Meatpacker produced a pair of binoculars and they lay on their bellies while he studied the castle. After a while he took the glasses from his face and handed them to James.

"Take a look," he said, "and tell me what you see. We'll find out how good an eye you have."

"All right," said James, and he looked through the glasses. It took him a moment to get his bearings, but he eventually found the tip of the castle roof and worked his way down, adjusting the focus so that the walls came sharply into view.

"At the end of the causeway there's a large gravel parking area," he said, describing the scene to Meatpacker. "Then you reach the main entrance to the castle across a small bridge, not a drawbridge—it looks permanent. The lower windows are all barred, but not the upper ones." He scanned the length of the causeway, following it to the shore. "There's a gatehouse, which has been repaired recently by the look of it, then the road carries on to a second gate in the new fence."

"See anything else?" asked Meatpacker.

"Oh, there's a sort of sentry box with somebody sitting in it with what looks like a hunting rifle over his knees. . . ."

Meatpacker grabbed the glasses back. "Is there, now? . . . I didn't see that, where is it?"

"It's set into the wall near the gatehouse; it's in shadow, but you can just make it out."

"By God, you're right, well spotted."

Meatpacker handed the glasses back to James.

"The place is better guarded than Buckingham Palace! Look to see if there's anything else I've missed."

As James looked again, he saw the heavy castle doors swing open and a man in bloodstained white overalls came out, carrying a large bucket. He said something to somebody inside the castle, then walked over to the edge of the bridge and tipped the contents of the bucket into the loch. James saw a filthy stream of bloody water pour out and then what looked like several pieces of raw meat and offal. He focused on the water and saw it surge and bubble up as some creature, or creatures, thrashed about just beneath the surface.

"There's something in the lake," he said. "Some kind of animal, I think."

"Well, that needn't bother us," said Meatpacker. "We're not here to study Lord Hellebore's pets. Come on, let's move on and see what's around the other side."

"Wait a minute," said James. "There's someone else coming out." As he watched, two figures walked across the bridge from the castle: George Hellebore and his father, carrying shotguns, broken across the elbow. Lord Hellebore seemed to be telling George off about something; he looked angry and George looked sullen and cowed. They stopped and Lord Hellebore gesticulated wildly before slapping George hard on the back of his head, knocking his cap onto the floor. When George bent down to retrieve it, Randolph gave him such a kick up the backside that he sent him sprawling into the dirt. Randolph offered his son a last, scornful look, then strode off. George brushed off his jacket, put his cap back on his head, picked up his gun, and followed his father.

They were met by a third person, who came from the gatehouse. He was a very small man with long arms and a stooped back that made him resemble an ape. He had a long nose with a bulbous end, like a Ping-Pong ball on a stalk, and wore an incongruous, battered bowler hat. His face was so weather-beaten it looked purple, and it was impossible to tell his age, although he seemed as old as the craggy rocks around the loch. Four tatty, mean-looking Jack Russell terriers darted around his heels, and he let fly a kick at one of them, but the dog was obviously expecting it and leapt out of the way.

The monkey-man touched the brim of his hat and took the gun from Hellebore, who said something to him before walking on; in a few moments all three of them had disappeared into the gatehouse.

After this, all was quiet, Meatpacker and the boys waited for a while before cautiously leaving their hiding place and skirting the edge of the hills until they arrived at the road, which was a wide dirt track, deeply rutted by tires. They found a spot where a bend between high banks hid them from the buildings, and darted across to the safety of the hilly ground on the other side. They made it to the cover of some rocks just in time, as a lorry came rumbling down the road from the direction of the castle and thumped and banged its way toward Keithly, mud flying up behind it from the wheels.

"That was close," said Meatpacker. "We'd best be on our toes from here on in. Now, let's go see what we can see."

They moved through the higher ground until they had a good view of the castle compound, where a second fence had been erected about ten feet behind the wire one. It was a solid, wooden affair some twelve feet high and topped with spikes. There was a makeshift guardhouse here, next to a gate, and behind the gate was a high lookout tower where two men stood, smoking cigarettes, silhouetted against the darkening sky.

"I told you he was a secretive beggar," said Meatpacker. "And look over yonder."

He pointed to an open patch of ground behind the hills where the grass was closely cropped and a twin-engined airplane stood beside a large, tin-roofed shed.

"An airstrip. Quite a setup this guy's got himself. Now, let's take a look-see what's behind that fence." Meatpacker climbed up into a twisted, stunted rowan tree to try to get a better look, but he was too big and ungainly and managed only the first couple of branches before he got stuck and had to come down.

Once again he passed the glasses to James.

"Here," he said. "You've got good eyes, shin up there and tell me what's what." Meatpacker yawned and settled down with his back to the tree.

James was a good climber and was soon at the top, from where he had a fairly clear view over the fence. He could see the ugly, new, concrete buildings that had been visible from the other end of the loch. They were clustered around a couple of older stone structures and an open cobbled area where three lorries were parked in a row, one of them being unloaded.

"What's a lorry?" said Meatpacker after James had described the scene.

"A truck," said Kelly. "You'd call it a truck."

"Yeah, I got you," said Meatpacker. "And what are they unloading?"

"I'm not sure," said James. "It looks like animal feed of some sort."

"Animal feed?"

"Yes, and over at the back there's a row of what look like animal pens."

"I guess he has to feed his little army," said Meatpacker.

Indeed, it did resemble an army barracks. Men walked busily about the place, dressed mainly in tweeds with flat caps, but occasionally a figure in white overalls and rubber boots would hurry from one building to another.

"Any clues as to what the buildings might be?" asked Meatpacker sleepily, and he yawned again.

"A couple of them are dormitories, I think," said James, who had seen beds through the windows. "And a guardroom of some sort. The larger ones nearer the castle could be small factory buildings, but if you ask me they're not making anything as big as a tank or an aeroplane. . . ."

But Meatpacker said nothing; instead, James was

answered by a long, rasping snore. He looked down. Meatpacker had fallen asleep.

James climbed out of the tree and smiled at Kelly.

"'We Never Sleep!'" he said, and they laughed. The noise made Meatpacker open his good eye.

"I ain't asleep," he said, "just resting." He hauled himself up and stretched. "Tell you the truth, this country air makes me tired. I'm a city man. I'm used to busy streets and crowds of people. I don't know what to do out here. After all, you can't take fingerprints off a tree trunk. You can't ask a sheep if they've seen anything. . . . And the locals . . . they don't want nothing to do with me. Lord Hellebore's pumped money into the place; he's their hero. So what if he lives in secret up here?"

James looked up at the sky and realized that it was getting late.

"If Kelly and I are going to get back before it's dark, we'll have to set off fairly soon," he said.

"Yeah, you'd better get going," said Meatpacker.

"What are you going to do?" asked Kelly.

"I'm going to keep on the case. Camp out up here, watch their comings and goings, get a feel for their routine. You two fellers can help me out. Ask as many questions around the place as you can. People'll probably be more happy to talk to a couple of kids than to an old scrapper like myself. And remember: Don't do anything else until you hear from me. I get paid to take risks."

As James headed off with Kelly, he couldn't help thinking that Meatpacker Moran wasn't at all equipped for a night on the moors, unless he'd already built a camp somewhere nearby with a tent and provisions. But he seemed happy enough, and he'd obviously dealt with worse situations than this in his time.

Kelly's imagination had been fired by the day's events, and on the way back he entertained himself with all sorts of lurid imaginings as to what Lord Hellebore might be up to in his fortress in the hills.

But all James could think about was that one lonely footprint and the boy who had made it. . . . And the man in bloody overalls tipping the bucket of dead stuff into the seething moat.

CHAPTER 14—THE MASSACRE OF THE INNOCENTS

The magnificent stag stood proudly on the hillside, its front legs up on a granite boulder that was almost completely covered by a cushion of pink-flowered moss campion. It was a big red deer standing nearly five feet high, with wide, heavy antlers. It looked as if it was posing for a picture—*Monarch of the Glen*. It sniffed the air, then roared once. It knew that there was danger nearby.

Red deer are cautious beasts, with excellent eyesight and sense of smell, and one wrong move would send this fellow skittering and leaping away across the rocks.

Three figures waited patiently in the shadows of a narrow corrie, dressed in gray hunting gear. At their head was Lord Randolph Hellebore, lying stretched out on the ground in a bed of alpine speedwell, peering intently through a small telescope. Behind him was George, staring sullenly at the back of his father's head, and behind George, crouched by a rock, his ever-present bowler hat squashed onto his tiny head, was the man in charge of hunting and fishing on the estate, Randolph's gillie, Cleek MacSawney.

MacSawney was pouring three cups of whiskey from a bottle. George looked at him with disgust. He was pickled in whiskey—he drank it for breakfast, lunch, and supper. George had never seen him eat, only drink. His skin had the appearance of boiled ham; the fat squashy end of his long nose had great gaping pores and the whites of his watery eyes were permanently pink.

"Look at him," breathed Lord Hellebore, wriggling back on his belly and sitting up once he was sure that he was out of view of the deer. "There are fourteen points on those antlers. He's an imperial."

"He's a fine, braw fiadh," grunted MacSawney, and he passed a whiskey to his master. Randolph drank it in one gulp as if it were water.

George sipped at his—he hated the taste, he hated the way it burned his throat, and he hated the way it sat in his stomach like acid—but he had no choice. If he was going to be a hunter, if he was going to be a man, he would have to keep up with his father.

"What's the distance?" Randolph asked.

"Eighty yards," said MacSawney bluntly.

"Do we risk a shot?"

"It's now or never," said MacSawney, drawing the cover off a rifle and passing it to George. "The land's too open from here on up. We're way above the treeline, and if we follow the fold in the rocks we'll get on the weather side of him."

Randolph turned to George and smiled, showing his big, white teeth beneath his golden mustache.

"Go on, then, son," he said. "He's all yours."

"I don't know, Dad," said George. "It's a long shot."

"No. It's about time you shot yourself a deer. This is your day."

George sighed and got down on all fours. He was tired

and hungry and soaking wet. They had been stalking the deer since first light that morning. It was now nearly dark, and all they had eaten was oatcakes.

They were out on Angreach Mhòr, far above Loch Silverfin and the castle. It was bleak and barren up here, and the cold, thin rain had completely soaked through his hunting tweeds.

George looked down the sights of his rifle and picked out the figure of the stag, which was taking fitful snatches at young heather shoots and grass, all the while on the alert.

George had no desire to shoot the poor animal, but he knew his father demanded it. To his father, this was the most worthwhile activity a man could undertake. How many times had he heard him praising the joys of stalking? "We're like Indians," he would say. "Forget all the feeble trappings of civilized society. This is man against beast. This is man taking his rightful place in nature. Man is a hunter. We forget that nowadays, but it's how we started. To stalk a deer you need energy, strength, perseverance, patience, a steady hand, and a quick eye."

As George watched, the stag turned and trotted warily up the mountain.

"He's moving too much," George whispered.

"Ach," MacSawney spat. "If you sit there long enough, laddie, he'll walk right over the top of yon mountain and be halfway to Glen Shiel. Ye've one shot. Make it count."

George was all too aware that MacSawney didn't like him. Apart from Lord Hellebore, MacSawney didn't like anyone. He was a vicious, sharp-tongued drunk. The previous laird had been strict with him and had kept his nature in check, but Randolph gave him a free hand and more power than he had ever had before, so he had become an invaluable right-hand man. In fact, Lord Hellebore was slightly in awe of him. To Randolph, MacSawney was a village elder, a wise, old man full of country lore, who knew all there was to know about the land and the animals on it. But George knew that MacSawney had no love for animals. To him they were just his livelihood, no more deserving of kindness or respect than a rock or a tree.

When it came down to it, as far as George was concerned, MacSawney hated animals and needed no excuse to shoot, trap, poison, or sometimes even club them to death.

"Kill him," MacSawney hissed. "Do it. It's your last chance."

George centered his sights on the deer's foreleg and took a deep breath.

He knew what to do, and muttered the advice to himself. "Bring it up the leg and when you see brown, fire. . . . Bring it up the leg and when you see brown, fire. . . ."

He nervously tried to steady the gun, gently squeezing the trigger, still holding his breath. The deer moved. George exhaled and cursed silently. He knew how furious his father would be if he let the stag get away.

There was nothing for it. He quickly lined up his target again, closed his eyes, and pulled.

He felt the gun hammer back into his shoulder, heard the deafening crack echo off down the valley, and when he opened his eyes there was no sign of the deer.

Had it fled? Had he missed completely or, worse still, only wounded it?

"Well done, boy, well done." Randolph clapped him on the back and passed him the telescope.

George took it and raked the hillside until he spotted the lifeless body of the stag.

"A clean shot," MacSawney conceded, and the three of them tramped up the mountainside toward their prey.

When they arrived, Randolph knelt down and studied the wound in the animal's chest.

"Right through the heart. He won't have felt a thing." His dipped his hand in the blood that was oozing out across the animal's fur, then stood and wiped it across the boy's face.

"First blood. Good boy."

George blinked. The blood felt sticky and hot.

MacSawney grinned at him. "Now you look like a proper red Indian," he said.

MacSawney gralloched the deer—slitting open its belly and removing the innards—then they lugged it down the mountain and loaded it onto a waiting pony.

That had all taken place six months ago—last October—and now the stag's head was mounted on the wall of the castle dining room. George Hellebore was looking at it now, at its dead, glassy eyes, and remembering that day. Because it was then, trudging down the mountainside through the drizzle, the blood washing down his face into his mouth and eyes, that a terrible thought had first struck him.

He missed his mother.

He was lost and lonely and confused, and he missed her terribly.

And once he realized it, he couldn't put the thought

out of his mind. So that now he missed her more than ever.

It was this castle that did it. He hated it. Its gloominess, its darkness, its tiny windows and huge, heavy walls. He had loved it at first, of course; for a young boy it had seemed an impossibly exciting and romantic place, with the turrets and the causeway and all its secret passages and hideaways. He had imagined knights there, and great battles, Highland warriors in kilts waving claymores. It was a fine place to play. But he had never had anyone to play with, to share it with, and he had slowly lost interest in his solitary games. Now, playing knights no longer appealed to him, and the castle had come to seem more of a prison than a home. There was nothing comfortable here, nothing soft and warming. Everywhere you looked, there were guns on the walls, dead animals, stuffed fish, and huge, heavy furniture that didn't invite you to sit upon it. It was full of men and men's things. Even the kitchen staff were all male.

George shivered, although it wasn't particularly cold. The dining hall was the same temperature all year-round, due to the thickness of the walls. They kept in the heat in winter and kept it out in summer, though there was always a log burning in the hearth, whatever the weather.

Two suits of armor stood, one on either side of the fireplace, above which hung a huge oil painting, darkened with age. It was violent and upsetting and very Victorian, showing one of the classical subjects the Victorians loved so dearly— the Massacre of the Innocents, when Herod, warned that a future king of the Jews would be born in Bethlehem, ordered that every male child under the age of two be slaughtered. The painting showed a group of men, some dressed as Roman soldiers, some half-naked in billowing robes, attacking a group of women and children with short swords and long knives. The women were screaming in terror and trying to protect their children. One man in the center of the painting held a boy up in the air, and several babies were trampled underfoot.

George had often wondered whether this violent and disturbing picture was a suitable decoration for a dining room, but he doubted whether his father had even so much as glanced at it. George often studied it, however—because of the woman.

She stood off to one side, her face just visible between two silver blades, and there was something in her expression . . .

He had no pictures of his mother, nothing to remember her by, and he hated the idea that this terrified woman might be all that he had to remind him of her.

When he and his father had left America and moved to England five years ago, they had left her behind, and Lord Hellebore had said to him bluntly: "You will never see your mother again."

They had been walking on the deck of the great steamship SS *Holden*, crossing the cold, gray Atlantic in midwinter. It had been stormy that morning and the deck was lashed by stinging rain and the spray from the huge waves that heaved all around them and smashed into the ship's hull with a noise like cannon fire. There was nobody else on deck—nobody else would be crazy enough—but Lord Hellebore insisted that every morning at nine they walk five times around the ship for exercise, whatever the conditions. George was horribly seasick and had to keep breaking away in order to vomit over the railings, but his father was untouched by either the weather or his son's condition. He might have been strolling through Central Park in New York on a sunny afternoon, discussing baseball, for all it affected him.

But he wasn't discussing baseball. He was discussing George's mother.

"She was a weak woman," he shouted into the wind.

"You talk about her as if she were dead," said George miserably.

"As far as you are concerned, she is," said Randolph bluntly. "We have no need of women in our lives."

George hadn't really understood. He had been kept out of things and had picked up only scraps of information from his nanny's hints and what he could understand from the forbidden newspaper reports he sneakily rescued from the garbage and read when his father was at work.

He knew that there had been a court case that involved another man, his mother's lover, and that his father, using the most expensive lawyers, had kept "custody" of George.

George hadn't known what "custody" meant at first, but he soon learnt. He learnt that it meant that he was to live with his father and never see his mother again.

George had been younger then, too young to care. He had worshiped Randolph and was happy to be with him, and for years he hadn't thought twice about the woman they had left behind in America, but suddenly, wiping the dead stag's blood from his face, watching MacSawney and his father dragging the animal through the grass, he had grown aware of an emptiness within him, as if a part of him were no longer there.

He couldn't say any of this to his father—he couldn't say

it to anyone, they would think him a sissy—the worst insult of all. He had once woken, crying from a dream about his mother and had lain awake all night, too sad and frightened to go back to sleep; when he'd told his father about it at breakfast, Randolph had beaten him with a cane and told him not to be so weak and to put such childish thoughts out of his mind.

Sitting in the great hall, eating his supper, he remembered that beating, he remembered the unjustness of it, as if any person could have control over his own dreams!

There were three of them at the table: himself, his father, way down at the other end, and his father's chief scientist, Dr. Perseus Friend, a thin, pale man of thirty who was already losing his wispy blond hair and was forever polishing his wire-rimmed spectacles. Perseus was the only other person who ever ate with them. Randolph worked all hours of the day and night, and he liked to discuss his progress with Perseus over supper.

Perseus Friend had been born in Germany of an Irish father and a Russian mother. His father had worked for the German army and, during the war, had developed poison gas for use in the trenches, working with chlorine, phosgene, and mustard gas.

After the war, the defeated Germans had been banned from maintaining any real army, and work such as Professor Friend's was strictly forbidden. So Perseus's father had traveled the world, selling his services to the highest bidder, and everywhere he went, Perseus went too, learning all he could along the way.

They had gone first to Japan, then to Argentina, and

finally to Russia. The Russians had suffered twice as many losses from the Germans' gas attacks in the war as any other army and were keen to develop weapons of their own.

Perseus had been a fiercely clever child and had followed his father into science; but, whereas his father had been a chemist, his own interest lay in biology. He had become intrigued by the use of germs and germ warfare; using diseases to fight the enemy. The two of them made a formidable combination, and eventually Lord Hellebore heard of the brilliant father-and-son team working in the Soviet government laboratories at Saratov.

Once Randolph had built his new operation here in Scotland, he had hired their services, but an accident at the Russian laboratory, shortly before they were due to depart, had left seven scientists dead, poisoned by their own gas, including Professor Friend. Perseus had always suspected that it was no accident at all; that the Russians had wanted to silence Friend and keep his secrets, and it was only by sheer luck that he himself hadn't been in the laboratory at the time. So he had left silently and furtively and came to Scotland as quickly as he could.

Perseus's only interest was his work—it was all he talked about, it was all he thought about. He had no curiosity about any other human activity and was utterly unfeeling toward other people. He never experienced love, or hate, or sadness, or happiness or even anger—unless an experiment went wrong, or his work was interrupted by some inconvenience. Women held no interest for him, so this isolated castle was the ideal place for him to live and work.

George looked at him now, cutting up his meat as if he

were dissecting some hapless creature on one of his slabs. There was something horrible about the way he ate, talking incessantly, oblivious to what exactly he had just pulled off the end of his fork with his neat little teeth, chewing with his mouth open, with no apparent enjoyment. It reminded George of a lizard eating, its eyes looking around, surely not relishing the taste of a spider or a beetle.

Tonight, it was roast beef. The centerpiece of every meal was some boiled or roasted meat. George remembered the days when his mother had had some influence over their food and his diet had been more varied and less heavy.

No. He must stop thinking about his mother; it only made him unhappy. But the alternative was to listen to Dr. Friend droning on about Germany. His voice was very irritating, slightly high-pitched, dull, and unmodulated; it droned on like a train along a track, with no light and shade and certainly no regard as to whether anyone was actually listening to him.

"This Adolf Hitler, the new chancellor of Germany, is an interesting man," he was saying. "I have been reading his book, *Mein Kampf,* and various articles and pamphlets that I arranged to have sent over. Herr Hitler has some very modern ideas about biological purity and the selective breeding of humans to create a master race. You should meet him, Randolph. His National Socialist Party will make some big changes. I can assure you that he would be most interested in our work here, and a friendly and cooperative government that understood our aims would make it much easier to obtain live subjects for our experiments. . . ."

George put down his knife and fork with a clatter and

interrupted him, as much to shut him up as anything else. "I thought the Germans weren't allowed to develop their army," he said.

"Hitler will change all that," said Dr. Friend without looking up from his plate. "Hitler will make the country great again, and we will be there beside him to reap the benefits. I was reading the *Hamburg Scientific Journal* just last night, and there was a fascinating article about twins, apparently . . ."

"Are you not eating, George?" boomed Randolph from half a mile away, at the other end of the black oak table, while Dr. Friend carried on talking over their conversation, oblivious to the fact that somebody else was speaking.

"I'm not very hungry this evening, Father."

"You must eat. Meat is good for you, gives you iron, builds your muscles and bones."

Before George could say anything in reply, there was a knock at the door and Cleek MacSawney came in. He looked distastefully at George and Dr. Friend, before lurching over to Randolph.

Halfway across the room, one of the laird's dogs jumped up and padded over to sniff the newcomer, but MacSawney lashed out with a foot and caught it in the belly. It whimpered and scurried under the table, its tail between its legs.

MacSawney murmured something in his boss's ear and Randolph's face darkened, his brow creasing in a heavy frown. He wiped his mouth on his napkin, pushed his plate to one side, and stood up.

"Finish your supper," he said tersely, and left with MacSawney.

Through all of this, Perseus had not stopped talking and eating, and he didn't even look up from his food as Randolph went out.

". . . genetics is the answer, but it is still too poorly understood, we have progressed hardly at all since Mendel. Of course, we cannot get the eels to breed, the simple fact is— we need people. . . ."

After dinner, there was no sign of Lord Hellebore, so George sneaked into his office. He knew that if he was caught his father would thrash him, but he didn't care anymore. At one time, all he had thought of was trying to please him, but since the sports day at Eton he knew that, no matter what he did, he would never please him, never come up to his standards. So he had stopped trying.

George started searching through Randolph's desk. It wasn't locked. Nothing was locked in here. It was forbidden for anyone to enter, and the servants were too terrified of the laird to disobey his orders. However, George didn't find what he was looking for in the desk, so he went over to the filing cabinet that sat near the tall, barred window.

He looked down the labels on the drawers:

ESTATE BUSINESS. That was no use.

SILVERFIN.

His father had borrowed the name of the loch for his latest research project. The SilverFin team was headed by Perseus and worked in secret behind the locked steel door of the laboratory under the castle. George wasn't interested in that.

The third drawer down was marked PERSONAL and he yanked it open.

He rifled through the contents and eventually found what he was looking for—a folder of legal documents and letters. He pulled the folder out and searched quickly through the papers. Nothing—nothing—nothing—there it was!

The address of his mother's house in Boston.

He read it several times to memorize it, then carefully placed everything back how he had found it and, after checking that the coast was clear, he hurried out and up to his room.

Once there, he sat at his desk, filled his pen with ink and wrote the address down while he still remembered it. Then, keeping an ear cocked for any sounds outside, he took out a sheaf of writing paper and began to write.

Dearest Mother,

I know I have never written to you before, but lately I have been thinking about you a great deal. . . .

There was a crash from down below and he stopped, his hands hovering over the letter, ready to hide it away in an instant. The huge front doors had slammed shut and he heard shouts and commotion. He waited for the noise to die down then carried on, his heart thumping.

It was a risky business. He would have to write this letter in total secrecy, then go to the post office at Keithly and post it himself; but just writing those few simple words had cheered him up. Not for the first time, he wished that he had someone to talk to, someone to share all his fears with, to dispel his loneliness. With a pang of guilt he recalled spotting James Bond at the circus. For a moment, when he'd seen him, his heart had jumped. He had smiled—here was someone he knew, a familiar face—and then he'd remembered that Bond was supposed to be his enemy, that he'd beaten him in the race, and all the bitterness and regret had bubbled up inside him like poison until a red veil of anger had fallen over him. How different things might have been if he had gone across and shaken his hand and called a truce. But no, the habits of his short lifetime were too powerful, and he had paid those two thugs to go and beat up the younger boy.

His thoughts were interrupted by further commotion coming from below, more angry shouts and another voice, crying out as if in pain. Maybe it was one of the workers being disciplined. His father was very strict, and anybody who stepped out of line was dealt with very harshly by the brutal MacSawney.

George tried to block the sounds out. At least if someone else was getting it in the neck, he was safe for a while. As the noises died away he carried on writing. For a long while there was silence and he lost himself in the letter, trying to say everything he had wanted to say to his mother since he had last seen her, but then he heard something snuffling at his door.

He knew what it was and for a moment he was revolted. This place, it was awful. He couldn't bear it anymore. The sniffing continued. He pictured wide, wet nostrils and a drooling mouth. He stared at the door and waited for the thing to go away.

After a while he heard footsteps shuffling off down the corridor, and he was alone again. He picked up his pen and put the nib to the paper. . . .

Please, mother, I can stand it here no longer. . . .

"Okay?" said Max. "Do you think you're ready?"

"As ready as I'll ever be," said James.

"Then let her go!"

James slipped the car into gear, released the brake, and moved slowly forward down the driveway. For the past couple of days he had been driving around the field in the mornings and learning about the engine in the afternoons, helping Max to strip down the various parts, then cleaning and replacing them, so that he had slowly gotten to know how the whole thing worked.

Max had shown him the oil sump, the gearbox, the two separate axles for the front wheels, the driveshaft, and the differential, which made the rear wheels spin at different speeds. At first James hadn't understood the need for this, but then Max demonstrated how, when turning a corner, the outer wheels on a car have to travel farther than the inner ones and so have to spin faster to keep up.

What had at first seemed horribly confusing was now beginning to make sense, and he appreciated just what an extraordinary machine a car was.

Eventually, Max reckoned that James was competent enough to leave the field and try the road again. So here he was, nervously negotiating the rutted track, his hands gripping the wheel, his hair blowing untidily in the wind.

This was very different from the paddock. He was all too aware of the nearness of the trees on either side and, as he picked up speed, they swished past angrily. But he made it to the gatepost without any mishaps and swapped seats with Max so that he could turn the car around on the main road.

"That was perfect," said his uncle, sliding back across so that James could take the wheel again. "Now, let's try it a little faster on the way back, eh?"

Since returning from the castle, James had heard nothing from either Red or Meatpacker and he was growing restless. Learning to drive was keeping his mind off things, but thoughts about the Hellebores were never far away and he was anxious to be doing something more about Alfie. But they had promised to do nothing until Meatpacker got in touch.

For the next hour, James drove up and down the drive, growing more and more confident, until Max suggested that this time he really went for it.

"She's a fast car, James. She needs to be driven hard. Really put your foot down. You can do it. Just feel the car, and feel the road. . . ."

James prepared himself. He knew the driveway quite well by now. He pictured the bumps he had to avoid, the straights where he could accelerate safely and the bends where he would have to slow down.

He imagined himself on the racetrack at Brooklands, lined up with the other cars, a crowd of spectators cheering. He revved the engine, hearing its growl fill the valley. He had no other thoughts in his mind now, except the car and the road. The castle wasn't there and Eton was a million miles away.

He selected first gear and pulled away smoothly. He was quickly into second, then third, then he had to shift down on the first corner. He grinned—now there was a good, long stretch and he made it up into fourth gear before he hit the bend, shifting down and applying the brakes at the same time, then accelerating into the curve to pull him around.

But then.

Panic.

There in front of him, in the middle of the road, rearing up and whinnying, was a huge black horse, its hooves flailing the air. James just managed to swerve around it and brought the car to a skidding halt, ten feet away.

He sat there, his heart pounding, his breathing quick and shallow. That was close.

He turned around.

It was Wilder Lawless on Martini. The horse was still jittery and prancing about in the road, but she brought him under control and with excellent horsemanship was able to calm him down.

"Sorry," James called out.

"So you should be," said Wilder, who was obviously rattled.

"Didn't you hear me coming?" James asked, getting out of the car.

"I couldn't get out of the road."

James looked. There was dense, impenetrable growth on either side.

"Sorry," he said again, and introduced her to Uncle Max.

"What are you doing here anyway?" James asked, patting Martini on the nose to settle him.

"I came to see you," she said. "I didn't expect you to try to kill me." With that, she dismounted, keeping hold of Martini's reins. She had relaxed a little and her manner was softer. "Will you walk a way with me?" she asked.

"Sure," said James with a shrug.

"I'll take the car back," said Max. "See you for lunch."

Max drove off, and James and Wilder walked Martini up the drive to where a track led away into the woods.

"Can you ride?" Wilder asked.

"Pretty well," said James casually.

"You should come out with me sometime. I could fix you up with a pony."

"Maybe."

"But that's not what I came to talk to you about," said Wilder, turning to him, her vivid green eyes bright and excited. "After I saw you, I spoke to Sergeant White about Alfie Kelly, in Keithly Police Station."

"Did you find anything out?"

"It turns out that Lord Hellebore never passed on what I told him that day up by the loch. You remember? About spotting Alfie up there."

"Did the police think it odd?"

"Och. Sergeant White won't hear anything said against the laird. He thinks he's Father Christmas, Buffalo Bill, and Saint Michael all rolled into one."

"Who's Saint Michael?"

Wilder laughed. "The patron saint of policemen."

They were walking between high earth banks along the

bed of a dried-up stream, the sunlight filtering down through the leaves of the big alders and ancient oak trees that grew here.

James snapped a stick off a fallen branch and swished it absentmindedly, like a sword.

Martini had relaxed and now ambled happily behind them, his big hooves thudding on the soft ground.

"When the last laird died, everyone thought it was going to be the end for this town," said Wilder. "But Randolph has thrown money about the place, and now people walk around with big, stupid grins on their faces. As I see it, he pays us to keep out of his way. You won't see much of him but, make no mistake, he pretty well owns this place."

"But will the police look into what you told them, do you think?"

"What? Our Sergeant White?" Wilder looked amused. "Have you ever met him?"

"No," said James.

"Well, he's fat as a pig and lazy as an old cat, and every Christmas he gets a nice big hamper of food from the castle. I told you, he's not about to start upsetting the laird by asking a lot of foolish questions. No, James, you'll have to be your own policeman, because our Sergeant White is about as much use as a pork pie on legs when it comes to getting things done."

"I'd already pretty well decided as much myself," said James, trying to sound worldly wise and grown-up.

"But be careful, James," Wilder said, putting a hand on his arm. "Despite what most people around here think, Randolph Hellebore is not a very nice man."

"What do you mean?"

They had come to an open patch of land where grass and young bracken grew. Wilder let Martini go and he bent his head to feed, tearing clumps of grass up with his huge teeth.

"My dad used to be the estate manager for the old laird," said Wilder, sitting down on a small mound. "He ran the place. He liked Hellebore at first, when he first took over. He made a lot of improvements. He had money to spend on the estate. But the more he got to know him as a person, the less my dad liked him. He found him a bit of a bully, and cruel with it. They argued. One day they were out riding, inspecting a new fence that was being built, and Hellebore's horse stumbled and threw him. He flew into a terrible temper and started to whip the horse terribly. My dad tried to stop him, and Hellebore sacked him on the spot. That was that. My dad was out of a job. He works over near Glencoe now; he comes back some weekends, but mostly he's too busy. It's all changed up there now, new people, no locals. I don't like him, James. I don't like any man who's cruel to animals, especially horses."

"I think it was Alfie you saw that day," said James. "I think he went up there to try to fish on the loch. Do you think Hellebore might have caught him? Do you think he might have done something to him?"

"I wouldn't put it past him. You've seen what it's like up there. Hellebore's got some kind of secret he doesn't want anyone to know about. The police won't touch him."

"I might go back up there with Red," said James nonchalantly, tapping his boot with the stick.

"Say," said Wilder, with a broad, open smile, "why don't I

help you? The three of us would make a good team. Specially as I've got Martini, I can get about the place quicker than you two, and—"

James cut her short. "But you're a girl," he said. "We don't want a girl along with us. This is man's work."

Wilder looked at him for a moment with her mouth open in surprise, then she tipped back her head and laughed loudly.

"Look at you," she said at last, "the big man with his stick. Why, you're nothing but a wee lad, James. 'Man's work' indeed. I'm older than you and I'm bigger than you, and I've no doubt I'm stronger too."

James snorted.

"Listen, you, I spend hours every day lugging great heavy bales of straw about the place," Wilder went on, "and grooming Martini, and mucking out the stables, and riding for hours on end. I've arms as strong as any man, and with three pesky brothers I've had to learn to fight."

"Oh, yes?" said James.

"Yes," said Wilder, and, before James knew what was happening, she grabbed him by the shirt, put a leg behind his leg, and neatly tipped him backward into the dirt. He sprang up and tried the same trick back, but Wilder was ready for him and the two of them toppled over. They rolled on the ground, wrestling for a while, until Wilder got the better of him, pinned him down on his back, straddled his chest, and stuffed his mouth full of dead leaves.

She leant very close to him and laughed in his face, and he saw that there were golden flecks in her green eyes.

"There," she said. "That'll teach you not to laugh at lasses."

So saying, she jumped up, sprang into her saddle, kicked her heels into Martini's flanks, and galloped off into the trees.

James propped himself up on his elbows and spat the leaves out of his mouth. Wilder wasn't like most of the girls he'd met, all fussy curls and pretty dresses that they never wanted to get messy. He couldn't imagine Wilder playing with dolls or having pretend tea parties.

He had to agree with Kelly: Wilder Lawless was quite a girl.

That evening after supper, armed with a hand-drawn map from Aunt Charmian and a flashlight from Uncle Max, James went into Keithly to find Red. His talk with Wilder had made him realize how impatient he was to find out more.

Annie Kelly lived in a cramped two-up two-down, in a gloomy backstreet of gray terraced houses.

James knocked on the door and Red himself answered it.

"All right, Jimmy?" he said, when he'd gotten over his surprise. "Come on in."

Annie Kelly was sitting in the tiny front room with three skinny children. It was dimly lit by a single gas lamp, and smoke from a sputtering coal fire filled the air. It reminded James of his little room at Eton. There was hardly any furniture and a bare stone floor.

Annie jumped up and asked him if he wanted any tea, but he declined, explaining that he'd just had supper and, after an awkward conversation, Red took him out into the backyard, where they sat on the wall next to the outhouse.

"Have you heard anything from Meatpacker?" James asked, looking up at the starry night sky.

"Not a Dickie," said Kelly, and he spat over the wall into the neighbors' yard. "I've asked some questions about the place, like he told us, but I ain't found out much."

"What have you found out?"

"All right. To tell you the truth, I've found out nothing. Except that Lord Hellebore's a good egg and everyone loves him to death. All right, so he doesn't like company, but maybe we're barking up the wrong tree."

"I don't think so," said James, and he told Red about his conversation with Wilder.

"So what do you think we should do?" asked Kelly. "Should we give Meatpacker a couple more days, and if he still ain't turned up . . ."

"I think we should go back up there ourselves," said James, "as soon as possible. Forget about Meatpacker."

"What do you reckon's happened to the silly sod?" Kelly said with a sniff. "Was he just giving us the brush-off? D'you reckon he never had any idea to come back and find us?"

"I don't know," said James. "Has nobody else seen him?"

"Nah," said Kelly. "I found out where he was staying. There you go! I did find out something. It wasn't hard. There's only the one place around here—the pub. I think he was very at home there. His room's paid up for the month, but they ain't seen him since we did."

"It could mean one of three things, I suppose," said James. "That he's done a bunk and gone off without saying anything. That he's still up there finding stuff out . . . or that—"

"Something's happened to him," said Kelly darkly, and he mimed slitting his throat.

CHAPTER 16—NOBODY CAN HOLD A BOND FOREVER

When James got back to the cottage, he found Aunt Charmian in the kitchen and he asked her if he could go off camping for a couple of nights with Red. After some debate she decided it would be all right as long as he was sensible and didn't cause trouble for anybody else or do anything silly that might put them in danger.

James said nothing about Alfie, or Meatpacker, or Lord Hellebore. This was between him and Kelly and the big American, and he was worried that if he told his aunt she wouldn't let him go. Also, some of Meatpacker's Pinkerton secrecy must have rubbed off on him.

They were interrupted by the arrival of Max, shuffling into the kitchen wrapped in a blanket. He looked deathly pale and utterly exhausted.

"I heard voices. Can't sleep," he wheezed.

"You should get back to your bed," said Aunt Charmian.

"I know I should," said Max with a great sigh, "but sometimes it seems such a waste of one's life, sleeping."

"Well, it may seem a waste to you, but I'm dog-tired," said Charmian, lighting a candle, "so I'm for my bed. I'll see you tomorrow. Don't keep the boy up too late."

"Shan't," said Max with a wink to James.

"I'll pack you some lunch in the morning," said

Charmian on her way out. "And I'll put together a first-aid kit for you, James. Good night."

"I know what you mean," said James, when Aunt Charmian had gone. "I hate going to bed sometimes, I always feel I'm missing out on so much. . . ."

"I remember one time when your father and I were boys," said Max. "We decided it would be the thing to stay up all night. We tried everything to keep ourselves awake, but in the end we both fell asleep, and in the morning, of course, we both pretended that we hadn't."

"I can't really picture you and Father as boys like me," said James.

"Oh, we were, you can believe it! And before that we were babies, and before that . . . we were twinkles in your grandfather's eye."

Max stared into the fire and James watched him. Somewhere behind the yellowish wrinkled skin and the black-rimmed eyes, he saw the boy that Max had once been.

"It's a funny thing, growing up," said Max. "We none of us think that it will ever happen to us. I still feel like a small boy most of the time, and then I look in the mirror and— Who's that?—it's as if a magician has stolen up on me in the night and turned me into an old man. And it'll happen to you, James. One day you'll be an old codger like me."

"You're not an old codger," said James.

"I feel like one," said Max, and he coughed quietly into his handkerchief.

After that he was silent for a long while, and they sat there, sharing each other's company, until Max at last spoke again.

"Do you have any idea what you'd like to be when you're grown up?" he asked.

"I haven't really given it much thought," said James.

"Not an engine driver or a fireman or a soldier?"

"I don't know. Maybe an explorer. I'd love to see more of the world."

"That's a good ambition."

"Or a spy like you," said James.

"Oh," said Max, and he quickly changed the subject. "You did well in the car today," he said. "Same thing again tomorrow? And then maybe in the afternoon some more fishing. I'm itching to get back on the river."

Once again James had to disappoint Max, and he told him of his plans with Red.

"Ah, so that's what the packed lunch and the first-aid kit are for," said Max. "That sounds like a grand plan. I used to love camping. . . ."

Then he fell silent, the light from the fire dancing on his face.

At last he spoke again, and his voice was so soft and quiet that James could barely hear him. "You asked me the other day if I was ever caught during the war," he said.

"Yes," said James. "But I didn't mean to be nosy."

Max stared into James's eyes. He had grown even thinner since James had arrived and had virtually stopped eating altogether. His skull was visible beneath his flesh, and his lips were blue and very dry. "I've never talked about this to anyone," he said. "I've tried to bury the memories, but, talking to you by the river, something stirred . . . and now . . ."

"Honestly, Uncle Max, if you'd rather not talk about it . . ."

Max coughed briefly and prodded the fire with the poker, sending up a spray of glittering sparks that lit the room red. "I suppose it must happen to all spies in the end," he said. "They can't remain hidden forever. And one night, they came to where I was staying. It was a small hotel in Flanders. There were four of them, big German soldiers. Didn't say much, just threw me into the back of a lorry and carted me away from there in my pajamas. I don't mind telling you, James, I was scared. Absolutely petrified.

"Their headquarters was a big old ugly medieval fortress made of black stone, and I knew that there was only one way out of that place—in a coffin. I'd been rumbled, and as a spy I could be shot . . . and worse . . . ."

Max stopped and rubbed his arms under his blanket.

"They didn't treat me very well, did some pretty ghastly things to me, but I wouldn't tell them anything. Not that I had much to tell that was of any military importance. But I had my contacts, d'you see? My friends—and I didn't want to give them away. Although I knew that sooner or later I'd have to tell them something. Sooner or later every man will break. That was the most frightening thing of all. But I didn't want that, I didn't want them to know that they could do it to me."

"But you escaped," said James. "You must have done or you wouldn't be sitting here, telling me about it now."

"Ah, yes," said Max. "Nobody can hold a Bond forever. . . ."

The fire was dying down in the grate. Dark patches crawled across the glowing red-and-orange embers and died away. Uncle Max dropped a couple of smaller sticks and a fresh log on and watched the flames spring to life and curl up the chimney.

"The Germans threw me into a tiny, windowless stone cell," he said quietly, as if the memory of his capture and imprisonment as a spy caused him actual pain. "And every few hours they'd drag me out for . . ." He paused, choosing the words carefully, "for questioning. I lost track of time. I had no idea if it was day or night. Sometimes they let me use a lavatory—they weren't complete beasts. The room had a tiny barred window, no chance of escaping there; but I noticed that where the pipes came through the wall on one side, it was damp. The place was ancient and the plumbing had probably been leaking since Napoléon's time, so all the plasterwork was rotted. I picked away at that wall with bleeding fingers and found that behind the plaster there was no stonework, only the stuff they use to pack stud walls with, a filthy mass of sodden horsehair and straw and old wooden laths so rotten they gave way like paper. I left it alone that first time, but I started to hatch a plan. I think that's what kept me going—having a plan—in some small, hidden part of my brain I still had control over my fate. And so, every time they let me use the lavatory, I worked on loosening more plaster. The last time they threw me in there, I worked like a dog and managed to kick a hole just large enough to fit into. I had no idea what was on the other side, but it was my only chance, so I wriggled through.

"It was hard work—I was fearfully weak and covered in cuts and bruises—but I made it. I found myself in a long dark room with a small, dusty window at the far end. The water tanks for the whole building were up in there, gurgling and clanking away. Well, I knew I had only seconds to get away, but I wanted to leave them something to think about, and I just had the strength to wrench a couple of pipes loose and start a flood. The water gushed out of the tanks in a great torrent, and I hobbled to the window, forced it open, and looked out into the night. . . . I was five floors up and it was snowing."

"What did you do?" asked James, picturing his uncle standing there in his rags, peering down at that long drop.

"I didn't stop to think," said Max. "It was only a matter of time before my guards opened the lavatory door and found me gone. Even though the outside of the fortress was cold and wet and slippery, I climbed out and somehow managed to grab hold of an old drainpipe, which I slithered down. I did all right until one section of it broke away and I fell the last twenty-odd feet onto the hard cobbles of the yard below. When I tried to walk I realized that I'd broken my leg, but that didn't stop me. I didn't look back, I hopped and stumbled across the yard for dear life, ignoring the pain, all the while expecting to feel a bullet in my back."

"Where were they?" said James. "What was happening?"

"I don't know. Maybe they were all sheltering from the snow or searching for me inside the building, maybe the flood had distracted them, but I didn't see a soul. Thank God, the back gate to the yard was open where a narrow roadway led to a small bridge. The bridge spanned a canal of some sort and as I got there a long barge full of neeps was passing underneath. So, without a second thought, I scrambled over the side of that bridge onto the great pile of neeps and buried myself in them."

"Neeps?" said James.

"Turnips! That's what my great adventure boiled down to: a raggedy, freezing scarecrow of a man hiding under turnips. Still want to be a spy, lad?"

"I don't know," said James. "But it does sound more exciting than being a bank manager or a postman."

Max gave a short, wheezy laugh. "I would have given anything, that night, to be a postman," he said. "Going about his rounds in some leafy village street. . . . I nearly died on the barge, James. It was bitterly cold and my broken leg was burning hot and feverish. I ate some of the raw turnips to keep me going—haven't been able to touch one since. But somehow, I made it till morning and a weak sun warmed me a little. We chugged along all that day and the next. I had no idea where we were going, and didn't much care, I was delirious, slipping in and out of sanity. Then, when we stopped at a lock, I must have had a brief lucid moment and I realized that the longer I stayed on that barge the more chance there was that I would be spotted. So I jumped ship and hid out in some woods. . . . Once again I lost all track of time, days came and went, waves of fever passed over me, sending me mad, but I must have been alone in the woods for two, maybe three weeks, trapping wild game, eating roots and berries, little better than an animal.

"I stole some clothes from a logging camp, strapped my leg up as best I could, but I was growing more desperate and weaker by the minute. How long could a man survive like that? In the end, I was saved by the most unlikely angels—a group of German deserters, of all people."

"Germans?" said James. "Really?"

"Yes. They were soldiers who had grown sick of fighting. They'd run away from the war and were living in the woods like savages. They fed me and looked after me until I was strong enough to set off through the mountains to Switzerland. And that was the end of my glorious war. No medals, just a limp."

"I had no idea," said James. "I knew you had hurt your leg, but . . ."

"As I say," murmured Max, "I've never told anyone. Your father knew some of it. And I don't know why I'm telling you, James, except, perhaps, to say—don't ever be a spy. War's a dirty enough business as it is." He poked at the burning log on the fire. "Now"—he straightened in his chair and put the poker down—"let's see if we can't find you some stuff for your trip. I've an old two-man tent from my army days that you can dig out of the shed, and I think you'll find a pair of binoculars and a decent water flask in there. Oh, and here you are, look, have this. A boy always needs a knife." He hobbled over to the mantelpiece and fetched his folding knife and handed it to James.

"Thank you," said James. "Thank you for everything. I've really enjoyed the last few days, learning to fish—and learning to drive, of course."

"Well, I suppose they're all things your father would have taught you. He was keen on fishing when he was a lad. The two of us were always out on the river near Glencoe. I do miss my big brother sometimes." He stopped and looked into the fire, his eyes clouded. "It was a terrible thing that happened. A boy needs a father, and I'm no substitute, an old wreck like me."

"You're not old," said James. "And you're not a wreck. You're still a demon behind the wheel of a car."

"Don't make me laugh," said Max, clutching his chest.

"When I get back," said James, "let's spend a whole day fishing."

"We will," said Max, his face brightening. "I'll show you how to Spey cast, and then we'll see if you can't beat your record to the gatepost and back." He lit a cigarette and coughed as he inhaled the smoke. Then he studied his battered, old, gunmetal cigarette lighter.

"Here you are," he said, giving it to James. "Might come in useful for lighting fires and whatnot."

"Won't you need it?" asked James.

"Not anymore." Max smiled at James, and James saw something unspoken behind his eyes.

"I'm going to take your advice," he said hoarsely. "As of tonight, I'm giving up smoking."

The two of them laughed, then Max rested his hands on James's shoulders.

"You take care, now," he croaked. "Don't get into any scrapes, and when you get back we'll see if we can't land ourselves a champion salmon."

"**R**ight," said James, slipping his knapsack off and retrieving Max's binoculars from a side pocket. "If you were Meatpacker, where would you make your camp?"

"In the pub," said Kelly, and James laughed.

"Be serious."

They had stopped at the pass at Am Bealach Geal and were sitting down, scanning the countryside with Max's binoculars. Ahead of them and below was the lake, to the right were the low hills that curled around to the castle at the far end. To the left were the craggy rocks and cliffs that over-hung the loch on that side, and above them the great brood-ing pile of the mountain, Angreach Mhòr, its peak hidden by clouds.

"We didn't see anything on our way around to the right, did we?" said Kelly.

"No," said James. "There wasn't a lot of cover, and when Meatpacker found us he must have been coming from over to the left, or we'd have seen him."

"Left it is, then," said Kelly.

"I agree," said James. "Let's go down and take a look."

They followed the path down to the fence where the dead animals were hanging, and then skirted clockwise around the wire until their way was blocked by a largish thicket of scrubby shrubs and half-dead trees. It looked particularly uninviting, and they poked about the edges until they found what looked like a way in through the tangled, thorny undergrowth.

"Look here," said James, pointing to the broken ends of some brambles and small twigs, "someone's hacked their way in here not so long ago."

Cautiously they went in. It was dark and cold and smelled of damp and decay, but somebody had certainly been this way before quite recently. In the center of the thicket was a small clearing that had obviously been recently enlarged; there were more broken sticks and branches here, and a few smaller saplings had been uprooted and tossed to the side. There were also some scattered ashes, though they had mostly been kicked into the soggy earth. Tiny black flies whined in the thick air and landed on the boys' skin in dark clumps.

"What do you think?" said James, swatting a patch of flies, which left a dirty smear on the back of his hand. "Looks like this could have been his camp, don't you think?"

Kelly was inspecting the ground.

"It's been raked over here," he said. "But look, there's some holes that could have been made by tent poles or something." He scratched his ankle where he'd been bitten by an insect. "If he *was* here, either he's tried to cover his traces, or somebody else has."

"What's this?" said James, looking deep into the undergrowth and trying to make out an object in the gloom. "There's something glinting."

He picked up a long stick and poked around with it, exposing more metal and a leather strap. He hooked the stick through the strap and fished it up.

"It's Meatpacker's binocs," said Kelly.

They brushed the earth off the binoculars, which looked undamaged. Kelly peered through them. "He wouldn't leave them behind on purpose, would he?"

"No," said James, and they both jumped as some animal scuttled noisily away through the bushes.

"Come on," said Kelly seriously. "Let's get out of here. I don't like this one little bit."

It was a relief to get back out into the daylight, even though the sky was now almost completely overcast and gray, with only thin, weak sunlight filtering through here and there.

"Okay," said James, shivering. "*We* found his hiding place easily enough, so it wouldn't have been too tough for Hellebore's men. We'll need to pitch our tent somewhere else. It's not safe here."

"You wouldn't catch me putting up a tent in there," said Kelly with a shudder. "The more I see of the countryside, the less I like it. Give me houses and walls and concrete anytime."

"The only houses near here are at the castle," said James, "and I don't suppose you want to spend the night there?"

"I don't think I want to spend the night up here at all," said Kelly. "Maybe we should just go back, eh?"

Half of James wanted to agree with him—he was beginning to grow scared—but the other half, the reckless half, the half that longed for adventure, wanted to carry on.

"No," he said decisively. "We've come this far; we're not giving in. Let's go and take a look at the castle and then plan our next step."

"If you say so, boss."

So they went back the way they had come. First to the fence, then around behind the cover, until they found the hill from where they'd spied on the castle with Meatpacker. They crawled up it on their bellies, and now that they had two pairs of field glasses, they both focused on the stark, gray building together.

Nothing was happening. It was all quiet. Apart from the bored-looking sentry with the hunting rifle at his post, there was nobody around.

"This is a waste of time," said Kelly. "You know what we've got to do?"

"What?" said James.

"We've got to get in there and have a look around the castle."

"Isn't that dangerous?"

"Yeah," said Kelly. "But you said it yourself—we've come this far. We're not going to find out much more skulking around out here, are we?"

"Yes, but you don't just go breaking into places . . ."

Kelly smiled and gave James a sly look.

"Oh," said James. "Maybe you do."

"Let's just say I've had a little experience with that sort of thing," said Kelly.

"You mean you're a burglar?" said James, who had always suspected as much.

"I'm not a bleeding burglar," said Kelly, "though I have

broken into a few houses in me time, when the need arose."

"You *have* burgled?"

"I've told you what I've told you. But it's simple, Jimmy. Once it's dark, I can get us both in there, we can snoop around and be out again without anyone noticing. Piece of cake."

"Piece of cake?"

"The only thing I ain't figured out is how to get past the fence."

Just then they heard the sound of an engine, and they wriggled back down the hill and crouched behind some rocks, squinting down the narrow dirt road that wound its way across the moors toward Keithly.

"It's a police car," said Kelly, and James focused his binoculars on the fast-moving black vehicle, which was throwing up a spray of dirt and water behind it. There were the shapes of two policemen in the front.

"Come on," said James. "Let's see what they're up to."

From their hiding place on top of the hill they watched the car pass through the gatehouse and stop. The guard had come out of his sentry post, but now there was no sign of the rifle he had been holding before. He was all smiles. He pointed the car toward the castle and it moved slowly down the causeway and parked at the far end, where a small group of men was gathered on the bridge, peering down into the water. As the policemen got out of their car, the castle doors opened and Lord Hellebore appeared.

He strode purposefully over the bridge to the new arrivals and shook their hands.

One of the policemen was young and skinny; the other was older and quite fat, his too tight uniform straining at the seams.

"That must be Sergeant White," said James.

"Yeah," said Red. "I seen him in Keithly. That's a man who likes his pies."

Sergeant White smiled at Lord Hellebore and nodded his head while the younger policeman took notes with a pencil. Hellebore pointed to the water several times with one big hand and shrugged every now and then as Sergeant White asked him a question. Finally, one of the men by the bridge shouted, and everyone hurried over.

James now saw that the man who had shouted was fishing in the moat with what looked like a boathook. He had evidently caught hold of something, because he started to pull. Two other men joined him, and eventually they hauled a large, soft object out of the water and up onto the bank.

It was a man's body.

"Bloody hell," said Kelly, who had his eyes pressed tightly against his binoculars. "Would you look at that."

The body was still dressed and, although it was covered with a fair amount of filthy green slime and the clothes were badly torn and stained, James could still make out an unmistakable pair of tartan trousers. One leg was pulled up and he could clearly see a small, pearl-handled pistol strapped to the sock.

"It's Meatpacker," he whispered.

Amazingly, he seemed to be still alive. At any rate, the body was moving.

Several of the men now broke away and hurried off,

holding their mouths and noses, so that James got a better look. But he immediately wished that he hadn't.

For the first time James saw Meatpacker's face.

Only it wasn't a face anymore. The flesh had been stripped away. And in a moment James knew what had done that to him, as a long, fat eel, as thick as his arm slowly squirmed out of Meatpacker's shirt collar and onto the ground, where it slithered away into the water.

James realized there were more of them, tangled in Meatpacker's hair like living locks, twisting and writhing. He wanted to look away but couldn't. He was mesmerized by the sight.

The man with the pole now poked Meatpacker's body, and the buttons on the front of his suit gave way and the clothing opened, releasing a great, tangled mass of gray and black eels. That was what James had seen moving. It was ridiculous that he had imagined that Meatpacker could still be alive.

James thought of the gun. What use would that have been against these fish?

The men by the castle had all backed away now. Nobody could bear the hideous sight. Sergeant White was consoling the younger policeman, who appeared to be sobbing. Several of the other men were being sick, and James felt the gorge rise in his own throat. But he fought it and kept his eyes jammed to the glasses, because he wanted to see the reaction of one particular man—Lord Hellebore.

He stood there, tall and stiff-backed, staring at the corpse, and the expression on his face was not one of horror, but one of fascination.

James turned to say something to Kelly, but then saw that he too was being quietly sick.

James rolled onto his back and lay there, looking up into the darkening sky. He took long, slow, deep breaths of clean, fresh air and tried to put the image of Meatpacker's ruined body out of his mind. But it was no good—he knew that it would haunt him for the rest of his life.

"There you go, Mr. Bond," said Kelly with the voice of a snooty shoe-shop assistant, and he gave James back his boot. "Nobody'll ever know it's in there."

James studied Kelly's handiwork. "That's amazing," he said, and smiled.

Kelly had spent the last half-hour fashioning a secret compartment in the heel for James. He explained that he often needed to hide things, back home in London, and James didn't ask too closely why. Using his penknife, the older boy had carved out the heel and made a space large enough to fit James's small, folding knife, and then fashioned an ingenious cover for it from the top layer of the heel.

They had stayed near the castle long enough to watch the arrival of an ambulance. By this time most of the eels had left Meatpacker's body and slithered back into the water. But the last few were helped on their way by some of the less squeamish men, who kicked and prodded them across the ground. The two horrified ambulance men wrapped up the body, which was little more than a skeleton clothed in filthy rags, put it on a stretcher, and loaded it in the back of their vehicle, before driving slowly off. There was no hurry. After all, Meatpacker was beyond needing a doctor.

Sergeant White and the young constable had gone

into the castle with Lord Hellebore and, after that, nothing else happened until the policemen left, nearly an hour later.

When evening came, the two boys had left their hiding place and searched for a good spot to make camp, as far away from the castle and any human activity as they could find. They had worked their way back around the loch, passing Meatpacker's thicket and carrying on until they found a suitably sheltered spot, beneath a tall overhanging rock among some birch trees whose roots helped keep the ground relatively dry.

James slipped his boot back on and laced it tightly.

"Do you think it's dark enough yet?" he asked.

"We'll give it a bit longer."

"While we're waiting, would you teach me how to fight dirty?" said James. "It might come in useful."

"No such thing as fighting dirty, really, Jimmy," said Kelly. "There's just fighting to win. Use whatever you like, you can forget about rules, you've got to kick, scratch, bite, punch, claw with your nails . . . What you've got to do, see, is *hurt* your enemy as bad as you can as quick as you can, before he hurts you. Go for the soft bits, the eyes, nostrils, armpits, belly and, of course . . . well, you know where a bloke hurts worst."

James looked down and winced.

"Exactly," laughed Kelly. "You get a bloke down there and he's out of action for the rest of the day. You want to know how to win a fight? You've got to get over your fear."

"Your fear of getting hurt?"

"No, Jimmy, your fear of hurting someone else. It takes a

lot of guts to smash someone up. To bust their noodle or knee them in the family jewels. That's why most blokes only fight when they're drunk. Of course," he said seriously, "the best skill you can learn is how not to get into a fight in the first place. But sometimes you won't be able to avoid it, in which case you need to get it over with as quickly as possible."

Kelly demonstrated some tricks to James—how to throw someone, how to get out of a stranglehold, how to punch without hurting your hand—and they spent a happy hour fighting each other.

At last they stopped, and Kelly looked up at the sky. There was a bright half-moon and the stars were starting to come out.

"Time to go, I reckon," he said.

"Have you figured out what to do about the fence?" said James.

"Yeah. There's no point trying to find where Meatpacker got in, 'cause they'll have fixed that."

"So what, then?" asked James, checking the flashlight that Aunt Charmian had given him last night.

"There's them lorries," said Kelly.

"How do you mean?"

"They're in and out of there a fair bit. If we could just get in the back of one of them."

"That sounds pretty risky."

"Everything's bloody risky!" Kelly snapped. "But we've got no wire-cutters to cut through the fence and no spades to dig under it, so the best bet is to just breeze through the gates in a chauffeur-driven charabanc. It's worth a look, anyway. I reckon it's plenty dark enough now."

A shudder of excitement passed through James. His heart was beating fast. He felt more awake than he ever had before.

"Come on," he said, jumping up. "Let's go, then."

It took them a good forty minutes to make their careful way around behind the hills to the rear gate by the compound; it was lit up bright as daylight, by high floodlights mounted on posts.

While Kelly scouted the area, James hauled himself up into the tree to get a look over the high wooden fence through his binoculars.

Kelly soon came back and asked him what he could see.

"It's still fairly busy, with men coming and going, but the lorries all seem to be parked for the night," he whispered as he got down out of the tree. "How about you?"

Kelly led James to the edge of the barbed-wire fence.

"See that ditch there?" he said. "It runs all the way along to the road by the gate, then goes underneath it, through a pipe. Nobody'd ever see us if we crawled along it. You'd be able to get right up to a lorry."

"If there were a lorry," said James. "Maybe we're too late, maybe we should have tried earlier."

"Yeah, maybe," said Kelly, climbing into the ditch. "But let's sit it out and see what occurs."

For an hour nothing happened, and the two of them were just thinking of trying something different when they heard the distant sound of an approaching vehicle.

"Ready?" said Kelly.

"I'm still not sure about this."

"You've had long enough to think about it."

"I've had too long," said James, but Kelly was off, wriggling along the ditch on his hands and knees toward the gates at some speed. James was right behind him.

The ditch was fairly deep and had two or three inches of water at the bottom, so they were soon drenched up to their elbows and hips, but James barely noticed.

Ahead of them, a big dirty lorry trundled up to the gates and stopped. The driver got out, slammed the door, walked over to the guardhouse, and spoke to the man inside.

The lorry's engine was ticking over noisily and clouds of choking fumes were pumping out of the exhaust into the damp night air.

Kelly signaled to James to stop, then turned and whispered to him. "Wait here."

He scrambled up out of the ditch and disappeared around the back of the lorry.

A few moments later, he beckoned to James, who scurried up after him.

There was a canvas flap above the tailgate and Kelly had quickly undone it just enough for them to squeeze through. It struck James that Red must have done this sort of thing before.

Kelly went in first, and James just had time to get in after him before the lorry moved forward and rumbled through the gates into the compound.

Inside the lorry it was dark and stuffy and crammed with sacks of something knobbly.

They climbed over the sacks until they were sure that they'd be hidden if anyone opened the back of the lorry and looked in.

This was madness. It had all happened so fast that James hadn't had time to think, and now here he was, entering Lord Hellebore's castle. He looked at Kelly, who grinned at him and gave him the thumbs-up.

James opened one of the sacks and looked inside—turnips.

He smiled and shook his head.

The lorry waited for a moment at the inner gate, then carried on through and half a minute later they stopped again and the engine was switched off.

They heard the driver get out, and then voices and laughter. The flap was tugged open, and the back of the lorry was flooded with light.

"I don't fancy shifting this lot tonight," said a harsh voice in a thick Scottish accent.

"It can wait till morning," said a second voice, which sounded American. "I'll fix you up with some grub, and then what do you say to a drink?"

"Sounds grand," said the first voice, and there was more laughter as the two men went away, chatting.

"Phew." Kelly sighed theatrically. "So far, so good. But we'd better get out of here sharpish and find somewhere a bit safer."

He cautiously peered out of the back, made sure it was all clear, and climbed down.

They were in a large shed where three other lorries were parked next to a couple of cars, a tractor, and a motorbike. Stacked against the back wall was a pile of boxes and crates.

The two boys crept toward the open doors, keeping close to the wall, and looked out into the compound. It had quieted down since they had first arrived, but the occasional figure still crossed from one building to another.

Kelly timed his moment, then darted across to the shadows of a long, low building that was less well lit. James stayed close behind him.

From their new vantage point they could see that only the center of the compound was this bright; toward the castle it was much darker.

Kelly pointed and James nodded, then they quickly moved away to the edge of the compound. They had one nasty shock when a door opened right in front of them. They instinctively dropped to the ground and pressed themselves against the base of the wall, but the man who emerged didn't see them; he simply threw out a bucket of dirty water without looking around, and went back inside.

James was relieved when they reached a deserted area behind the main buildings that was completely unlit. The two of them pressed their backs against a wall, slid down, and sat on the floor.

James's throat was so dry, it felt as if he'd swallowed a cupful of sand, and his heart was beating so hard and fast it hurt. He was terrified and thrilled at the same time and was already exhausted, even though they hadn't come very far.

"We need to find somewhere to hole up," whispered Kelly. "And wait till everyone's gone to sleep."

"You won't catch me arguing," said James, and he looked across to where the great dark bulk of the castle loomed up over the nearby buildings. A few of the high, narrow windows showed lights and, as James watched, one of them went out. He thought of George Hellebore and his father in there

. . . and what else? Who else? What secrets did it contain?

They rested for a while, until they felt confident enough to set off again, creeping through the darkness, hunched over and alert, scuttling across the occasional pool of light. Soon they came to a low wall, and James remembered seeing what had looked like animal pens when he had first spied on the compound from the trees. There was certainly a strong animal scent in the air.

On the far side of the pens was a large, unlit area, and James pointed it out to Kelly.

"It's worth a look," he said, and climbed over the wall. Almost immediately he swore.

"What is it?" asked James, climbing down behind him.

"I've trod in something. Careful where you walk."

James stared at the ground and saw several piles of stinking excrement. So these were definitely animal pens, but what sort of animals? Cautiously he made his way to a low, concrete shed at one end and peeped in. A fat sow lay there with a litter of piglets snoozing restlessly by her side, snuggled against the warmth of her belly. In the way that some pigs have, it looked as if there was a big happy grin on the mother's face.

"Dirty animals," grunted Kelly, wiping his boot, and James suppressed a laugh. What with the tension and his tiredness, he was on the verge of hysteria.

Suddenly they heard a cough and a spit and, almost as if they'd rehearsed it, they both vaulted over the wall into the next pen and pressed themselves to the ground, not caring what they might be lying in.

James saw a crack in the wall and shuffled forward so

that he could see through it. A man was coming into the first pen. James recognized him immediately—it was the short man with the long arms and the bowler hat James had seen with Randolph and George the other day.

He was muttering under his breath and appeared to be drunk. He rocked from side to side as he walked on his little bowed legs and, up close, he looked even more like some kind of grotesque monkey than before.

"Come on, you wee porkers," he sang, and stooped down to get into the shed where the pigs were sleeping.

Immediately there came a frightful whining and squealing, and the man emerged, carrying a wriggling piglet by the back of its neck.

The big sow and two or three more of her litter, all making a terrible din, followed him out.

"Get back in there!" the man shouted, and let fly a kick that took the sow on the side of her head. She shrieked and backed away, but the short man was laughing now and he took aim at one of the piglets. He got it with the toe of his boot and it flew across the pen and smashed into the wall of the shed, where it lay still. The man waddled over and picked it up. Its back was broken. He studied it and licked his lips.

"You'll make good eating, laddie."

He chuckled and left the pen carrying the two piglets, one dead, the other very much alive and kicking. The last thing James heard was a string of insults aimed at the living piglet.

The boys waited there until they were sure that the man wasn't coming back, then they jumped up and managed to climb over the rest of the pens without further mishap. They soon found themselves by the loch's edge, looking over at the island with the castle on it.

"I don't fancy swimming across that," said Kelly, staring uneasily into the black water.

"Me neither," said James. "He doesn't need watchdogs with those eels to look after him."

"Don't mention the bloody eels," said Kelly. "I never want to see another eel as long as I live. I used to like a nice jellied eel. Never again."

"Look," said James, and he nodded along the water's edge toward a derelict area which was fenced off by rusting chicken wire that had mostly fallen down. It looked like a makeshift rubbish dump and was full of old boxes and tin cans and piles of rotting paper. In the middle of the dump stood the big old Scots pine that they'd seen from the far end of the loch. It looked diseased and uncared for and was probably dying.

Past the tree was the tumbledown ruin of an abandoned building.

"What do you think?"

"Worth a look," said Kelly.

They trotted over, pushed down a section of chicken wire and picked their way through the rubbish toward the building. It was made of dirty red brick and was covered with ivy and moss. All the windows were smashed and only one story of it was still standing. The door was padlocked shut, but the wood was so rotten that they easily levered it away from the screws with a penknife. They tried to open it without making too much noise, but a sharp creak suddenly echoed out into the night as its rusted hinges complained. They froze. To them the noise had sounded as loud as an explosion, but they saw nobody, and nobody came. All that happened was another light went off in the castle.

They swiftly went inside. The roof was largely missing, though it did offer some shelter in one corner where there was a pile of reasonably dry boxes and empty sacks. There were some abandoned bits of decayed iron machinery in here, whose use James could not even guess at, and more dumped rubbish.

With the intention of building a secure hiding place they began to rearrange some of the boxes and sacks and, as James shifted an old crate full of broken bottles, he discovered a wooden trapdoor in the floor.

Kelly helped him clear enough stuff away to one side so that they could haul the door open, then the two of them went down a flight of stone steps into the darkness.

They swung the door shut above their heads and James got out the flashlight and switched it on. They were in a forgotten cellar. It was clean and dry and, apart from a shelf of empty glass flasks and a row of ancient barrels, it was empty.

"Bingo," said Kelly. "This is perfect. We can make a halfway decent camp down here. Let's get some of those sacks for beds and lie low until everyone's asleep. Come on."

A quarter of an hour later they had made a cozy little den, and they lay down to rest. James turned off the flashlight, and the cellar became utterly black.

"Not scared of the dark, I hope," said Kelly.

"Never have been," said James. "I like the dark. I've always felt that if *you* can't see the monsters, then *they* can't see you."

"I thought monsters could see in the dark," said Kelly with a chuckle.

"No," said James forcefully. "They can't."

James drifted off into a troubled sleep, filled with dreams of eels and water and drowning and the sound of a boy screaming, and it was a relief when some time later Kelly nudged him awake and shone the flashlight in his face.

James sat up.

"What time is it?" asked Kelly, who had no watch of his own.

James looked at his wristwatch; it was half past twelve.

"Then we'd best get going," said Kelly.

They carefully opened the trapdoor, left the derelict building, and crept back outside. It was very still and very quiet, though the big floodlights still burnt in the compound.

Bats flitted in the air above them, swerving and dive-bombing after all the insects that were attracted by the lights.

The castle was absolutely dark now. All the windows were black slits.

"Shall we risk the front door?" said Kelly. "It's always worth trying. . . ."

But James was looking up at the Scots pine, which leaned drunkenly out over the water toward the castle walls. High above them was an open window with a low stone balustrade outside it.

"Look," he said. "That window's open."

"Oh, that's ideal," whispered Kelly sarcastically. "All we need is a ladder and a boat to get across the moat."

"No, we don't," said James. "All we need to do is climb

the tree. Don't you see? That big branch up there goes almost right up to the window."

"Don't be daft," said Kelly. "We're not climbing up there, we'll break our bloody necks."

"No we won't. It's not that high. Don't tell me you've never climbed a tree before."

Kelly looked sheepish. "I've climbed a few drainpipes, and I'm no stranger to a ladder, but . . . well, there's not a lot of trees around where I live."

"Well," said James. "As you would say—it's a piece of cake. Just follow me and do exactly as I do, and you can't go wrong."

"Seriously, James," said Kelly. "I don't like heights and I don't trust trees."

"Follow me," said James, and he walked over to the big Scots pine.

The hardest part of climbing a tree is usually getting up to the lowest branch, and this tree proved no exception. After a few minutes of fruitless scrabbling and jumping, Kelly made a stirrup with his hands and boosted James up, then James dangled down and grabbed Kelly by the hand.

"Ready?"

"Heave away!"

In a moment the two of them were sitting there, safely in the arms of the pine.

From here the next few branches were relatively easy, and they quickly gained height, but the tree was taller than it had looked from below, and the window much higher than they had assumed.

The tree had a strong, piney smell and was oozing resin,

and soon their hands were sticky and filthy. Kelly was cursing and struggling, nervously testing branches that James had clambered up easily, and every now and then he chose to use a different branch altogether. The higher they went, the thinner the branches became, and they were covered in small, sharp twigs.

"I'm not sure about this, Jimmy," said Kelly. "I'm not sure I can go on. . . ."

James looked down; Kelly was perched on a very thin, dead branch that James had purposely avoided.

"Don't use that one," James said. "It's too weak. Put your weight on that one there."

But Kelly seemed frozen, his face almost white in the moonlight.

"Come on," said James. "You'll be all right, so long as you don't look down."

"I can't look down," stammered Red. "I can't look up, I can't . . ." There was a terrible snap, Kelly swore, and then he was falling—down through the tree, smashing and bumping into branches as he tried to grab on.

PART 3—THE CASTLE

CHAPTER 19—ALONE

James climbed down the tree as fast as he could after Kelly, praying that he would be all right. Kelly crashed from branch to branch and finally managed to grab hold of one near the bottom. He hung there for one agonizing moment, looking up at James, before, overcome with pain and weakness, he let go and thudded to the ground in the middle of a pile of rubbish.

He must have been terrified when falling through the tree, and it must have hurt like hell as the branches bludgeoned and whipped him and tore at his grasping hands, but he never once cried out or made any sound.

As James scrambled down after him, he wondered if he would have been so brave in Kelly's place. He was about to jump from the last branch when Kelly gestured to him to stop.

"Don't," he hissed. "You'll never get back up again."

"Are you okay?" James asked as loudly as he dared.

"No, of course I'm not okay." Kelly's clothes were ripped and his hands and face bleeding from several nasty cuts and scratches. "I think I've broken my leg."

James thought of his Uncle Max, falling from the drainpipe in Germany.

"I'm coming down," he said.

"No!" hissed Kelly. "You go back up and carry on. I'll get to the den and strap myself up with something. You'll be back in less than an hour. In the meantime, I'll try to think of some way out of this mess."

"Are you sure?"

"Go on." Kelly crawled away through the rubbish toward the abandoned building. James waited until Kelly was safely inside, and he was sure that nobody had heard them, then he started to climb back up the tree.

It was quicker and easier the second time, since James knew the good branches and which ones to avoid. He was soon higher than he had reached before, but the higher he got, the harder it became. The branches were much closer together up here and getting dangerously thin. He had to go slowly and choose his route with care.

He broke a couple of dead sticks that were in his way, and squinted through the clusters of pine needles to try to get some idea of how close to the window he was. It had looked easy from below, but he now realized that the building was much farther away from the tree than it had appeared from across the water, and what he thought might be strong branches were mostly too thin and bendy to carry his weight.

He decided that he would have to try to climb above the window and hope that a higher branch would bend down toward it.

He struggled on up through the tangle of small twigs and young limbs, feeling like Jack climbing the beanstalk toward the giant's castle. At last, after some careful searching, he found a suitable branch. In fact, it was probably his only hope, because it was the last branch that looked as if it would be strong enough to support him. He lay down on it, gripping it with his legs, and slowly slid himself away from the trunk and out over the loch.

He looked down at the black water, so still now, but he could picture the eels beneath the surface, lying in the stinking mud at the bottom, their wide snouts sticking out, waiting patiently. His one consolation was that if the fall didn't kill him, it would at least knock him unconscious, and he would know nothing about sinking down through the dark water toward those slimy mouths.

He suddenly felt very lonely. If he fell, Kelly wouldn't come, and nobody else knew he was here. He was utterly alone.

He forced his eyes away from the water toward the wall ahead of him. The branch was bowing sharply now, and he found himself crawling downward toward its tip, so that there was a very real danger of slipping forward and off the end. Best not to think about that.

Slowly he shuffled along. The castle was six feet away, five . . . four . . . the branch was swaying alarmingly. He felt like he could tip off at any moment.

He stopped.

The wall was still three feet away. . . .

He didn't move.

He knew it wasn't going to work. The branch wasn't long enough. It was too thin. If he went any farther, he would be past the point of no return. He'd be stuck.

He glanced down: He was over the ground now, at the foot of the wall. That would be worse than hitting the water, eels or no eels. He closed his eyes and slowed his breathing, trying to calm the mounting panic.

And then he heard it.

First a creak, like a loose tread on a staircase.

And then a crack.

He felt the branch shudder. . . . It was splitting.

He looked hopelessly around for the break, but could see nothing. There came another crack, louder than before, and the branch jerked downward another few inches.

He had no choice now; he had to get off the branch as quickly as he could, and that meant going forward. Quickly he pulled himself along. The branch had bent so much that he was now to the left of the window and below it. He could see the stonework of the wall quite clearly in the moonlight. Thankfully, it was more uneven than it had appeared from a distance so, if he could get to it, he might just be able to hold on. . . . He had been rock-climbing a couple of times and knew roughly what to do, but how could he get any nearer? The branch wasn't going to reach.

There came another crack and the branch jolted so quickly downward that his legs were thrown off, and he was dangling in the air, fifty feet above the ground, with the branch slowly slipping between his fingers. There was only one thing for it—he kicked out and swung toward the wall. His feet brushed against it, then he swung away, back out over the water. With all his might he swung forward again. Maybe the branch would hold, maybe it would break completely; it was in the hands of God now. He swooped up and his body slammed hard into the stonework. He grunted but, before he had a chance to try to grab on, he had swung back. The air rushed in his ears, and the ground below was a blur. He reached the end of the arc, stopped, hung there for one agonizing moment, then swung forward, faster this time; but as he went he felt the branch above him shudder and snap completely. He let go of it and it dropped away. He thudded into the wall, arms and legs outstretched in a star shape, and desperately clung with his fingertips and toes.

It was no good. He was slipping downward.

He gripped harder and groaned between clenched teeth. A terrible image came into his mind: of his own father, clinging to a rock in France and letting go and falling and . . .

He stopped. He wasn't falling. He was stuck to the wall. His feet had found a tiny ledge.

He let out his breath and pressed his face into the cold stone. His fingers were bleeding, the nails ragged, but he was secure.

All right. Now upward. There was a handhold just within reach above him. Gingerly he stretched up for it, gripped tight, then moved one foot up, probing for a crack. Yes. He felt a piece of jutting stone. He tried it. It would hold. He pulled himself up. Good. Now another handhold, and another. That was all he had to do, just keep finding the holds and not think about anything else. One hand, one foot, then the other foot. . . . At last his right hand felt something different. He looked up and saw a stone balcony, which offered him a couple of good, firm grips. He dragged himself up, held on with one knee, pulled, scrabbled, swung his other leg up and, thank God, there was the window. He grabbed the sill and hauled himself inside.

He'd done it. He was safe.

For a long while he didn't move; he just lay there, face down, on a dusty, threadbare rug, breathing heavily. He felt sick. His head was pounding and sweat was pouring off him, stinging his eyes.

Then it slowly dawned on him that, in fact, he was far from safe. If anything, he was in a more dangerous position than before.

Jack was inside the giant's castle.

What was he going to do? Without Kelly he was lost. Their whole plan was shot to pieces. He knew nothing about creeping around houses in the middle of the night. Yes, he was in all right, but somehow he had to get out again. He couldn't go back the way he had come. He had to find some other exit from the castle, and he had to find it without waking anybody.

He forced himself to his feet. There was just enough light from the moon through the open window to show him that he was in a short corridor that ran from the window into the heart of the castle. There were dark paintings hanging on the walls, and heavy oak doors were set into the cold granite walls on either side.

The building was absolutely quiet, like a mausoleum— which meant that at least nobody had heard him. He crept along to the first door and put his ear to it. Nothing. Not a sound. Carefully he tried the heavy iron latch. It popped up with a small click and the door opened. James boldly pushed it back. The room was in total darkness. He fished Max's flashlight out of his pocket and shone it into the blackness.

He jumped back in fright as the beam fell on the snarling face of a large wildcat.

Then he let out his breath and relaxed. The cat hadn't

moved. It was stuffed, frozen in anger, and falling apart. One back leg was missing and sawdust was spilling out from a long tear in its belly. James raked the room with his flashlight beam. There were several more stuffed animals: some small deer, a couple of foxes, and a collection of birds in a dusty cabinet. On a rail near the window hung a row of moth-eaten fur coats.

The rooms up here all seemed to be used for storage. Behind other doors he found old clothes and hats, battered sports equipment, moldering books, paintings disfigured by patches of damp and mold, dull mirrors, broken furniture, boxes of papers that had been chewed by mice . . . the forgotten junk of countless generations of Hellebores. So when he came to the last door, he casually pushed it open and shone his flashlight in, expecting to find more rubbish.

Instead, the beam shone directly into George Hellebore's sleeping face. James instantly shut the flashlight off, but not before George had stirred and mumbled something in his sleep.

James pressed himself against the wall and stayed utterly still, trying to quiet his breathing. George shifted uneasily in his bed and then slowly settled down again.

James's eyes gradually accustomed themselves to the dim light filtering through the thin curtains. He could make out a huge black wardrobe, a desk, an ancient four-poster bed, and there, in the middle of it, George, wearing a striped nightshirt.

James felt for the door handle, then delicately opened it and slipped out.

Without stopping to think, he hurried along the corridor and through the door at the end.

He found that he was near the top of a winding stone stairway, on a wide landing. This part of the castle was lit by gas wall lamps that gave off a dull, flickering, orange light. It was freezing and the air smelled of gas and damp. He shuffled forward and leant over the banisters. Far below was a marble-floored hallway with a black-and-white checkerboard pattern. All he had to do was go down the stairs and across the hallway, and he would be at the front door.

But what if it *was* open? What if he *did* get out without being seen? What would he have achieved? Could he really go back to Kelly and tell him that all he had discovered was a stuffed cat, some old furniture, and George Hellebore asleep in his bed in a striped nightshirt? What would his friend say?

But then again, what exactly had he hoped to find? Alfie Kelly's body hidden in a cupboard? A handwritten confession from Lord Hellebore lying on a desk? The real world didn't work like that. You didn't hide behind a door and hear the chief villain telling a crony exactly what he'd done, how he'd done it, and what he was going to do next. It struck James that he had come up here unprepared, that he had had some vague schoolboy fantasy of solving a mystery with no real thought as to how he might do it.

He needed a plan.

A stupid thought popped into his racing mind. A joke, a riddle: *A man, a plan, a canal, Panama!* It was a palindrome; it read the same backward as forward.

Well, he had a joke, but not a plan.

Don't get hysterical, James. Keep your mind alert. Keep it focused on what has to be done.

He made a deal with himself: He would go down and see if there was an easy way out through the hallway and, if there was, then he would set himself a time limit—say twenty minutes—to explore the castle before escaping. Yes. That was a good compromise.

All right.

And what if there wasn't a way out? What if, as was more likely, the front door was locked or even guarded by one of Hellebore's men? What then?

Then he would explore the ground floor until he found another way out.

Okay. There it was—a plan.

Luckily, as the stairway was made of stone, there was no danger of creaking steps. Apart from the faint hiss and an occasional sputter from the gas lamps, the building was deathly quiet. In less than a minute he was at the foot of the stairs, and he could see that there was nobody around, no armed guards, nothing.

As he had thought, this was the main hallway. The front door was reached via a smaller, wood-paneled porch. He took a step toward it and then froze.

It was a footstep. He was sure of it. He stood there without moving and strained his ears. Was his mind playing tricks on him? Feeding on his fear and creating phantoms?

No. There it was again. But it was no ordinary footstep. There wasn't the click of a shoe; it sounded softer, more like a slap. There it was again, a definite slap and then a sliding sound. Maybe it was someone in bare feet? But whoever it was, James didn't want to find out. He ran to the huge front door and grabbed the handle.

It was locked. Of course it was locked. And now he had wasted time. He hurried back into the main hall. The footsteps were getting nearer.

There were several different corridors leading off from here. James looked feverishly from one to another, but had no clear idea of where the sound was coming from.

Most of the corridors were relatively well lit, but underneath the stairs was a low arch, beyond which was empty darkness. He darted through the archway and waited.

For a moment there was silence; the footsteps had stopped. Then, from far away, James heard what sounded like some large beast sniffing the air. Could the man have a dog with him? No. A dog didn't sound like that.

Suddenly, the footsteps started again, much quicker now. James glanced into the hallway and saw a shadow lurching along a corridor, off to the left. The shadow of somebody large. And then he heard wet, sloppy breathing. It sounded labored, as if it were bubbling up through a pipe of water, and behind it was a high-pitched, wheezing tone.

James didn't wait to see who it was; he turned and ran blindly down the corridor through the darkness, with no idea where it led. He turned three corners, bumping into the walls, and came to a dead end. He stopped and listened. Whatever it was, it was still coming after him, *slip-slop*ping along the stone floor, its horrible breathing echoing off the walls.

James quickly backtracked, feeling his way along the wall until his hand touched the cold metal of a door handle. He opened it and went through, closing the door quietly behind him.

He was in a huge kitchen. A battery of brass pots and

pans hung from the ceiling, and there were two big stainless steel sinks off to one side. In the middle of the stone-tiled floor stood a gargantuan scrubbed wooden table with various utensils laid out neatly on it, ready for use, including several razor-sharp chef's knives. James grabbed one and ran out of the far end of the room, past a range that glowed red in the semidarkness.

The room he found himself in was smaller and colder than the kitchen. It was a larder of some sort. Several animal carcasses were suspended from hooks, and James could smell the meat.

What am I doing? he thought, staring at the knife in his hand. He put it down and looked for another way out.

Returning to the kitchen, he spotted a small side door opening into a dark passage. He hesitated before going any farther, but then he heard a snuffling at the other door and he plunged into the darkness without another thought. He brushed against a row of coats, nearly getting himself entangled, and, as he flailed around, his hand caught a light pull and switched on a dim, bare bulb. Past the coats he saw a narrow, twisting staircase, and he started up it. Behind him, he could hear the wet slap of footsteps again, and he cursed himself for wasting time in the kitchen.

One floor up, James came out into what must have been a servants' passageway, long and thin and twisting. He belted along it as quickly and as quietly as he could, hoping against hope that he would lose his unseen pursuer. But it was no good; still it came after him, steadily and silently. Why didn't it cry out? Why didn't it try to raise the alarm? Call for help?

James was beginning to panic. He was completely disoriented; he had no idea which way he had come or which way he was going. It was like being lost in a nightmare maze, with a monster after him.

He came to another stairway. Had he been up it before? Or had he come down it?

No time to think.

He leapt down the steps three at a time, but lost his footing in the dark and went tumbling head over heels, smashing his head against the wall. When he finally landed at the bottom, he was stunned. There was a horrible throbbing in his right temple. He felt nauseous and waves of dizziness passed through him. But he managed to get to his feet and made himself walk. Come on, one foot in front of the other—it wasn't so hard. He could do it. . . . he stumbled. He was very wobbly and had bruised his legs badly in the fall. Then he saw a light ahead and, like a moth, he went toward it, hoping that it might offer a way out.

The light was burning above a large metal door. He wrenched it open and went through.

He came out onto a platform overlooking a huge, windowless room, which, he thought, must have been underneath the castle. It was lit by glowing, violet lights and was chillingly cold. There was an animal stink mixed with a fishy smell and the cloying scent of chemicals.

Below him were row upon row of glass tanks with things swimming in them, plus steel tables, almost like hospital operating tables, with taps and shallow basins at one end. It reminded him of one of the science rooms at Eton, but on a huge scale.

Off to one side were some cages, and he could hear a snuffling, grunting sound coming from them. And there, he hadn't seen it at first, laid out on one of the tables, was the body of a pig, split open down the middle, its insides pinned out around it.

James tried to take it all in, but his head was spinning and the room spun with it. He grabbed hold of the iron railing to stop himself from falling over. He closed his eyes for a second—and then something grabbed him from behind. Two great, slimy, wet hands closed over his face. He felt cold breath on his neck and that horrible, wet breathing close to his ear. . . .

Then he let go and sank into unconsciousness.

CHAPTER 20—THE SARGASSO SEA

When James awoke, the first thing he was aware of was the cold. There was cold air on his face and filling his lungs. There was cold seeping into his back, where he was lying on something hard, and there was a cold, wet patch on his right temple.

Even though he felt very weak and still only half-conscious, he tried to move, but found that he couldn't. He forced his eyes open and saw through the slits that his wrists and ankles were strapped to one of the steel tables in Hellebore's laboratory.

He still felt faint and closed his eyes, but they almost immediately snapped open again as a searing pain jolted through his head.

He found himself looking up into the expressionless face of an unassuming young man with blond hair, glasses and thin, pale lips. He was holding a wad of cotton wool and a small glass jar full of yellowish liquid.

"Did I hurt you?" he said with the trace of a German accent.

"Yes," said James, and the young man studiously wrote something down in a small notebook that he'd taken from the pocket of his grubby white lab coat.

James wished he could free one hand and rub his scalp

where it stung, but it was out of the question. He couldn't move an inch.

"I'm afraid you hit your head rather badly," said the young man, putting down his book. Then he held open James's eyelids with chilly fingers and peered into his eyes. "Do you know your name, and what day it is?"

"My name is Bond, James Bond," said James with a note of irritation in his voice. "And it's Wednesday—no, Thursday morning. Now, undo these straps and let me up."

"James Bond!" boomed another voice, and James turned his head to see Lord Hellebore leaning against a nearby glass tank and watching him. "I thought I recognized you. You're from Eton, aren't you? I met you with the Head Master."

Lord Hellebore came over and looked down at James, rubbing his jaw. James was overwhelmed by the animal smell of him and the heat that his body gave off.

"You punched me in the mouth," he said.

"Yes," said James sheepishly. "But it was an accident."

"Then you went on to win the cross-country, I seem to recall. . . . You're Andrew Bond's son?"

"Yes," said James with relief. "That's right." He forced a smile. "Now, will you let me up?"

"You are secured there for your own good," said Hellebore, returning to the tank, where he tapped the glass and studied a long, black eel that swam up and down in the murky water.

"We didn't want you to harm yourself. Hitting your head can be a nasty business. It can bring on fits. Once we're sure you're okay we'll let you up." He turned away from the tank and smiled at James. "Now, in the meantime, why don't you tell us exactly what you were doing, wandering around my home in the middle of the night?"

"I came to see George," said James, making up the only lie he could think of quickly.

"George?" Randolph raised a mocking eyebrow. "You came to visit my son at two o'clock in the morning? That seems a little unlikely."

"I was hoping to surprise him," said James limply, and Randolph laughed.

"Well, hell, I'm sure he would have been surprised!" he roared, then he came over and leaned down to sniff James's hand.

"Pine resin," he said. "You climbed that goddamned tree, didn't you?"

James said nothing.

"I always knew we should have cut that tree down."

The laboratory was in semidarkness, lit by pools of light from the violet lamps overhead, and James felt detached from reality. He might have thought it was a dream, except there was an awful stink in the room, and you never smelled anything in dreams. Suddenly there came a terrible inhuman shriek, and a snorting, grunting sound that James couldn't identify.

"Please believe me," James said, trying to hide the desperation in his voice. "I came to see George. I got stuck up in the tree and it took me much longer than I expected. I meant to—"

"All right," Randolph snapped. "Have it your way. MacSawney!" he shouted. "Go and get George from his room."

James saw the short, apelike man in the bowler hat move out of the shadows, take one look at him, grin like a chimp, then cross the floor and hurry up the metal steps, which clanged beneath his feet.

Randolph began to undo James's straps. "I have to be a little careful," he said. "You may think me slightly overconcerned with security, but all sorts of people come here to try to spy on my work, steal my secrets, and"—he tried to inject a tone of sincerity into his voice—"it's very dangerous for them. Why, only yesterday we found a man from the Pinkerton Detective Agency floating in our moat. Poor fellow must have been snooping around and slipped in. You were damned lucky that that didn't happen to you. A man could fall in there and never be seen again."

"Or a boy," said James. "A boy like Alfie Kelly?" He watched Lord Hellebore closely and was pleased to see that, for the first time, his cool exterior was ruffled.

"What do you know about Alfie Kelly?" he said, and paused before undoing the last strap around James's left ankle.

"Only that he came up here to fish," said James, "and never returned."

"That's an interesting theory," said Randolph with a pleasant smile, and he unfastened the buckle, freeing James's foot.

James swung his legs over the side of the table and sat up, gingerly touching the lump on the side of his head. He felt woozy and dog-tired.

"A very interesting theory," Randolph continued, "but sadly, one that can never be proved."

Behind Randolph the eel pushed itself against the glass

wall of its tank and snaked upward, as if trying to escape, then it flopped back down into the water and continued to swim up and down, tireless and unthinking. James was mesmerized by it.

"You like my eels?" said Randolph. "Pretty things, aren't they? Perfectly adapted. There are no unnecessary embellishments on an eel. They haven't changed for millions of years. They don't have to. They're extraordinary creatures, you know." Randolph took James over to the tank and they stood side by side, watching the fish looping and twisting in the green water. James could see Randolph's face reflected in the glass, his eyes shining. He rubbed a finger thoughtfully across his perfect white teeth.

"*Anguilla anguilla*, the European eel," he said. "They spawn in the Sargasso Sea, thousands of miles away in the North Atlantic." His voice was quiet and reverential. "The Sargasso Sea, that strange, dead place, caught between ocean currents. It sits there, perfectly still and flat, its surface clogged with sargassum weed, and beneath that surface, through the black depths, come the eels. What a sight that must be—though no man has ever seen it—a huge, boiling mass of eels, engaged in their dance of love."

Randolph led James past more tanks, each with a solitary eel in it, some only a few inches in length, some more than a foot long—one monster nearly three feet long and as thick as a man's arm.

"All the eels of Europe are born there," said Randolph. "All these eels were born there. Every one of them came from eggs laid in the Sargasso Sea, where they hatch and then set off home."

Randolph stopped and turned to James.

"You wouldn't recognize them," he said. "They're tiny things, completely transparent and shaped like a willow leaf. At that stage they're known as "thin-heads," and as thin-heads they embark on their unimaginable voyage to the freshwaters of Europe, across the hostile ocean, past numerous predators, and, when they arrive, they have grown more like eels, but they still don't look like these big fellows. Look here . . ." Randolph pointed to a larger tank, where thousands of tiny transparent creatures swam, with heads too large for their bodies and eyes that were nothing more than black pinheads, each about two inches long.

"Glass eels," said Randolph, "like tiny splinters of glass. When they reach the river's mouth they wait there, growing, darkening, until they become young eels at last, and then they swim, in their millions. Oh, you should see them coming up the rivers, a torrent of them, you can dip your net in and pull out bucketful after bucketful. Nothing can stop them, they are too many. Up, up the riverways they come, to the lakes and ponds. My God, they will even slither over wet grass in order to get to where they want to go, and there they'll stay, growing older and wiser, fatter and longer, year after year, waiting in the mud, until one day, nobody knows when or why, they get the call and decide that it's time to go back, and they set off—back down the rivers into the ocean and onward, mile after mile, to the still Sargasso Sea, where they spawn; and then they die, and their bodies fall slowly down, down through the darkness to the seabed."

Randolph reluctantly tore himself away from the tank of glass eels and turned to James, with fire in his eyes.

"Have you ever caught an eel?" he said. "An adult? A really big one? They are awesome beasts; their skin is so tough you can make boots out of it. And have you ever tried to kill one? By God, it takes a lot to kill an eel. They are frighteningly strong and quite ruthless. You put ten small eels in a tank; the next day there'll be nine, the next day eight, and in no time at all, there'll be only one eel left. A big, fat, tough beggar." Randolph laughed. "We think we're kings of the world, top of the food chain, masters of all beasts, but compared to eels we're puny, frail, and neurotic. Ah, here's George."

James saw two sets of feet coming down the steps and saw that one pair belonged to George. He looked pale and disoriented. He yawned and rubbed his eyes, and when he saw James his face dropped.

"You know this boy?" his father asked bluntly.

"Yes," said George guardedly, and James remembered when he had watched the two of them together at Eton. He remembered how George had seemed petrified of his father.

"He says he's a friend of yours," said Randolph, staring at his son.

George hesitated before replying.

"Well?" his father barked.

"I know him," said George. "I know he has an uncle in the village."

"That's not what I asked you. I asked if he was a friend of yours."

Again George hesitated. He looked at his father. He looked at the floor. He didn't look at James.

"No," he said at last.

James's heart sank—but, after all, what had he expected? Now that he thought about it, saying he knew George was just about the worst thing he could have done. George hated him. If only his head had been clearer, he might have come up with a better story.

"Do you have any idea why this boy might have come here?" asked Randolph.

"No," said George.

"Very well," said Randolph. "You may go to your room."

James saw a flicker of concern cross George's face.

"What are you going to do with him?" he said.

"Don't worry yourself about that," said Randolph affably. "I just need to get to the bottom of this. Now go and get back to sleep."

"Maybe I should stay," said George.

"It's late," Randolph snapped. "Go back to your bed. This need not concern you."

George's eyes met James's, and James was sure that something passed between them, some tiny thread of companionship.

"Dad . . . ?"

"You are not needed here."

George nodded and turned away.

James ran to him and grabbed his arm. "George," he said urgently, "you have to help me."

"I can't," said George quietly as MacSawney stepped forward and pulled James away from him, his powerful hands digging into his arms.

George didn't look back. He walked briskly to the stairs with his head bowed and went back up.

James's position looked hopeless. He heard the door above slam shut, and it felt like the lid of a coffin closing on him.

"I'm going to tell you something now, Bond," said Randolph when the echo of the door had died away, "because it will help you to understand what is going to happen to you."

A chill passed through James; his stomach lurched and a lump of fear rose in his throat. He looked around wildly, but all he saw was the bland face of the young German, smiling pleasantly at him. The scientist stroked the side of his nose with a long, bony forefinger, then he sniffed and made a note in his little book.

"He looks strong," he said. "That is good."

James felt physically sick. He was shaking. He clenched his teeth and fought for self-control. He wouldn't give Hellebore the satisfaction of seeing him break down.

"Cheer up, Bond," said Randolph. "Console yourself with the fact that you are going to be a huge help to the advancement of science and the understanding of the human body."

"People know I am here," said James desperately.

"Do they?" Hellebore gave James a patronizing look. "Did you really tell someone that you were going to come up here and break into my house? Who exactly did you tell? The police? Your uncle? It's no matter if you did, though, I can keep you hidden for as long as I wish. This castle has countless secret rooms, and I'm sure you saw our security on your way in."

"Yes," said James. "Your guards are really first-rate, apart from the small fact that they let a schoolboy get past them."

Randolph's eyes narrowed, and he puckered his lips peevishly.

"That will be looked into," he said, and then he walked across and held James's face in one of his huge fists. "I made a fortune in the war," he said, "selling arms to the United States government and her allies, but I also fought in it."

"I know," said James. "I heard your speech at Eton."

Randolph struck a heroic pose, his chest thrust out. "I didn't have to fight, Bond. A great many other businessmen spent piles of money ensuring that they didn't go to war—ensuring that they were considered too important to get blood on their hands. But not me, I joined the army. I came over to Europe. I fought for a year. My brother, Algar, was perfectly capable of running the company while I was away. But do you know why I fought? Was it patriotism? Was it a belief that our side was right and their side was wrong? No, sir. I fought because I wanted to see war firsthand, I wanted to taste it, I wanted to confront death and spit in his face."

The gleam of madness was burning fiercely in Randolph's eyes. Why was he telling James this? Why did he feel the need to show off to him?

And then James realized—Randolph couldn't tell anyone else. It was all secret. But he could talk to James. He could talk to James, because—James gripped his knuckles together and bit his cheek—because James wasn't going to live to tell anyone else.

"And I wanted to test myself," said Randolph, passionately. "To see if I was a man."

"And are you?" said James with false innocence. If he was already doomed, it didn't really matter what he said or did anymore.

"Don't try to mock me, boy."

"Please," said James. "It's late and I'm tired, and you are, frankly, beginning to get a little boring. If you're going to punish me, could you please get on with it."

"All in good time. I am just now coming to the interesting part."

"That remains to be seen."

"Be silent!" Randolph snapped. "When I returned to America after the war, I set to work. I had seen a lot of things on those muddy, bloody battlefields of Flanders. I had seen with my own eyes the frailty of human beings. I saw how weak they were, how useless, how easily they came apart and perished. It struck me that the future of warfare was not in making better weapons; it was in making better people— stronger, bigger, more fearless, more ruthless. But it's damned hard, experimenting on human beings."

"I wouldn't know," said James.

"Oh, spare me the disapproval. You're all the same. They didn't appreciate what I was doing in the United States. Americans can be very sentimental. They said it was immoral, inhuman. What did they know about humanity? The generals with all their fancy medals thought it was just fine to send millions of young men off to die in a war, but they couldn't spare me a handful to study in my laboratory. I had to become more and more secretive, I had to surround myself with more and more layers of protection; but the hardest thing was always finding living specimens to work with."

James was starting to get some idea of where all this was going, what his fate might be—and he didn't like it one bit.

Now that his head was clearing he tried to focus his mind and look around for a possible way out of this hellish room.

"It wasn't just me," Randolph went on. "My brother, Algar, was the true genius. I had the ideas, but he was the one who knew how to put them into practice. He was a brilliant scientist, totally dedicated to his work—nothing else mattered to him."

"But he objected to what you were doing, didn't he?" said James. "And you killed him."

Randolph paused for a moment, staring at James, and then burst out laughing, his voice bouncing off the bare walls of the laboratory and setting off a strange, animal echo, like the laughter of demons.

"I didn't kill him," said Randolph. "I did nothing to him. He did it all himself. As I say, we had problems finding humans to work with, so Algar used the only body he could . . . his own. Perhaps you would like to meet him properly. MacSawney, bring out my brother."

MacSawney nodded, then shuffled to the back of the room, where James heard him unlocking something. There was a pause and an angry shout, and then there came that horrible shuffling and wheezing sound that James knew so well, and a huge, hideous shape lumbered into view.

James recoiled, but then forced himself to look at what had once been a man. Algar was taller than Randolph, though stooped over. His arms were enormous, and great knots of swollen muscle showed through his thin, filthy shirt, but there was something ruined about him, as if he could hardly carry his own great weight. His skin was smooth and shiny and gray, stretched tight over his vast frame, and it glistened with oily sweat. The face was wrecked: it looked as if it had been split down the middle and forced apart, so that the nose was flattened and stretched, the teeth had separated and the eyes had curved around almost to the sides of his head.

The eyes were the worst part. They were dark and wet, and James saw in them, not murder, but sadness and pain.

It was then that James realized that Algar's feet were chained together and MacSawney was pointing a shotgun at his back.

"My dear brother." Randolph laughed. "You know, the irony is, we are twins, near as dammit identical. But there was always a difference between us. . . ."

Randolph went over and stood next to his brother, beaming at James.

"Algar was considered the better-looking one. Ha, ha, ha, ha!"

CHAPTER 21—HELL WILL ENDURE

"The road to hell is smooth, Bond, and the doors are always open." Randolph grinned. "What's the motto of that snobby school you boys attend? 'Eton will endure'? Well, I have no doubt that it will; it's been there for a few hundred years; it'll probably stand for a few hundred more. But do you know what is really certain? Death. As long as men walk the surface of this earth, there will be pain and death and suffering. Death will endure. War will endure. Hell will endure, and, as long as its gates are open, I'll be in business. As long as one man wants to bash another man's brains out, I'll be standing, ready to sell him a club."

Food had been brought in, and James was sitting at one of the laboratory benches with Lord Hellebore and the young scientist, who had been introduced as Dr. Perseus Friend.

They seemed keen for him to eat, even though he had no appetite. He forced down a couple slices of ham but they stuck in his throat, and his saliva felt like glue.

"It's not my fault that men are the way they are," Randolph went on. "And only a fool would fail to profit from it. Men were born to kill. It's what we do best. And I'll help them in any way I can. Now, how can anyone say that that is wrong?"

"I had the same problems with my work before," said Dr.

Friend. "Nobody appreciates a visionary. Some of the diseases I perfected were quite beautiful."

"What you are doing is evil," said James, pushing his plate away.

Randolph laughed. "Evil? What a quaint idea. As if a dead man cares whether he's killed by a nice clean bullet, or a cloud of gas or the plague. Our governments make up the rules for warfare. It's okay to do this, but it's not okay to do that. And you're telling me that that somehow makes the whole damned thing acceptable, does it? Pah! They can dress it up pretty, they can try to pretend it's civilized. It ain't. War is dirty. I should know, I was in one."

Randolph stopped and stood up. MacSawney was still standing off to one side, keeping one eye, and the barrel of his gun, fixed on Algar. Randolph walked over to the creature who had once been his twin, and Algar cowered away from him.

"How much do you know about the human body, Bond?" Randolph said.

"Only what I've learnt at school."

"You know about the nervous system, then? The network that sends electric signals around your body, to activate the muscles, to feel pleasure . . . and pain."

He raised his fist, and once again Algar shrank away from him.

"Well, there's another system—the endocrine system—which is even more important, but is still only poorly understood. The messages in the endocrine system are sent as chemicals, which are produced in various glands and travel through your body in the blood."

"Hormones," said James. "My aunt taught me a little about them, but I've forgotten most of it."

"Hormones is right," Randolph nodded. "And they affect us in many different ways. Some tell us when to wake up, or when to sleep. Others tell us when to be excited, when to scream and run, and when to fall in love. Others tell us when to grow and when to stop growing. Up in your skull, in a small concavity on the sphenoid bone, sits a seemingly unassuming little gland called the pituitary. Now, I could tell you that the pituitary gland is connected to the hypothalamus by the infundibulum, but that would mean nothing to you. All you need to know is that the pituitary gland controls the whole system—and, most important, it controls your growth."

Randolph raised his hand again but, instead of hitting Algar, he stroked his brother's slimy cheek.

"When you are young, your pituitary gland sends out growth hormones that worm their way into your cells and tell them to divide and multiply, and when their work is done other hormones come along and tell the cells to stop. Are you following me?"

"I had hoped to have left school lessons behind for the holidays," said James, trying to appear uninterested but concentrating hard so as to glean any clues he could about his fate.

"But this is fascinating stuff, Bond. Fascinating," said Randolph, his face alive with emotion. "Just imagine what can happen when the system goes wrong and becomes unbalanced. A child can grow up to become a dwarf or a giant; he can become immensely fat . . . or immensely strong.

Well, that got me thinking—what if we were able to manipulate the endocrine system ourselves? What if we could control the hormones and tell the muscles to grow? Tell the bones to grow?"

Randolph turned excitedly to his brother, who looked at him through his dull, bulging eyes.

"That was the area we were fascinated by, wasn't it, Algie? Hmm? So what did we do? We set about studying glands and the different types of hormones: amines, peptides, proteins, and steroids."

"Am I supposed to know what you're talking about?" said James. "Or are you just showing off that you know a lot of clever stuff?"

"Be quiet," snapped Hellebore. "You won't be able to understand half of this. Just so long as some of it sinks in."

Dr. Friend interrupted. "We have been looking into ways of synthesizing hormones, making our own versions, extracting them, combining them, altering them . . ."

Randolph took up the story again.

"Our idea," he said, his voice crackling with excitement, "was to turn an ordinary man into a superman."

James looked at Algar. He stood there, breathing with difficulty through his ruined nose, snot dripping down and mixing with the saliva that hung from his mouth in a thick rope.

"Well, you failed," he said quietly.

"No!" yelled Randolph, slamming his hand down onto the table and rattling the cutlery. "At first the experiment appeared to have been a huge success. After the initial injections, Algar began to grow, to become stronger, and he felt so healthy and energetic he used to describe it as a feeling of tremendous power raging inside him, as if he had swallowed a lightning bolt. So I increased the dosage . . . but it was then that things started to go wrong. His mind become hazy, he became forgetful and clumsy, awful spasms shook his body. He complained of headaches and muscular pains, and slowly we realized that he was changing, physically altering. We had somehow upset his endocrine system. His musculature had become monstrous. His bones were growing at an alarming rate, and he developed a form of acromegaly. His skull widened, his skin thickened, his thyroid gland was destroyed, his vocal cords ruined. His salivary glands and his sweat glands became overactive, and terrible rages gripped him. In the end, we had to have him sedated. But, with a series of injections and treatment over the years, I have been able to calm him. And now? You're as gentle as a lamb, aren't you, Algie?"

Randolph patted Algar on top of his slimy, hairless head. "Tonight we found him carrying you across the hallway, Bond. He almost got away."

"What do you mean?" said James.

"He wasn't trying to harm you, Bond. He was trying to help you—the poor fool—to rescue you, to take you away from this place."

"But why?"

"There was a previous time, another boy—Algar rescued him from drowning in the loch."

"Alfie Kelly."

"Yes. A big around of applause for the boy! Your theory proved correct after all, Bond. Algar brought Alfie to me, to nurse him, but we had other plans."

"We needed a human being," said Dr. Friend casually, wiping his spectacles on his lab coat.

James felt his throat tighten and his head pounded as he tried to take in the full implication of what Dr. Friend had said.

A strange whine escaped from Algar's blubbery lips.

James looked from one brother to the other, and he knew which one was the monster. Not the ugly, misshapen one, the one who had become deformed and difficult to look at, but the other one, the handsome one, with his golden hair, his bristling mustache, his clear, tanned skin, perfect white smile, and china-blue eyes.

In the process of their experiments, one had gained humanity and the other had lost it.

"Take him away, MacSawney," said Randolph, "and lock him up in one of the pens. We can't risk him interfering again."

The squat gillie waddled over and gleefully prodded Algar in the back with his gun. Algar hobbled away, and Randolph wiped his fingers on a cloth, before straightening his hair and preening himself in the glass of a fish tank. He then took a small silver box from his pocket, opened it, tapped out two tiny white pills into his palm, and tipped them into his mouth. He swallowed.

"You think we've failed?" he said, approaching James and rubbing his hands together. "Quite the opposite. We are nearly there. Already we have developed pills that increase the body's capabilities."

"That's what you gave to George, didn't you?" said James. "I saw you at the sports day."

"George had been taking the pills for some time. He refuses now, but then . . . they made him stronger and faster. The cup was to be my first triumph. Of course, there were the usual side effects: increased aggression, a short temper, a small loss of intelligence. But that is of no consequence, and in a soldier would all be admirable qualities."

"You did that to your own son?"

"Why not," shouted Randolph angrily, "if it had made him win?"

"But he didn't win, did he?" said James. "Because you'd sent him crazy. What with the false starts, and trying to attack me on the cross-country . . ."

"Be silent! He didn't win because he is fundamentally weak. As you can see, I take the pills myself, and they do me no harm. They keep me like this—a perfect physical specimen."

"You're not worried that you will slowly turn into your brother?"

"My brother was a fool. He tested the serum before it was perfected, and in too high a dose. Our concoctions are enormously powerful. They can turn a sniveling coward into a hero with the heart of a lion, they can turn a feeble weakling into a Hercules with the body of a bull—why, they could even turn a woman into a man."

"And what did they turn Algar into?"

"What does he look like to you? My wretched brother?"

"I don't know," said James miserably. He just wanted this night to be over. He wanted to be back at the cottage, in his own bed. He wanted to be safe.

"Look!" Randolph exclaimed, and he pointed at the eel

in the tank. "An eel! Algar has become an eel. It's uncanny, isn't it? The resemblance."

"How can you talk like that?" James shouted. "How can it not affect you? You're crazy. You're all crazy!"

"Scientists are not like other people," said Dr. Friend calmly. "Algar was a scientist, a pure scientist. He saw beyond today, beyond our insignificant little lives. He understood that the end justifies the means. History will prove us right."

He stopped and cleaned his spectacles for the hundredth time.

"People aren't important," he went on, "it's what they leave behind that matters. Look at the great artworks of Renaissance Italy, paid for by murderous villains. Nobody remembers their victims, but everybody marvels at the paintings and the sculptures and fine buildings. The great doctors of old were considered monsters for experimenting on dead bodies, but now they are heroes!"

"There's a difference," said James, "between experimenting on dead bodies and experimenting on live ones."

"It is academic," said Dr. Friend.

"This is the perfect site for a factory, you know, Bond," said Randolph. "Just as it was the perfect site for a castle, directly over a freshwater spring on an inaccessible island in a loch. Loch Silverfin. You know the legend? It' Airgid? The big fish that ate all the little fish? The biggest, toughest fish of them all. Silverfin. Seemed like an apt name for my project. Especially as this lake has played such an important part. For some time we have been pouring all our waste into it: failed serum, the dead bodies of animals we had experimented on, the blood that is daily sluiced out of this place, all manner of waste chemicals and drugs. It all goes into the loch, where the greedy eels devour the lot. And do you know what happened? In a remarkably short time it started to get into their systems. Because they are so primitive, so tough, they thrived on it, and their nature changed. Ordinarily, an eel is not a hugely aggressive creature. Oh, it's true they are ruthless and uncaring, but they're not sharks, they're not barracuda, their teeth are not sharp, they're little more than grinding plates. Once they bite on something it's the very devil to make them let go, as they try to screw the flesh loose, but they're not dangerous to humans. They eat leeches, nymphs, shrimp; they'll eat the fresh corpse of almost anything, although they're rather fussy about stale meat; but they're not really fearsome predators. Not usually. Our waste, however, turned the placid local eels into killers—bloodthirsty, ferocious, and unstoppable. Yes, my drugs were turning them into the sort of fighting machines that I had been trying to create. So I speeded up the process, pumping the water full of drugs, then trapping the eels and removing from them what I needed. They have endocrine systems, like any vertebrate. Their glands are easy enough to extract."

Randolph fetched a small net and dipped it into a tank. After a few moments he fished out an eel and brought it to James. Then he grabbed it by the neck, removed it from the net and pinned it down on the tabletop, where it thrashed about, scattering food with its tail.

"Look at him. One taste of blood and he'd be on you like a tiger. That loch is teeming with his brothers and sisters. I even erected a complicated system of nets and barriers so that eels can get in happily enough, but they can't get out again.

Oh, of course the odd few escape, they're tenacious beasts; but on the whole the population here is growing and growing, a population of bloodthirsty, powerful killers."

"But what about the trout, the local salmon . . . ?" said James, appalled at this tampering with nature. "They'll be wiped out."

"Who cares about a few fish, Bond? They are long gone; that lake is a vast aquarium now, my own laboratory."

"It's cheating," said James.

"Cheating? You are full of such quaint notions," said Hellebore.

"Yes," said James angrily, "cheating. To think that a man could simply take a pill and he would be stronger and faster than another man. It's not right."

"We are living in a new age, Bond, forged in the horrors of war, and your ideas about right and wrong, good and bad, no longer have any value. Now there is only weak and strong, quick and slow, the living and the dead, the rich and the poor. And, given the choice, which would you rather be? Strong, quick, rich, and alive, or weak, slow, poor, and dead?"

"I would rather be anything than a stinking cheat!" shouted James. "I don't want to live my life among bullies and freaks."

"Well, hats off to you, Mr. Bond, but don't blame me if your life is miserable and short."

So saying, Randolph picked up a spike, and with one swift movement he stuck it through the eel's head, securing it to a wooden dissecting board on the tabletop.

CHAPTER 22—THE GADARENE SWINE

"Look at him go," said Randolph, marveling at the eel, which was twisting on its spike, smearing the table with thick slime and blood. "Imagine, if you could combine the characteristics of an eel with those of a human! We could make a fighting man who was not only bigger and stronger, with a hide like steel, but also simpler, more obedient, unquestioning, and unstoppable. He would be magnificent, wouldn't he? Utterly ferocious and terrifying! Soon, James Bond, soon, I will have perfected my serum. I will have the correct balance of growth hormones, adrenalin, testosterone, and all the countless other chemicals that I have extracted from my eels. Soon I will be able to create an unkillable soldier."

Hellebore dragged James up out of his seat.

"Let me show you something," he said, and he led James across the laboratory, threading his way between the workbenches on which half-finished experiments were set out: dead pigs, dissected eels, unnameable body parts, gray bits of flesh in jars, microscopes, and paperwork scrawled with numbers and symbols.

They arrived at what looked like a row of low animal pens, built right up against the wall. The heavy steel-framed doors were all padlocked.

As they got nearer, the grunting noise that James had been trying to identify since he had woken up grew stronger, as did the animal stench. Then, as he peered through the mesh in one of the doors, he realized what the source of it all was.

Staring miserably back at him was a live pig.

It was no ordinary pig, however. For a start, it was a giant, maybe twice the size of a normal pig, but all out of proportion. Its head looked tiny, with a bony growth on its forehead like a short horn. It could hardly support itself on its stumpy, twisted legs, and it was shivering horribly.

James quickly glanced into the next cage and saw a similar deformed creature, this time with jutting, dinosaur teeth in a grotesquely swollen lower jaw, and a head far too large for its malformed and elongated body. The rest of the pigs were no better. Some had shriveled bodies, some were missing eyes, some had bulbous, puffy trotters, some were drooling, some chewing at their cages, and in all of their faces were madness and pain.

MacSawney came over to join them and James noticed that, as he drew near, the beasts became agitated and some shrank back in fear. One or two threw themselves at their cages as if trying to smash their way out.

Hellebore laughed. "They can smell you, Cleek," he said.

The wizened goblin gillie kicked at a cage. "Quiet down, you ugly brutes," he spat.

"With no people to test our work on," said Hellebore, raising his voice to be heard over the agitated squealing and grunting from the pens, "we have been forced to use pigs."

Dr. Friend now joined them. "I have injected all of them with different versions of the SilverFin serum," he said, "with varying effect, as you can see. But if you look along the line from left to right, you can compare the earliest results with the latest. The animal in pen number one dates from January, and the chap here"—he pointed to where a pig lay on the concrete floor in the half-darkness of his filthy cage—"he started his course of injections earlier this evening at seven thirty-six. He's subdued at the moment, and you will not notice any visible changes for a few more days, but as he grows we can increase the daily injections. We are still a little way from total success and can have no exact idea what the effects would be on an actual human being, but we are confident that within a short time we will have perfected the serum so that we will be able to take an ordinary soldier and turn him into an unstoppable fighting machine within a few weeks. This fellow next to him is our most successful experiment to date."

James looked into the next cage and saw a pig that, at first glance, appeared to be a magnificent animal. It had a massive, well-proportioned head on strong shoulders and sturdy, muscular front legs. It might have been an ordinary pig—albeit a massive and incredibly strong one—except for its skin, which resembled the thick, rough hide of a rhinoceros, and its expression of pure murder. James had never seen such a human and hateful expression on an animal, and, as the pig shifted its gaze to him, he jumped back, expecting the beast to burst out of its cage and sink its yellow teeth into him. But then the pig turned around, and James saw that its back legs were stunted and next to useless. They dragged along the floor behind it, spreading feces and uneaten food across the concrete.

James couldn't look anymore. He turned away from the cage and pressed his hands to his aching forehead, but then he heard a familiar wheezing hiss and turned back.

Sitting in the next cage was Algar, hunched over, the back of his head scraping the ceiling. He had a pitiful, defeated expression on his face, and James saw that he was cradling something. James looked closer and realized that it was the piglet MacSawney had removed from the pigpen outside. Algar was cuddling it like a doll.

"Are you familiar with the biblical story of the Gadarene swine?" said Randolph.

James said nothing.

"You may recall how demons had possessed this old guy and sent him crazy, ranting and raving and smashing the place up, like my brother in his prime. And then here comes Jesus Christ to the rescue, and he chases those demons out of the old guy and straight into a nearby herd of pigs, who become crazed and throw themselves into the sea. Well, my pigs are possessed by demons all right, and our job is to trap those demons and breed them."

James felt sick.

"What did you do to Alfie?" he said.

"He was a feeble specimen," said Dr. Friend mildly.

"What did you do to him?"

"These godforsaken locals," snapped Hellebore, "they're weak and undernourished. What did we do to him? I'll tell you what we did to him. We fed him and watered him. We put some meat on his bones."

"But he was still too weak for the serum," said Dr. Friend. "The first injection was too much for him. His heart gave out."

"Or maybe," said Hellebore, "maybe he died of fright."

"This was a terrible tragedy." Dr. Friend paused for a moment and shook his head sadly. "Because we hadn't had time to test the SilverFin properly. But afterward he was still able to help us, we cut him open and—"

"Stop it!" yelled James. "Stop it. I don't want to hear anymore. Stop it!"

"I only want you to understand," said Lord Hellebore. "We didn't tell the Kelly boy what we were doing. We simply convinced him that he was ill and needed our help. But in retrospect we think that it would have been better if he'd known what was really going on. You are older than him, and stronger, and our experiments have leapt forward since he came to us. I have no doubt that you will live a lot longer."

James stared in horror at Algar and the other freaks in the cages, then a red mist of anger descended on him and he lashed out, kicking Hellebore in the knee. Hellebore yelped and clutched his leg and, while he was distracted, James broke away and sprinted across the laboratory floor.

He made it to the metal stairway and leapt up the steps four at a time, but when he reached the metal door at the top he found that there was no handle, no possible way of opening it without a key.

He swore and looked around for some sort of weapon. If they were going to take him, he would hurt as many of them as he could before they succeeded. He would make them pay. But there was nothing up here. He wished he'd grabbed something from the laboratory: a scalpel, or a jar of acid, any-thing. He ran back. Halfway down the stairs was a door to one side with the warning: DANGER! HIGHLY FLAMMABLE. He smiled. There might be something in here he could use. But then the smile died on his lips. This door was locked as well.

"They're all locked," shouted Lord Hellebore from below, "and made of reinforced steel. There are no windows, and you have no friends here. There is no possible escape from this room. And please don't make it difficult for your-self, because we don't want you to be harmed in any way. We need a perfect physical specimen."

MacSawney was coming slowly up the stairs in a crouch, chuckling, his long, ape arms outspread.

"Come on, laddie," he said. "I'm ready for a fight."

James retreated up to the platform. For a brief moment he thought of cheating them, of hurling himself off the bal-cony and killing himself, but in the back of his mind was a spark. It may have been only tiny, but it burnt fiercely and told him not to give up, to keep fighting; it told him that somehow he would find a way.

"What do you think you are going to do, Bond?" yelled Randolph, putting as much amusement into his voice as he could. "Really, I mean? Come on, you're just a boy. A little boy. Please don't imagine that you could ever succeed in doing anything to harm me or my work in any way. And please don't imagine that you are ever going to leave this castle!"

MacSawney was at the top of the steps now and was creeping toward him along the platform, his pink eyes glint-ing, his tongue exploring his lips and teeth like a parasitic animal. James waited until he was nearly on him, then charged, butting him in the stomach with his head. The air was forced out of MacSawney's lungs with a hiss, and he collapsed onto the floor.

James scrabbled past him and down the steps, toward Dr. Friend and Hellebore, not sure what he was going to do except hurt them as badly as he could.

And then he saw it. Hanging on the wall. A safety ax, next to a small sign that read IN CASE OF FIRE. He switched direction and raced toward it, but he hadn't noticed two more of Hellebore's men, who had hidden themselves beneath the steps. Before he could reach the ax, they jumped out and grabbed him from behind, holding him fast.

"Good work," said Hellebore. "Now, that's enough fun and games for one night. Secure him to the bench, if you would, please. And, Perseus, fetch the SilverFin."

James kicked and struggled with all his strength, but it was no good, the men were too strong for him. It still took them several minutes to get him strapped down, however, and then he was unable to move on the cold steel table.

"You are lucky that I don't want you damaged in any way, Bond," said Hellebore, leaning across and breathing over him with his rank breath, "or I would hurt you now. Hurt you a great deal."

"Don't worry, Lord Hellebore," said Dr. Friend. "The injection will hurt him well enough. I would advise you, boy, not to struggle or tense your muscles too much, or the needle will have trouble getting in and it could be very, very painful indeed. Also, if it were to snap off . . ."

James closed his eyes and tried not to think about what

was happening to him—what was going to happen. But all he could see in his mind's eye were the hideous pigs. Then he felt a rubbing and a cool wetness on his arm where Dr. Friend was cleaning it. After that there came the sound of a rubber stopper being removed from a glass bottle.

James clenched his teeth and tried to relax his arm.

Perseus and Hellebore talked in quiet voices.

"One hundred and seventy-five milligrams should be sufficient for a primary dose . . ."

". . . we will increase the doses by ten milligram increments every twelve hours . . ."

". . . we must prepare a strict and regular diet . . ."

". . . here . . ."

Suddenly James felt a sharp sting and a cold, numbing pain in his arm, as if someone had punched him. He cried out, picturing the spike being driven into the eel's brain. He shook his head and waited for the agonizing ache to go away, which it slowly did, only to be replaced by a terrible feeling of heat and pressure within him. It pressed on the back of his eyes, forcing them out of his skull. It pressed on his teeth, which seemed to rattle loose. It crushed his heart against his ribs and squeezed his lungs. It was as if someone were filling up his body with air from a bicycle pump. He could feel his fingers swelling like sausages, his stomach bursting, the blood thumping in his head and ringing in his ears. He strained against the straps and opened his eyes, to find the whole room spinning. He was overcome with dizziness and felt horribly nauseous. He retched and tasted blood in his mouth. Pressing the side of his face against the slab to try to cool it, he saw Dr. Friend, calmly making notes in his book.

James closed his eyes again.

As the long minutes ticked away the pressure eased slightly. His breathing slowed and a feeling of drowsiness crept over him.

At last Hellebore reckoned he was strong enough to be moved. The two men came over and gently released the straps.

This time James didn't resist in any way but, as they got him to his feet, he vomited onto the floor and saw with satisfaction that some of the mess had splashed onto Hellebore's smart shoes.

To the sound of Hellebore's cursing, James went meekly with the men up the stairs, too sick and weak to try anything. Then the door was unlocked, and he was dragged through the winding corridors of the castle. They eventually arrived in the hallway, where they took a narrow side passage and, after several sharp turns and a clumsy descent down a dark, damp spiral staircase, they came to a massive door. MacSawney took a rusting key that must have been at least a foot long and fitted it into the lock, which clunked open.

The door swung back and James was pushed in.

"Don't think I've forgotten what you did to me," said MacSawney, rubbing his belly, his voice slurred. "There's plenty of time to get my own back on you . . . plenty of time. Now good night, and sweet dreams."

He laughed and closed the door.

James stood there and stared with little emotion as the key turned in the lock.

He didn't care anymore.

He didn't care about anything.

CHAPTER 23—INTO THE DARK

James sat and stared at the ancient, gray, granite walls, slick with damp and stained with blotches of green and yellow fungus. Miserably he clutched his knees to his chest and felt the cold stone floor beneath him, chilling his bones.

So this was it, then. It was all over.

He was deathly tired. He wanted to curl up in the corner of the room and go to sleep forever, to become as cold and still as the stones. . . .

No.

He shook himself and stood up. He mustn't give in, because then Hellebore would have won. He thought of all he'd been through to get this far: the trek up to the castle with Kelly, crawling along the ditch, hiding in the back of the lorry, crossing the pigpens, climbing the great pine tree, and the mad scramble up the wall. . . . Then being chased through the dark passageways by Algar. . . . How long ago was all that? Was it really just last night? Another wave of tiredness washed over him and for a moment he wanted with all his heart to sit back down and rest.

No.

He started to pace the room, back and forth. He had to think. He had to make a plan. He had to do something, to keep active. Above all, he mustn't despair. He thought of

Uncle Max, and all he had had to put up with during the war.

He didn't want to let Max down.

Or Kelly.

Kelly was relying on him, waiting outside in the abandoned building for him to return. He couldn't let Kelly down. People had had to deal with worse situations than this. Max had had to escape from a German fortress; even tortured and beaten, he had found a way out.

Yes.

Nobody can hold a Bond forever.

There was always a way out of any situation, no matter how bleak it seemed. You just had to find it.

The first thing to do was examine his surroundings. He hadn't looked around properly since he'd been shut in here. That was careless.

The room was almost perfectly square, with very high walls, about twice the height of a normal room. James wondered if perhaps there had at one time been another room above—certainly there were square holes in the stonework where thick wooden beams might once have sat.

He slapped one of the walls. It was like slapping a mountain—it had to be at least ten feet thick.

There was only the one door, and—about twenty feet above his head—there was a single, narrow window with heavy bars across it. Even if he could climb up there, James doubted that it would achieve anything.

No light came in through the window, so it must still be night-time.

The room was lit by a bare bulb sticking out of a rusted fitting, high up on the wall opposite the window. The thick electrical cable snaked along the stones a little way before disappearing through a rough hole.

The floor was made of smooth paving slabs, worn and uneven after hundreds of years of use. From his memory of the layout, James guessed that this room was at the lowest level of the building, which meant that beneath the slabs would be the impenetrable rock on which the castle had been built.

The only other feature of this bare and cheerless room was a large iron grille, covering a hole in the floor. He walked across and peered down into it; there was a deep shaft cut into the bare rock, but it was too dark to tell how deep it went or what was at the bottom. James looked closer: The grille was cemented in place, but the mortar looked old and crumbling. He kicked off a piece and let it drop down into the black hole. There were a few moments of silence and then a plop as the chunk of cement landed in water, far below.

What had Hellebore said about the castle being built over a natural spring? Maybe at one time this had been a well shaft?

James lay flat and stared down the hole into the gloom until his eyes grew accustomed to the light and he could just make out a faint glint, but that was all. It scared him to think what might be down there in the darkness.

He shivered and jumped up. Well, he'd wasted some time, he'd kept his mind off his predicament for a little while—but, if anything, he'd now made himself more depressed than he was before. There was no way out of this prison. He was done for.

He sat down against the wall, drew his knees up to his chest once more, and stared at his boots.

His boots!

Of course. How could he have forgotten? He pulled off the left one and twisted the heel to reveal the secret compartment. His knife was still there. He took it out, gripped the blade between his fingernails and unfolded it. It felt good to hold this small weapon in his hand. It felt as if he were doing something at last.

But what? He laughed bitterly at himself. What could he do with this puny little knife? He was not about to dig his way through the solid granite of the walls.

What about the door, then?

Yes. That was an idea.

He jumped up and hurried over to it.

The door was massive, built of great oak beams that were as hard and black as the stones in the walls. The giant rivets and bolts looked strong enough to keep out an army. The keyhole was designed for a gargantuan key the size of his forearm. It was a giant's door from a fairy-tale castle; but, unlike Jack in the fairy tale, there was no magic harp or ogre's wife to help him. His heart sank. He was utterly alone.

Then, as he stared at the door, he noticed something. He squatted down. Two letters were scratched into the wood: *A K*—Alfie Kelly. James felt desperately sad. The poor boy. He must have used a piece of sharp stone, but he had barely scraped the surface.

What did James hope to do with his silly little knife? There wasn't any way he could pick the massive lock. If he tried to carve his way out through the wood, he'd be here for the rest of his life. He could picture himself with a long white beard, steadily chipping away at the impenetrable wood. He was going to die here, to die like Alfie Kelly.

And then he remembered the loose cement around the grille in the floor.

He went back to the shaft and examined the circular iron grating with its crisscrossing bars. He tugged at it—it didn't give even a fraction of an inch. But hadn't he kicked some of the mortar away? He jumped on the grille and noticed a piece of the cement wobble. Fired with the need to keep himself busy and not brood, he lay down and started to pick at the mortar with his knife. After a few minutes he felt a tiny grain of satisfaction as a small lump broke away. He poked at it some more, and soon another small piece came loose, uncovering a clean, shiny section of the grille beneath. Twenty minutes later, he had cleared away a sizable section and exposed about a fifth of the grille. Feverishly he carried on, losing all sense of time. He shut any other thoughts out of his mind and simply concentrated on gouging and poking and digging away with the knife.

Some time later—how much later he had no idea, an hour? Two hours?—he dug out the last piece of cement, uncovering the full span of the grille.

Once again he laced his fingers around the heavy bars of the grille and tried to lift it, and this time it came up—slowly. The thing weighed a ton, but he got it just high enough to shift it fractionally sideways, where he dropped it with a clang to the floor. He waited until he got his strength back, breathing slowly and deeply, then hoisted it up and slid it another couple of inches.

It took him several goes but, eventually he had it clear of the opening.

Now what?

He hadn't really thought this far ahead. He hadn't wanted to. It scared him. He looked down into the shadowy drop.

What was down there?

While he had been working, pieces of mortar had occasionally fallen into the hole and he had gotten used to the sound of them splashing into the black water below. He could tell by the echoes that there was a larger chamber of some sort down there, but what did that mean? Was he really thinking of climbing down there? If he got stuck, he'd be in a worse jam than he was now.

He had rashly assumed that this was an old access shaft down to the spring Hellebore had mentioned, but it could equally well just be a drain. And anyway, what if there *was* a spring down below, with water bubbling up from under the ground? That didn't necessarily mean that there would be a way out of it into the loch.

There was only one way to find out.

The shaft was just wide enough for him to get into, and it looked as if he might climb down quite easily. Maybe . . . maybe he could go down just far enough to take a better look, and if it was hopeless he could climb back up again. Let's face it, anything was better than sitting here and waiting for Hellebore and MacSawney to come back and finish him off. . . . And then, as he sat there with his head spinning with all the possibilities, he heard a splash, like a fish breaking the surface of the water, or an animal. . . . Had he imagined it?

No, there it was again. It was unmistakable, a splash of

the kind only something living could make. That settled it. If there was something alive down there, then the water had to be connected to the loch. There must be a link of some sort to the outside.

In the back of his mind was an awful picture, but he fought to keep it out of the way and not let it come to the front.

He knew what shape that picture was, though.

It was the shape of an eel.

All right. So there were eels down there, but, from what Hellebore had told him, there was no reason for them to attack him—he wasn't wounded, there was no blood. They were just eels, after all. Scavengers, not killers. He had to be positive. If an eel could get in, then it could get out, and if an eel could get out, then maybe a boy could too.

His mind was made up and, before he had time to think of all the terrible reasons he should never go down there in a million years, he eased himself into the shaft.

He groped around for a foothold and soon found one that could take his weight, then he wriggled down and wedged his feet and hands on either side. If he pressed hard enough, he ought to be able to stay in place, even if there was nothing to hold on to or to stand on.

Right, James, here goes. . . . Coolly and methodically, he began to squirm his way downward, moving one foot, then the other, then one hand, then the other, inch by inch. After a few feet, however, his boot slipped on the slick surface, and he had to find a grip in the rock with his fingertips, which were already ripped and sore from his climb up the wall. He grunted in pain, but managed to lodge himself securely, pressing against the walls with all his strength. He couldn't stay like this for long, though. His arms were growing tired from the constant strain, and he was shaking with the effort.

Don't think about that, you idiot, just carry on, you've put up with worse. . . . Another few feet farther and he decided he had to rest. Carefully and rather awkwardly, he shifted his position so that his back was against one side of the shaft and both feet were jammed against the other. He stayed like this for a while before he realized that it would be less effort to descend like this. By bending his legs he could shuffle down fairly easily, and it took the load off his arms, although it was still hard work. The jagged rock dug into his back and he was constantly afraid of slipping.

Down he went. He couldn't see anything below but, from the sound of the small pieces of rock that occasionally fell beneath him, he guessed that he must be about halfway. He looked up. The opening above him looked like a shiny penny.

The walls of the shaft were cold, but James was sweating from the effort, and the worst thing was that a big part of him wanted to go back up rather than carry on down into that dark unknown.

What was he doing? He must be crazy. He could get stuck down there, in that black water, alone and in the dark. But the only alternative was to wait in the cell for certain death.

His mind was racing, his whole body throbbing like an engine ticking over. He felt as if he were on fire. Pulses of energy rippled through him and excited his thoughts.

Maybe he had gone crazy?

No. The injection—the SilverFin. He remembered what those little white pills had done to George. What must this infinitely more powerful serum be doing to him?

Well, it had backfired on Hellebore, because James was getting away. . . .

He laughed, and the sound echoed up and down the shaft.

He was going to get away!

Go on, then, move, don't stop here like a wet blanket. As long as he kept moving, as long as he kept on doing something, he was all right . . . yes, he was all right. . . .

No, he wasn't.

He froze. He'd lost touch with the wall and one leg was dangling in midair. Quickly he pulled it back up and found the rock. He hadn't been concentrating, just staring ahead, not looking up or down. Not that it would have made any difference. There wasn't enough light down here to see anything. He felt with his foot again: it was as he had thought, this was the end of the line. The walls of the shaft ran out. . . . But what was below? How far was the water? How deep was it?

There were too many questions and no answers.

James suddenly had an image of the cell door opening and Hellebore coming in with the ghastly MacSawney, seeing the grille on the floor, looking down into the shaft and finding him here, stuck like a rat up a drainpipe. . . .

He let go.

There was a short painful moment as he scraped down the last two feet of the shaft and bumped his knees, and then he was in space, black space, like falling in a dream. . . . It lasted only a short, terrifying moment, and then the freezing water hit him like a great fist, and he was under it, not knowing which way was up or down.

CHAPTER 24—A LONELY DEATH

James had been aware of noise more than anything. First the wind rushing in his ears, then a great explosion as he hit the water, then a confused, muffled silence as he went under.

He was turning slowly in that inky silence now, stunned, lost in the darkness. Then suddenly, he broke the surface and heard his breath, very loud, echoing off the walls, mixed with the slap of the disturbed water and the reverberations from his splash landing that were still rumbling around the underground cave.

Luckily, although the water was icy cold, it wasn't quite cold enough to make him completely pass out as he smashed into it. As it was, he had an evil headache and his ears, nose, and eyes hurt like hell.

It was almost totally pitch-black down here. Only a tiny faint glow came down the shaft from above, and it did nothing to light the area. Reaching out with his hands, James swam slowly forward, feeling for something solid. It was hard work, swimming in his clothes, and his heavy boots weighed him down. It was as if he were inside someone else's body, a body that was clumsy and sluggish. But then at last his hands touched rock. He trod water for a few moments, then began to work his way around the edge of the pool, to see if there was a place where he could get out of the water and plan his next move.

After a while he found a narrow ledge, just wide enough to take him, and he hauled himself onto it. He lay there with water streaming out of his clothes into the pool.

So, he'd come this far—he wasn't dead, and he was out of the cell. He was alive.

He smiled. He was mad—mad as that lunatic Hellebore—and it was Hellebore's drugs that had done it. Already he could feel a fire inside his body warming him through.

Once he'd gotten his strength back, he stripped down to his underwear to avoid getting a chill in his soggy clothes. It would also be easier to explore the water like this. Although, if he did find an escape route, he'd have to take everything with him.

He knew that was the first thing he had to try to do—find a way out of this hole—but before he could do that, he needed to make a map in his head of the dark space around him, so that he could get his bearings. Closing his eyes to concentrate, he felt all along his ledge, learning its contours, then slipped back into the water and began to explore the edges of the cave, finding a distinctive outcrop here, a smooth stone just under the water there, and here a slimy patch where water trickled down the wall.

Around and around he went, until he was familiar with it all. Now, if he did find a passage out beneath the water, he would know exactly where it was in relation to his ledge, and he could easily find it again when he was ready to leave.

But was there a way out? Yes, there had to be, because he had heard the slap of a fish. Of course, the exit might be only large enough for a fish, but he had to find out.

This time when he skirted the edges of the cave, he did it underwater, taking a few feet at a time, swimming down, feeling all over the surface of the rock with his fingers until he was sure he had thoroughly covered each section of wall.

Luckily the pool wasn't very deep. It was worst in the center, where it was about eight feet or so to the bottom. Diving down here, he could feel numerous cracks and fissures through which the water bubbled in. But nearer the edges it was less than half that depth. It still took him some time, however, to make his way round, and the constant diving was making him very short of breath. Once he'd surveyed a fair amount of the pool, he rested again on the ledge and used the deep breathing exercise that Leo Butcher had taught him, until he felt almost relaxed. Despite the drugs inside him, the cold was beginning to get to him and it was making him weak, so that he was constantly having to fight off the despair that lurked in the corners of his mind, waiting to come out and swamp him.

He didn't feel at all tired, though, despite the fact that it must be about four o'clock in the morning and he had had no sleep. He had to make use of his energy while it lasted.

He sat up and slipped back into the water. This time—after only a few minutes, as his hands groped their way down the submerged rock face—he felt a small flow of water and, following it, he found an opening. In his excitement he nearly took in a mouthful of water and he quickly bobbed to the surface. He was laughing, triumphant. It was a large hole, definitely big enough to fit his slim body into . . . but would it stay as wide as its entrance for the entire length? He took a deep breath, ducked under, and swam a little way into it, arms outstretched. Yes, it certainly went some distance and it seemed to stay the same size. Also, he could feel the water growing slightly warmer, the farther he went. There was no doubt about it: this tunnel must lead to the loch.

But he wasn't ready to leave just yet. He pulled himself back out and swam to the ledge, which he could now do in the dark without thinking.

He sat there, elated, and pictured the look on Hellebore's face when he found the cell empty. Oh, Randolph had been so sure of himself, and so dismissive of James, and now James had the upper hand.

He decided to leave his jacket behind, but the rest of his clothes he would have to take with him, including the boots, as he wouldn't get very far outside without them. He unthreaded his bootlaces, then made two bundles—one with his trousers and the other with his shirt—and wrapped one boot in each. Then, using his belt and the laces, he tied the bundles to his waist. They'd drag in the water and there was a danger that they might get snagged, but it would be easier than swimming with them on.

Now that he was ready, he carried out his final preparations. He began to breathe very deeply and very quickly, which got rid of most of the carbon dioxide from his blood and pumped it full of oxygen. He was soon feeling light-headed and he knew that if he carried on much longer he might faint, but he was ready. Now, he would be able to hold his breath for . . . ?

For how long? How long could the tunnel be? Ten feet? Twenty?

Practicing holding his breath in his room at Eton, he

could manage nearly two minutes, thanks to Butcher's training, but underwater, with the extra pressure and the exertion? That was a very different matter.

And then there were the eels. The one thing he had been most desperately trying not to think about. This tunnel led to the loch. The loch from which they had taken Meatpacker's half-eaten body.

Well, he'd been bashed about and was bruised all over, but, so far, James hadn't cut himself. If he could just keep it that way, maybe they'd leave him alone. It was a slim hope to cling to, but it was his only hope.

It was best not to think about it. He should just get on and do it. He slid back into the water and paddled over to the tunnel entrance.

There was really nothing to it, he told himself, it was a piece of cake. There was nothing that could go wrong—except getting stuck in the tunnel and drowning, or possibly being eaten by eels.

Nothing to it.

Slowly, he filled his lungs to their fullest capacity and then plunged beneath the surface and into the mouth of the tunnel.

He sculled along, arms outstretched, feet kicking up and down, his clothes bouncing along behind him. For a little while he moved quickly, but then he felt rock on one side of him. The tunnel was narrowing. Never mind; he could always grab hold of it and pull himself along, which meant he could go faster. And he had to go faster—his lungs were already beginning to burn as they filled with the poisonous carbon dioxide being produced by his overworked body. He had to hold on to his breath for as long as he could, though, to extract as much of the precious oxygen as he was able and to maintain a certain level of buoyancy. But the pressure of the water was also crushing his lungs, and he knew he would have to release that pressure soon.

A little farther on, the tunnel narrowed still more, so that its walls were brushing against him on both sides. *Please, please don't become so narrow that I can't squeeze through. And please, please don't cut me with any sharp stones.*

He couldn't risk bleeding.

How long had he been down here now? Maybe thirty seconds. Maybe only twenty. It was impossible to tell. He just had to keep groping his way forward through the utter blackness.

He became aware of little tugs and pulls at the bundles of clothing, and then he felt something press against him, not something hard like rock, but something soft and slimy and alive. An eel. Then another. They were down here in the tunnel with him. It was their tunnel. He imagined them all around him, their inquisitive snouts sliding out of holes in the rock, tasting the water, tasting him. Was he cut? He had no way of knowing; his body was numb and growing number by the second. Not so numb that he couldn't feel another eel, though, as it slithered up his leg and nipped his belly with a sucking mouth. He twisted in the water and shook it loose.

He mustn't panic. He must keep moving.

Come on, eels, show me the way out. Lead me out of this trap.

The pain in his lungs was growing unbearable, and he let out a few bubbles. It felt a little better, but he knew that he didn't have much oxygen left.

A larger eel now slid along the entire length of his body, feeling him with its wide snout. A second one twisted around his left ankle and, as he stretched a hand forward, it fell on a fat, slippery body that wriggled out from under his fingers and, with a powerful swipe of its tail, shot away down the tunnel.

The eels had distracted James for a moment, and now he realized with a shock that he had arrived at a section of the tunnel that was only just wide enough for him to squeeze through. If he went any farther, there would be no turning back; he would only be able to go forward. Forward into what? Into a tunnel that could narrow down to a few inches for all he knew. And he'd be stuck there—unable to go backward or forward, with no breath left, surrounded by the waiting eels.

Would they wait until he was dead before they started feeding? Or would they begin while he was still alive?

Don't think about that. Just make up your mind.

Forward into the unknown? Or back into that dark cave?

He'd wasted so much time thinking, he wasn't even sure that he would have enough breath now to *get* all the way back to where he'd started. Especially as he would have to feet first, pushing with his hands, because there was no question of turning around.

The longer he hesitated, the less time he had, and the inquisitive eels were growing bolder by the minute, nudging him, smelling him, rubbing their long bodies against him. . . .

What the hell.

Every insane decision he'd made so far had paid off: going down the branch of the pine tree, swinging onto the wall, climbing down the well shaft, dropping into the pool. . . . He had to trust in his own crazy guardian angel.

He let out another bubble of air and pulled himself into the gap, which scraped him on all sides, grazing his spine. But—thank God—he could still go forward, wriggling like an eel himself, pushing with knees and elbows, crawling with his fingertips along the rock. He was going to make it. He'd made the right choice. He let out the last of his breath and squirmed forward, racing against time, his blood singing in his ears, his head wanting to explode, his lungs full of acid.

And then he stopped.

He could go no farther.

What was it?

One of the bundles had got caught behind him. He jerked his hips to try to free it. *Come on! Come on.* He couldn't get a hand back to untie his belt. He wormed his body backward to give the bundle some slack, then jerked forward again. He'd done it. He was free. He was moving again.

No. His fingers felt something. Solid rock.

He'd come to a dead end.

It couldn't be! To have come this far, to have risked so much. His guardian angel had let him down and now she was laughing at him. *See how I teased you? How I offered you escape? But you can't escape. All I really have for you is a lonely death.*

James was losing consciousness. Mad thoughts were playing in his mind. He opened his eyes. The sun was blazing in a deep blue sky, palm trees threw ragged shadows onto the white sand of a beach. What was going on? Of course—it was only a picture. And next to it he could see his picture of King George. . . .

He was back in his room at Eton.

But that couldn't be.

He shook his head.

Which was real, which was the dream? Yes—a dream, it had to be. This was all just a dream. He was in his bed at Eton, asleep, this couldn't be happening in real life, could it? It was too awful.

And then he saw his Uncle Max's face, smiling at him.

He wasn't at Eton, he was at the cottage, and Max was telling him one of his stories, but now he looked angry.

"James!" he yelled, and the sound came from far, far away. "Go on. Don't give up."

"Give up what?"

Oh yes . . . the rock, the tunnel, he was underwater. . . .

Freezing black water

But what could he do?

Nothing.

Don't be stupid. Don't give in.

He felt his way forward again. It was still solid rock; there was still no way out of here, and no air to go back. There was nothing he could do but lie here. Yes, just lie here. It would all be all right. He could sleep. All he had to do was open his mouth and breathe in a mouthful of water, fill his lungs with it and it would all be over . . . they said that the pain of breathing in water was less than the pain of having empty lungs. . . .

"James!"

Who was that? He turned to look, spun around, and saw a dim light . . . above him! There was a way out above him. How stupid. He had never looked up. He pushed off from the floor of the tunnel, drifted slowly upward until, yes, he could see the moon and stars, and . . .

Air.

Blessed, fresh air.

He was out. He was free. He filled his lungs, which hurt like the devil and made him cough agonizingly, but it didn't matter—he was out.

Painfully slowly, feeling as if he would sink at any moment, he swam to the bank, where he crawled out and was violently sick. The sodden bundles of clothes were tangled with writhing eels, but he didn't care, they were just eels. They flopped back into the water as he lay there on the grass, panting and shivering.

Four hours earlier, propping himself up with the aid of an old broomstick, Kelly had made it safely through the rubbish dump to the cellar in the tumbledown building, where he had deduced that he had broken his ankle. He'd strapped it up with some strips of canvas that he'd cut from an old tarpaulin and then he made a splint out of some pieces of broken packing case. Then he sat with his back against the wall, clutching a knife, ready for anything.

He had no idea how long he'd been here, drifting in and out of consciousness, fighting the pain in his leg. He had water, at least, and some food, but he wasn't sure how much longer he could last.

The he heard a sound. Someone was coming; he heard the trapdoor creak open. He tensed. He'd been in some tight spots before, but this wasn't his territory. Never mind, nobody was going to take Red Kelly without a fight. He clutched his penknife in one hand and the broomstick in the other and tried to see who it was in the dark.

"Kelly?"

It was James.

Kelly had never been happier to hear anyone's voice in his life.

"Down here, mate." He switched on his flashlight and was surprised to see a bedraggled, sopping, half-naked figure, carrying two bundles of wet clothes, his body grazed and bruised, his hair tangled and filthy.

"Bloody hell, what happened to you?"

"It's a long story," said James as he closed the trapdoor. "I'll tell you while we get ready. We've got to get out of here, Red. It's only a matter of time before Hellebore comes after us. So far, he doesn't know about you or this hiding place, but he'll be bound to look."

As James struggled back into his wet things, he told Kelly all that had happened. Kelly was amazed and kept stopping James and getting him to repeat what he had said, hardly able to believe him, while keeping up a constant stream of interjections—"You're kidding me . . . never . . ." and other phrases too obscene to repeat.

James's clothes were cold and clammy and they stuck to him annoyingly, but at last he was ready—or as ready as he could ever hope to be.

"So what about you, then?" he said, staring at Red. "Can you walk?"

"I've no bloody choice, have I?" said Kelly hoarsely. "I can hop at least, and I've got me stick, but you're going to have to help me."

"Of course . . ." James took a deep breath and looked at Kelly hopefully. "Have you thought of a plan?"

"A plan of sorts . . ." Kelly paused, and struggled to his feet. "What it boils down to, Jimmy, me lad, is we go out the same way we come in."

"You mean, in the back of a lorry?" said James.

"No," said Kelly. "In the front."

"The front?" James struggled to understand.

"From what you tell me," said Kelly, leaning on James's damp shoulder for support, "it's not dawn yet. So it must be five o'clock at the latest. There won't be anyone about. If we wait and try to hide out in the back of a lorry, it'll be too late: someone'll sound the alarm and they'll be swarming all over the place looking for us. Also, we don't know what lorries will be going to be going out when."

"I know," said James. "But I still don't follow you—"

Kelly interrupted him. "The gates'll be guarded all day and night, but one of them big lorries could smash through them, no trouble."

"Yes, but who's going to drive?" James felt dizzy and sat down, his head spinning.

"Well, it's not me, is it, Sherlock?" said Kelly. "With this leg."

"But I've only ever driven my uncle's car. I can't drive a lorry," James protested.

"You're going to have to try," snapped Kelly.

"Won't they follow us?"

"Not if we nobble the other trucks. It won't stop them for good, but it might just give us the time we need to get to Keithly before them."

"I don't know . . ."

"If you've got a better plan I'd like to hear it, mate," said Kelly forcefully. "I can't walk, you can't fly, but a lorry drives pretty much like a car. It's just bigger an' heavier, that's all."

James thought for a moment, then his body was hit by another wave of heat and his mind fizzed.

"Okay," he said, jumping up, his eyes wild. "Let's do it!"

"Oh, bloody hell," said Kelly. "I was hoping you was going to talk me out of it."

CHAPTER 25—SURE AS THE SUNRISE

Apart from the lone figure dozing by the gate, the compound was deserted; all the other men were sleeping soundly in their bunks.

There was a faint glimmer of brightness in the sky, and most of the floodlights had been switched off. James and Kelly skirted the edge of the yard and, as quietly as possible, entered the first of the two sheds where the vehicles were parked. Kelly had his arm across James's shoulders for support, and the two of them were worn out. Red sat down on a pile of sacks and got his breath back. His clothes were soaked with sweat and he was evidently in some pain.

"Now what?" said James.

"You still got your knife?"

"It's in my heel."

"Well, there's a lorry, and there's its tires, so what are you waiting for?"

James grinned, got out his knife, and set to. The sound of air hissing out of the ruined tires was music to his ears, and it was very satisfying watching the lorry tip over and sink down as they deflated. Kelly worked with relish too, cutting wires, removing spark plugs, slashing fuel lines.

It was a tense but exhilarating few minutes. James kept thinking that somebody would come in and find them, but they managed to sabotage every vehicle in the shed without being detected. There was a very strong smell of petrol and spilled oil, however, and James hoped that it wouldn't alert the sleeping guard.

"Why don't we start a fire?" suggested Kelly, a wicked glint in his eye. "That'd really give them something to think about."

"No," said James. "Too risky. It might get out of hand before we're safely away. Come on."

They checked that the coast was still clear and moved into the second shed, where they carried on puncturing tires, ripping out engine parts, blocking up exhausts with oily rags, and generally wrecking Hellebore's transport. They couldn't be sure that there were no other vehicles elsewhere in the castle grounds, but all the ones they'd found were well and truly out of action. One they left alone, however, a big Albion lorry with a tough-looking front end. On the radiator was the familiar sunburst badge and the legend SURE AS THE SUNRISE.

"She'd better be," whispered Kelly, as James climbed inside and checked the controls. Everything was bigger than in the car, but basically it looked the same. He just hoped he had the strength to control it. He remembered his fantasy about Jack climbing the beanstalk into the giant's castle. Well, this was the giant's car all right.

He helped Kelly up.

"Ready?" James said. "Once I start this engine, they're going to hear us."

"Let 'em," said Kelly, and James fired her up, pushing the accelerator right down to the floor. She roared and rattled, shaking the two boys on the seat. James glanced over at Kelly.

Kelly gave the thumbs-up. "Go on," he said, and James released the brake. For a moment nothing happened and James almost panicked before he realized that the Albion's controls were much heavier than those in Max's car's and he had to be brutal with the pedals, leaning on them with all his weight. At last the lorry jerked forward, bumping out of the shed and across the cobbles of the yard toward the gates.

James floored the accelerator and the sleeping guard was startled into action by the noise. He raced toward them, gesticulating wildly with his arms, but James didn't let up and at the last moment the man dived out of the way with a yelp of fright.

The tall, wooden gates were getting nearer and nearer and James wondered whether they were going fast enough to batter their way through.

Well, there was only one way to find out. "Hold tight!" James yelled, and closed his eyes. They hit the gates with a terrific *bang*. Splintered wood whipped across the bonnet and rattled against the windscreen, but the gates fell away and they were through. The lorry had barely slowed down at all and the second set of gates gave just as easily, although the windscreen was badly cracked by a large lump of flying timber.

"Yahoo!" yelled Kelly, and he leaned out his window to wave his fist triumphantly at the receding compound.

"See you later, you mugs!"

The engine whined and jerked, missing a beat. The boys were thrown forward in their seats, and Kelly looked anxiously at James.

"Is she all right?"

"Yes, sorry, wrong gear." James got the lorry back under control, and they howled off down the road.

Driving the Albion was similar to driving his uncle's car, except it was so much bigger and heavier. James had to be very careful on the corners to stop the thing from tipping over or veering out of control. It took all his strength to turn the huge steering wheel, and he seemed to have to wrench it endlessly around and around in order to steer through even the gentlest of bends.

But the farther they went the more confident he became. He loosened his grip on the wheel and relaxed his tense muscles. He couldn't relax too much, however, as the road was deeply rutted and the lorry bounced along uncomfortably, shaking the teeth in his skull.

The lorry's engine was big and powerful, but not fast, and the road to Keithly was by no means direct; it meandered over the moors, along the way connecting various tiny villages that were little more than clusters of one or two houses, most of which were abandoned and falling into ruin.

"Life on the open road, eh, Jimmy-boy?" said Kelly, putting his feet up and settling back into his seat with his hands behind his head.

"Don't get cocky," said James. "We're not clear yet. Even if we do make it to Keithly, we've still got to convince Sergeant White that we're telling the truth; and who's he going to believe, two boys who've stolen a lorry, or Lord Randolph Hellebore, monarch of all he surveys?"

"Well, Fatty White only has to go up to the castle and take a look around for himself."

"What'll he see? Eels in tanks? Some big pigs? A few scientists doing some obscure research? Randolph can blind him with science for as long as he likes."

"Yeah, yeah, all right," said Kelly grumpily.

"And that's provided we actually make it into Keithly," James went on. "What if Randolph telephones ahead? Calls somebody in Keithly? We could be trapped on the road."

"Stop it," said Kelly. "I was beginning to enjoy myself there for a moment."

So far, there was no sign of anyone else on the road. The lorry trundled along noisily, and with each mile they traveled they were closer to home. James should have been feeling happier, but he knew that he wouldn't properly feel safe until he was back in his bed at Max's cottage and Hellebore was locked up.

They passed two white-walled thatched houses, but no one was up and about. Then the road pulled around in a wide sweep and climbed the side of a fair-sized hill. When they reached the top, they saw that they had a clear view in both directions, so James stopped the lorry, opened the door, and jumped down to take a look.

It was a cold morning and had started to drizzle. The sky was an unbroken slate gray, and a miserable wind moaned across the lonely moors.

James shivered as his damp clothes stuck to him.

"Here." Kelly passed him the binoculars and he focused them on the distant, dark smudge of the castle buildings.

"Blast," he said.

"What is it?" Kelly asked anxiously.

Driving along the road at great speed was the big

Rolls-Royce that James had seen pick up George from the station in Fort William, and behind it were two other cars.

"They're after us," said James.

"How far away?"

"Quite a distance at the moment. They're only just leaving the castle, but they can go a lot quicker than we can."

"Can we make it, d'you think?" said Kelly, straining to look back.

"We've got a chance, but it'll be close."

"You still worried about the coppers?"

"Not much. Better a few days in a police cell than eternity at the bottom of a lake."

James swung around and scanned the road ahead, following its winding path across the moors. He lost sight of it now and then behind a hill or clump of trees, but he always picked it up again without any trouble. It was clear for a few miles, but then his heart sank as he saw a cloud of spray and exhaust fumes thrown up by a lorry, identical to those in the compound, racing along toward the castle.

"We're in big trouble," he said. "They're coming at us from both directions."

Kelly swore and hammered the lorry's interior with his fists.

"We'll find somewhere to ditch the Albion," said James, clambering back into the cab. "Then I'll have to risk it on foot. I'm a pretty good long-distance runner, and the ground here's too boggy for them to follow in the vehicles."

"What about me?" said Kelly "I can't hardly walk."

"They don't know about you, they'll only be looking for me." James wrestled the gear lever into first and set the lorry rolling forward. "You'll have to find somewhere to hide. Then, when they've gone, try to make it back to Keithly somehow. Even if it means hopping all the way. But go to my uncle's house, not the police. Okay?"

"Where'm I gonna hide?"

"I spotted a bit of a wood in the valley up ahead, and some farm buildings. We'll try there."

In a couple of minutes they were down the other side of the hill and crossing a narrow stone bridge over the Black River. A small crofter's farm, surrounded by trees, nestled in the secluded nook. James stopped the lorry in the middle of the road, cut the engine, and helped Kelly down. Sheltered from the bitter wind, it was very quiet and peaceful here. The water babbled happily under the bridge, birds were singing in the trees, and for a moment the two boys could forget all about the rest of the world.

But only for a moment.

They searched the buildings until they found a small, dilapidated barn, half full of straw.

"Under there," said James, and as soon as Kelly lay down he piled straw on top of him until he was completely buried.

As James hurried back outside, he ran straight into a short, wiry crofter with a huge gray beard and fierce, red-rimmed eyes.

"Whit d'ye think ye're doin'?" he said in a hard, thin, high-pitched voice.

"Sorry. I'm lost," said James, and the ancient crofter peered at him quizzically.

"Whit's yon stinking great lorry doing in ma road?"

"It's yours if you want it," said James, walking away.

"And whit would ah want wi' a dirty old lorry?" The crofter made a move to follow James, who turned and bolted, leaping over a wooden fence, down the riverbank and away through the trees, the angry little man scampering after him, yelling insults. James was reminded of something, and as he blundered through a vegetable patch he realized what it was: Mr. McGregor in the books about Peter Rabbit.

He grinned as he splashed across the stream and set off into open country.

Peter Rabbit.

That was from a different world. A world of safe childhood nurseries and bedtime stories about rabbits that wore little blue coats. That wasn't the world he was living in right now.

James felt weirdly light-headed. He wondered if he had the strength to cope but the human body is an amazing thing—it can surprise you with its resilience—especially a human body that has been tampered with. Instead of feeling tired, James was filled with a fluttering, pulsing, wild sort of energy. He was a superman, capable of anything. He could run forever if need be. It felt effortless.

It was a shame that he had bumped into that crofter, as he would be bound to point Lord Hellebore after him, but he had a good head start and was an experienced cross-country runner, so at least he had a small advantage.

He was heading into Am Boglach Dubh, the Black Mire. The ground here was very waterlogged and made for slow going, but it would be the same for Hellebore and his men, and they would definitely have to follow him on foot rather than in their cars. Also, James was lighter, so he didn't sink as far into the boggy ground as the men would.

But they were men. He was just a boy. He was kidding himself if he thought he could outrun them forever and it was a good five miles to Keithly.

It was raining harder now, so any drying out his clothes might have done in the lorry was thoroughly reversed. A million cold needles were pricking at his skin and his boots chafed against his ankles. They felt horribly heavy and were clogging up with mud. After a while he stopped, took them off, and slung them away. It was easier to continue barefoot.

None of this country was familiar to him; the path to the castle on foot from Keithly became a very different and more direct route. He could make out the hills around the Hellebore estate, way off to his right, and above them the watching face of Angreach Mhòr, which meant that Keithly must be to his left. The route was generally downhill from here, which would help, but it was still going to be hard work.

He looked behind him. A dirty cloud told him that the lorry coming from Keithly was approaching the woods by the croft, but he had no idea whether the party from the castle had arrived there yet. He didn't wait to find out, but turned and sprinted away across the grass, scattering a small group of scrawny sheep.

As he ran, his head cleared, all useless thoughts fell away, and he could concentrate properly on what was important.

First of all, what would be going through Randolph's mind right now?

He would link up with the men in the other lorry. He would talk to them. He would talk to the crofter. And then he would set off after James with most of his men.

Yes.

Given time, they could catch up with him, but there was a fair chance that he could outrun them at least as far as the village.

But Randolph wouldn't send all his men across the moors on foot, would he? No. He would send some on ahead in the vehicles to Keithly, and a second search party would set out from there.

James stopped dead in his tracks.

What a fool he was! He was in exactly the same position as he had been on the road: trapped between two gangs of men. Hellebore knew his name. They would easily find his uncle's house. They could be waiting for him there as well.

What was he going to do? For a start, he mustn't just stand here and wait for Hellebore to come and get him. He had to keep moving and he had to keep thinking.

Okay. So he couldn't go back to Keithly. What else could he do? Where else could he go?

Where wouldn't they expect him to go?

The moon?

Timbuktu?

The castle . . .

That would be the last place on earth they'd look for him. But why on earth would he go back there? What would that achieve?

It was then that James realized that an urgent thought had been nagging away at the back of his mind, and now it barged forward and yelled at him, obscuring all other thoughts.

Hellebore must be stopped.

It was as simple as that.

What he was doing was wrong. It was evil. But Hellebore had money and power and authority. James, as he had pointed out to Kelly, was just a boy. A boy who was also a vandal and a thief. Going to the police would achieve nothing—Hellebore would carry on as normal, James would be punished—but what if he destroyed Hellebore's work? What if he stopped him from ever finishing his research? Was he capable of that?

Without realizing it, James had changed direction. His feet had already made the decision that his mind was stumbling toward. He was going to go back to the castle, and somehow or other he was going to ruin Hellebore forever, no matter what the consequences. Most of the men would be out looking for him, or repairing the damaged vehicles and gates. If James could get back in and somehow destroy the laboratory and all it contained, then nothing else would matter.

He was running uphill now, toward Loch Silverfin, and it was a much harder route than his original downhill path, but he was filled with a grim determination. He wasn't human. He was a machine. He would carry on. He would finish this. Nobody would stop him.

The wind shifted direction and he heard shouts behind him.

Best not to think about that, best just to keep running.

The rain hammered against his forehead, stinging his face and blinding him; thorns and sharp stones cut his feet. There was a constant pain in his lungs and he was beginning to cough regularly, but still he forced himself on.

The minutes passed. He kept his head down, watching the ground slip past beneath his feet, feeling his breath grate agonizingly out of his throat almost as if the air were solid. His head felt disembodied, floating along, five feet above the ground. There was no feeling in his limbs. He was only dimly aware of them working away beneath him, but they belonged to somebody else. The ground was stonier here, and he had to avoid rocks and gorse bushes, which meant zigzagging all over the place and traveling twice as far than if he'd been able to go in a straight line. Once he came to a large outcrop of rock and had to go all the way around it, but still he hammered on as the rain hissed down relentlessly.

Some time later, it struck him that he hadn't heard anything for some while and he allowed himself the luxury of thinking that he had lost his pursuers. He turned to take a look and in that split second stumbled and fell, face-first, into a bed of moss.

It was then that his tiredness overwhelmed him, and he was buried beneath a great avalanche of exhaustion. Spots danced before his eyes. A black glove took hold of him and squeezed gently. Ever so gently. It was warm and comforting. He closed his eyes and in a moment was asleep.

It felt as if it had been only for a second, and he woke with a jolt of panic. He rubbed his temples, got shakily to his feet and staggered a few steps, before leaning against a rock to get his balance. Every breath was a struggle now and his heart felt as if it were working so hard, it might burst out of his chest like a bloody fist.

"There he is!"

James spun around and saw, less than a quarter of a mile away, down the hill, about ten men with dogs, and, at their head, his golden hair flapping in the wind, the unmistakable figure of Lord Hellebore, a riding crop in his hand.

CHAPTER 26—GO TO HELL

He must have slept for longer than he'd thought. How else could they have gotten so close? How could he have been so bloody careless? He had done exactly what he had told Kelly not to do—he had gotten cocky.

But James wasn't done for yet, he could still run. He urged his body back into action and trudged heavily up the hill, away from the men. After a short, grinding climb, the ground leveled out and he speeded up. The relief was only temporary, however, because he knew that his pursuers would also be able to speed up when they got this far.

Odd sounds drifted to him on the air. The harsh rattling croak of a ptarmigan launching into flight, stones bouncing over rocks, rain sleeting onto wet ground, a solitary shout, then, nearer to hand, his feet pounding the earth, his breath rasping out of his throat, and the sound of his blood thundering in his ears like crazy drumming.

After a long, level stretch, the ground climbed sharply again up to a rocky ridge. James came to the top of it and saw a nasty drop on the other side into a foul-smelling bog. He ran along the crest of the ridge, the stones cutting into his bare feet, and felt stupid that he had thrown away his boots, but he had been expecting to be running downhill, where the land was lush and grassy and not up here where it was more barren.

He glanced back at the men: They were strung out now, finding it difficult to keep up, but striding ahead of them was Lord Hellebore, his powerful arms pumping at his sides, his big white teeth bared. Hellebore was an athlete, and James knew that he was doomed. The man was closing the gap with every moment.

James slowed down and picked up two sharp stones, then carried on running as fast as he could, but it wasn't fast enough. With every second, with every step, Lord Hellebore was drawing nearer. James heard his footsteps horribly close behind him and turned to let fly one of the stones. Randolph ducked to one side and it bounced harmlessly away across the rocks. James threw the other stone, but it too went wide. He had no choice now. Randolph had nearly caught up with him—he would have to risk the bog. He found a suitable spot where the ground didn't look too steep, went over the edge, and started to make his way down the almost sheer slope on the other side. He slipped on the loose stones, picked himself up—and then the sun was blotted out as, with a ferocious yell, Randolph was upon him. The big man barged into him, and the two of them lost their footing and went tumbling down together into the bog.

The bog was only a couple feet deep, but when James stood up, spluttering and choking, he could barely move his feet in the thick mud at the bottom. He tried to run, forcing his way in desperate slow motion, and Hellebore followed, churning up the stinking water. For a few seconds James thought he might just get away, but then he felt the heat coming off Randolph and the cloying, animal reek of him, and a hand grabbed his face from behind and pulled him back under the surface of the bog.

James came up again, blinded by the yellow, peaty water. He wiped his face and opened his stinging eyes, to see Hellebore standing over him with the riding crop raised in his hand. Before James could do anything, Hellebore swung at him, cutting a deep gash into his cheek. James grunted and put a hand up to the wound. It came away bloody.

"Damn you, boy!" bellowed the lord. "Damn you to hell. You have caused me a great deal of trouble, and before I kill you I'm going to thrash every scrap of skin off your body."

James spat at him and got him right in the eye. Randolph cursed and brushed it away. "You should not have done that," he raged. "It will only make things worse."

James spat again hitting him in the exact same spot. He saw such a look of fury erupt in the lord's eyes, it was as if his very brain had become molten. Hellebore roared like a beast and raised the whip again.

James had been very aware of the thundering in his ears and he shook his head to clear it, but the sound only got louder. He tried to concentrate, to be ready for the next attack, and, as Hellebore swung the whip at him, James just managed to throw himself out of the way. Once more he plunged under the water, but when he fought his way up out of the bog, his mouth full of mud, he was amazed to see a horse splashing toward him. Randolph saw it as well—too late. He screamed as the horse reared up and knocked him sideways with its front hooves.

James recognized that horse—it was Martini—and he recognized the blond girl riding him.

"Get on!" Wilder Lawless shouted, and she held out a hand toward James, who grabbed hold of it eagerly. Wilder pulled him up into the saddle behind her, and the black horse thrashed away through the water.

James smiled—that's what the sound of thunder had been. It hadn't been in his head at all, it was Martini's hooves.

They pulled up safely on dry land on the other side and galloped away across the grass, leaving Lord Hellebore behind, floundering and cursing in the bog. Of the other men there was no sign.

"What are you doing here?" yelled James.

Wilder laughed. "You can thank your friend, Red Kelly."

"You've seen Red?"

"Aye. I was exercising Martini before breakfast, and who should pop out of the trees, leaning on a stick like an old hobgoblin, but your Mr. Kelly."

"Where was this?"

"About a mile out of Keithly. It seems he'd sneaked into the back of one of the laird's lorries and stolen a ride into town, but he had to jump ship before he quite got there."

"But he's all right, though? I felt bad about leaving him behind."

"Aye, he's fine, apart from his ankle. You need to worry more about yourself, James. You look like a dirty rag that's been through the wringer."

"I'm fine," James lied, clinging tightly to Wilder, his arms around her waist. He felt like burying his face in her hair and falling asleep.

"You're way off course, James," Wilder shouted. "It took me ages to find you up here. The sooner we get you back to Keithly, the better."

"We can't go into Keithly," said James.

"What?" Wilder pulled up the horse and twisted around in the saddle to look James in the face.

Once again he was struck by the intense green of her eyes, so clear and bright and clever, and the hint of a smile that always played around her mouth.

"What are you talking about?" she said.

"This is going to sound mad, I'm afraid," said James.

"Try me."

James explained his plan, and at first Wilder looked shocked, then dismissive, then intrigued, and finally very serious.

"Do you think we'd have a chance?"

"I don't know, Wilder, but we've got to try. Are you up for it?"

Wilder put a hand to his cut cheek and frowned. "Aye," she said quietly. "You know I've never liked the laird after what he did to my dad. And if what you say about him's true, then he's a rotten swine who should be taught a lesson. Come on, let's go."

She dug her heels in, shouted some words of encouragement to Martini, and they were off again. The big horse was steaming in the rain, but he was tireless and sure-footed and knew his way across the treacherous surface of the moors.

It was exhilarating, racing across open country, the sun in their faces, the powerful muscles of the horse pounding away beneath them. Martini easily carried the extra burden, but Wilder didn't want to ride him too hard, since they might have to make a fast getaway later on.

In what seemed no time at all they came to the hills surrounding the loch and slowed to a walk. They passed through the gap at Am Bealach Geal and could see no one, so they rode around to the boys' camp. Everything was as they'd left it. Hellebore's men had obviously been too preoccupied with other events to search for it and destroy it, the way they had Meatpacker's dismal den in the thicket.

James drank long and greedily from his water bottle, then he stuffed a dry and curling sandwich into his mouth. He had a change of clothes in his rucksack, including a pair of plimsolls, and Wilder turned her back as he undressed.

"Are you sure you don't want to rest for a wee while?" she said. "You look like death."

"No," he said, his voice hoarse with tiredness. "If I lie down to sleep, I think I'll never wake up again. Let's get this over and done with while I'm still standing."

Once he was dressed in warm and, blessedly, dry clothes, he began sorting through his kit for any useful items. He found his uncle's gunmetal lighter and flipped the top open.

"You still think this is no job for a girlie?" said Wilder with a raised eyebrow.

James smiled. "I'm sorry about that," he said, testing the lighter. "I'd have been stuck without you."

"You'd have been dead, my lad. Here, let me look at that cut." Wilder inspected the deep gash in James's cheek, which was still dripping blood.

"Do you have a first-aid kit in that bag of yours?"

James's face brightened. "Yes. Yes, I do. Aunt Charmian put one in."

Wilder cleaned the wound with some iodine, which stung like the blazes, then fixed a sticking plaster over it.

"There. You're as good as new."

"Thanks, Wilder."

Wilder quickly kissed the plaster. "Don't mention it."

James was going to say something else but he suddenly put a finger to his lips and signaled with his eyes for Wilder to be quiet and careful.

There was somebody coming, moving noisily through the bushes toward them.

James scrambled behind a tree and crouched down while Wilder stayed in the clearing, trying to look as innocent as possible. After all, she could hide herself, but she could hardly hide Martini.

The sound of breaking branches and rustling leaves came closer and closer, until James could make out the shape of someone crouching low, holding a shotgun out in front of him, pushing through the thin branches and twisted brambles.

The figure came even closer and still hadn't seen James, but then he spotted Wilder, straightened up slightly, and hurried forward.

It was George Hellebore.

A bitter gobbet of poisonous anger rose in James's throat. He had a sudden, overwhelming desire to fall on George and smash his skull into a thousand pieces; but he had to wait until he had a clear run.

George was in the clearing now and was confronting Wilder.

"Hello," George said, and James hurled himself on George's back, flattening him.

George yelled and fell, face-first, dropping his gun.

"Grab it," yelled James, and Wilder snatched the shotgun up off the ground.

"Stop it," George gasped, badly winded, as James pounded the back of his head with his fists. "Please, stop it!"

"I'm going to kill you, Hellebore," snarled James.

"No. It's all right, Bond, I'm on your side."

James laughed bitterly. "Oh yes, of course you are," he said sarcastically. "You have been from the start."

"No. Please. You can trust me."

"Why should I?" said James, and he twisted George's face around so that he could see him better. It was stained with tears; there was no fight left in it.

"I don't know what's happened to my father," said George sadly. "I can't stand it anymore. He's gone crazy."

"I repeat," said James, "why should I trust you?"

"I can help you. If you help me. I'm your only chance, James. We have to stop my father from doing what he's doing."

"I think he's telling the truth," said Wilder.

"You don't know him."

"True. But I've got the gun."

James looked over and saw that Wilder had the shotgun aimed steadily at George's head.

"Careful with that thing," said James, jumping up off George's back and scurrying backward out of the line of fire.

George sat up and rubbed his head. "Thank you," he said.

"Talk," said James.

"This morning," said George miserably, "when I woke and found that all hell had broken loose, I made up my mind. I wanted to help you last night, James, believe me I did, but I was scared. You don't know what he's like."

"Yes I do," said James quietly.

George stood up and brushed the dirt and leaves from his clothing. "I feel pretty bad about what's happened. How I've treated you."

"You feel bad? Well, hurrah. You think that makes up for what you've done, do you?"

"I've been crazy too, but my head's cleared now."

"The pills," said James. "The white pills. I know."

George looked at James and put a hand on his shoulder. "Are you okay?"

"No, I'm not," said James, shrugging the hand away. "But at least I'm alive."

"I'm going to make it up to you," said George. "I'm going to help you. I've been searching for your camp all morning, and then I heard voices." He looked from James to Wilder and back again. "What were you going to do?"

James stared long and hard at the American boy. He seemed genuine. Eventually, James held out his hand, and after a brief pause, George shook it.

"If this is a trick," said James, "I will surely kill you, George."

"It's no trick. I've had enough. I can't live like this any longer."

Twenty minutes later, James and George were hurrying along a hidden path in the undergrowth. The track led deeper and deeper into the woods, until eventually it came out by the fence. George pointed to a hole under the wire.

"I think a fox dug it originally," he said as he wriggled through and James followed. "Dad doesn't know about it, or he'd have had it filled in."

There was a steep bank on the other side, and they crawled down it through more dense and tangled growth, until they were able to climb down a small rocky cliff to the edge of the loch.

There was a rowboat tethered there.

"I rowed over, a couple hours ago," said George, stepping aboard and taking the oars. "Nobody saw me, I think, but we've got to be careful."

James boarded and sat down. Wilder had stayed behind with Martini to keep a lookout and provide a getaway if needed, and James hoped he had made the right decision to trust George. He looked at him now, pulling hard on the oars with strong and confident strokes, and prayed that he wasn't being led into a trap.

"Most of Dad's workers went with him," George explained, keeping close to the edge of the loch in the shadow of the overhanging rocks. "But there are still a few guys around, repairing the gates and cutting down the big pine tree."

"Already?"

"Dad doesn't hang about. When he wants something done, he wants it done now."

"What about the laboratory?"

"The scientists'll be in there right now. We'll just have to bluff it out. There's a small dock around the back of the island that leads straight into the lab." George's voice was strained from rowing. "There're some big old loading doors there, they're usually locked, but I swiped a set of Dad's keys from his office, so we should be okay. I'll go in first, and once I'm sure it's safe, I'll whistle and you can follow."

"Right. Then what?"

"Then we wreck the place. We should start with the paperwork, and all the completed SilverFin serum, which is kept in a strongroom at the back. We've got to do as much damage as we can before we're stopped."

James nodded. He was still feeling light-headed, as if all this were happening to somebody else. It felt extraordinary that they were calmly plotting to ransack the laboratory and destroy George's father's life's work.

But he knew George was right. It had to be done. If James didn't stop him now, before Hellebore was expecting it, then there would be no other chance. The man was too strong, too rich, too powerful.

James coughed, trying to stifle the noise and to ignore the burning pains in his lungs, as the brooding bulk of the gray castle loomed overhead.

A chill gripped him. He was lucky to have escaped from hell once.

Surely nobody ever escaped twice.

CHAPTER 27—THE FIST CLOSES

They came in under the shadow of the castle and moored the rowboat at a small stone pier. As they were tying her up, a blast of wind and freezing rain came in low across the loch and lashed their faces. James coughed and shivered, his teeth rattling in his aching head. His fingers were numb and his vision blurred. His head was throbbing. He felt as if he had the flu. He wondered how much longer he could carry on.

George took James over to where a pair of large wooden doors was set into the castle walls.

"They lead straight into the laboratory," he said. "It used to be a storage area and they'd bring supplies over by boat." He fished a set of keys out of his pocket. "You wait here, and remember—only follow me in when I give the all-clear. One whistle."

James nodded. His throat was too dry and raw for him to speak.

George found the right key, fit it into the lock, and turned it. There was a click, then the door swung open a little way. James saw George illuminated by the eerie violet light from within.

George took a deep breath, offered James a tight, grim smile, then pushed through the opening and went down a flight of stone steps, leaving the door open a crack behind him.

James crept to the door and peeped through. Had he been a fool? Was this a trap? Was George about to turn him over to the scientists again?

There were several men in there, wearing stained white coats. They were blinking at George and frowning, and James could just hear George's voice, trying to sound authoritative.

There was no sign of Dr. Friend.

"My father wants to see you all now."

The scientists looked confused.

George carried on. "As you know, we've had some problems last night and this morning. We are on full alert. Lord Hellebore needs to see you all now in his office."

"Why can't he come here?" said a tall gray-haired man who looked like an irritable Oxford professor.

"Because he's too damn busy!" shouted George. "Now do as you're told."

"This is most awkward," went on the gray-haired scientist. "I am halfway through an experiment—"

"Just do it," George snapped. "Or do you want to make him mad?"

With much mumbling and grumbling, the scientists tidied their work and drifted out in ones and twos. Once George was satisfied that he was alone, he whistled and James hurried in through the doors, shivering once again in the freezing air inside the laboratory.

"This way," said George, running toward the back of the huge chamber. "We may not have much time."

They threaded their way through the tightly packed tanks, and then past the cages of squealing and grunting pigs, some of whom threw themselves at the bars with mad cries and tried to bite their way out.

They came to a small steel door and George fumbled with the lock, trying to find the right key, his hands shaking violently. At last he got the door open, and they went into the strongroom, where George turned on the light.

It was even colder in here. And James still felt light-headed, as if his blood were freezing in his brain. He looked around.

One wall was filled with wooden filing cabinets, and opposite them was a bank of refrigerated, glass-doored lockers with row upon row of labeled test tubes in racks. This was the SilverFin.

"I'll sort this lot out," said George, unlocking the first door. "You see to the paperwork."

James pulled open a filing cabinet, grabbed a handful of files, and dropped them on the floor. He heard a smashing sound behind him and turned to see George hurling racks of tubes against the wall. It wasn't a trap—George was definitely on his side.

James's spirits lifted and he set to with fierce determination, ransacking drawer after drawer, pulling piles of paper out onto the floor until there was a mountain of it. George was stamping vials of SilverFin underfoot and spilling jars of pills everywhere. Once James was sure he had removed all the papers and that George had destroyed the last of the test tubes, he took his uncle's cigarette lighter from his pocket.

"Should I do it now, or should we wait?" he said.

"Start the fire," said George. "Then we'll wreck as much of the lab as we can."

"Okay." James knelt, picked up a handful of papers, flicked the lighter into life, and put the flame to an edge. The papers soon caught fire, and once they were blazing steadily he dropped them to the floor and started carefully feeding the other papers to the fire until the mound was burning strongly. The smoke very quickly filled the room and the two of them had to back out, coughing and choking.

The pigs had smelled the fire now, and were charging crazily around in their cages, screaming.

"Shouldn't we let them go?" said James.

"They're monsters," said George, "freaks. They won't live long anyway, they can't. Once Perseus Friend starts injecting them, they're doomed—none has ever lived more than a few weeks. And besides," he said with a shudder, "they'd kill us if they got the chance. Come on. It's kinder to let them die."

James suddenly put a hand on George's elbow. "Algar!" he said.

He ran along the row of cages until he found the one that contained Algar and the piglet.

The big man was sitting there, bent over, fear in his eyes.

"George!" James yelled. "We can't leave him here. . . ."

George reluctantly came over and looked at Algar, unsure what to do.

James snatched the keys from him and tried them in the lock, but he couldn't find one that would fit.

"We don't have time," said George, and he picked up a large spanner from under a workbench. "Stand back!"

He swung the spanner at the padlock, which broke off and clattered to the floor.

Algar pushed the door open and wriggled out of the

cage. He looked at the boys, and James was sure that he was trying to smile. Then he picked up the piglet, raced across the laboratory, and crashed out through the loading doors.

"We're running out of time," said George, looking back to where smoke was billowing out of the strongroom.

James remembered the fire safety ax hanging near the steps. He rushed over and grabbed it off the wall. "Ready?" he said, walking over to one of the eel tanks.

"Let's do it," said George, and James swung the ax against the glass. There was a terrific crash, and a flood of foul-smelling water gushed out. A long, fat eel flopped onto the floor, where it slithered away right under the door and into one of the pigs' cages, where it was instantly ripped to shreds.

George joined in, and they demolished as many tanks as they could before smashing open cabinets, pulling down shelves, and destroying the experiments on the operating tables.

The floor was soon strewn with broken glass and writhing eels and mangled equipment, but the smoke pouring from the strongroom was beginning to fill the main laboratory, stinging the boys' eyes and choking their lungs.

Covering his mouth and nose, James found another huge tank containing countless glass eels, and he had just raised his ax to shatter it when a shout came from the platform above.

"That's enough!"

They looked up to see Cleek MacSawney, armed with a hunting rifle.

"Put that ax down and come over here," he said, his voice filled with quiet menace.

"Make me," said James, getting ready to swing the ax again.

"With pleasure." MacSawney grinned and fired at James. The bullet ricocheted off the wall, two inches from his head. James ducked and scuttled out of the way behind a row of cabinets. The next shot exploded the very tank that James had been about to demolish, and MacSawney swore and clattered down the iron steps.

James peered through the smoke for George and saw that he'd climbed on top of one of the pigpens. He signaled for James to join him. James looked around but could see no sign of MacSawney and, keeping low, he darted over to George and shinned up the side of the pen.

As soon as James was up, George knocked the padlock off the cage with his spanner and it flew across the laboratory into a pile of broken glass. The door to the cage was instantly forced open, and a huge, deformed pig shot out like a bull into the ring. Its back legs were stunted and next to useless, but it pulled itself along on its enormous, muscular front legs, its vast, slobbering head hanging low to the ground between its shoulders. George swung the spanner again and an equally freakish pig lumbered out of the next pen, its mouth gaping.

They heard a shot and a squeal, then another shot, and the two boys hacked furiously at the padlocks until seven pigs were free.

The pitiful beasts had lived miserable lives of pain and torment, and somewhere within their small, crazed brains they wanted revenge, revenge on the people who had caused them pain. They smelled one of them now. The one with the hard boots. He was close. MacSawney.

The boys heard more shots, then two thuds in quick succession that were followed by a scream, long and thin, like a child's. Then there came a horrible snuffling and grunting and a sickening crunch.

James tried not to think what that crunch meant. But he had seen the powerful jaws of the pigs.

The laboratory was quickly filling with smoke now, and the boys could barely see, but they knew they had only moments to get out while the pigs were distracted. They jumped down from their perch and sprinted toward the stairs, slipping on the wet floor.

Halfway up the stairs, James stopped. He remembered the iron door with the sign on it showing a lurid illustration of flames and a skull-and-crossbones and the warning DAN-GER! HIGHLY FLAMMABLE.

"What's in here?" he asked.

"It's where they keep the preserving fluids and all the solvents and raw alcohol for their experiments," said George.

"Do you have the keys?" James coughed and clutched his chest.

"I think so."

George found the key quite quickly. Inside were jar upon jar of clear liquid. James looked at George, daring him to go all the way and risk burning down the entire castle.

George rose to the challenge. They grabbed two jars each and ran back out onto the steps.

They could see bright flames licking out through the strongroom door and already the air was growing hot. As James looked, the thick smoke parted and he caught a glimpse of something unreal, but it was for such a brief instant that he wasn't sure whether he'd only imagined it. In that one teasing moment of clarity he thought he'd seen MacSawney lying on the floor, but there was something wrong about him. James's brain tried to make sense of the fleeting image, but, no matter how he turned it in his mind, it seemed that the lower half of the gillie was missing.

James turned to George. He had seen nothing.

"Quick!" George shouted. "What are you waiting for?"

James hurled one of his jars. It flew across the room and landed near the flames, where it exploded like a bomb. They threw the rest of their jars and soon the room was an inferno.

They had done enough; Randolph's research was ruined, his experiments destroyed, his papers burned. SilverFin was no more.

They ran on up the stairs and into the castle, where they met a group of panicked scientists, running toward them in some confusion.

At their head was Perseus Friend.

"What's happening?" he said.

"Everything's gone," croaked James, and Dr. Friend looked at him uncomprehendingly.

"What do you mean?" he said, his voice high-pitched and tremulous.

"You're not going to hurt anyone or anything ever again," said James.

"No!" Dr. Friend ran to the door and looked through, his face lit red by the flames. "No!"

"It's too late, Perseus!" yelled George.

"What have you done?"

Before anyone could stop him, Perseus ran into the laboratory and disappeared. The other scientists were more careful; they hung around the door until they were driven back by the smoke and one of them had the sense to push the door closed.

A thin, gray haze hung in the air and drifted through the twisting corridors of the castle as James and George made their way as quickly as possible toward the exit.

There were more confused men in the entrance hall, running around and trying to find out what was going on. They ignored George and James, who hurried across the tiles, wrenched the big front doors open, and burst out into the sunlight.

For a moment they were blinded by the brightness. Shielding their eyes with their hands, they stumbled onto the driveway, where they collapsed to the ground, gasping clean, fresh air into their lungs.

All the tension, all the stress, and all the fear inside James now dissolved; he felt as if a tightly wound piece of elastic inside him had suddenly snapped. He started to laugh, sitting up and clutching his chest.

"So much for the ultimate fighting machine," he said, and turned to George.

But George wasn't laughing. He was staring at something, his face deathly white, his mouth hanging open.

What was it?

James looked around.

Lord Hellebore stood there, his shotgun pointing at the boys.

"I've two barrels," he snarled as James jumped to his feet, "one for each of you. Then I'll feed your useless bodies to the eels."

"Father, for God's sake," pleaded George. "It's over."

Randolph laughed bitterly. "It is far from over," he said. "You can't stop me."

"You're crazy," said James, simply. "That's why you never could have succeeded, that's why you never will succeed. Madmen never do."

"This is nothing," Hellebore spat. "A minor setback. I'll move on. I'll go to Germany, or Russia, somewhere where they'll appreciate my genius. By the time they find your skeletons, they'll have been picked clean, and I'll be long gone."

George Hellebore was crying.

"Stop your sniveling, boy," said Randolph. "I always knew you were weak. You have too much of your mother in you. Look at you, crying with fear."

"It's not fear," said George. "It's not that at all. Despite everything, I still love you. You are my father."

"Oh, stop it," said Randolph harshly. "You'll break my heart."

"You won't get very far," said James. "The police are on their way."

"Are they? Or are you trying to bluff me, Bond? Either way, it doesn't much matter. My airplane is fueled and on the runway, and all my research is in here." He tapped his head and grinned, showing his immaculate white teeth. "You may have destroyed my laboratory, all my work, my papers, and experiments, but every bit of it is stored away, up here. I can have a new laboratory set up within weeks, and I can have fresh serum ready in days after that. I know how to do it, Bond. And I *will* do it. I will create a master race of soldiers, and we'll come back here one day, and we'll destroy this precious little country of yours." He cocked the twin hammers on his shotgun and his tone became very businesslike. "Now, I *would* ask you to say your prayers, but it should be abundantly clear to you by now that there is no God." He smiled. "No God but me."

"You can't do this," George sobbed.

"Yes I can. I hold the power of life and death. You mean nothing to me, George. You see, the thing of it is, I couldn't breed the perfect boy, I couldn't breed a boy who would grow up to be the perfect man: strong and fearless and ruthless. I failed there. But why bother trying to *breed* one when I can *make* one? The men I create will be my true sons. I will create an army of sons who will crush the soft underbelly of Europe beneath their feet. But first, I have to get rid of a small annoyance."

He raised the shotgun and pointed it at the boys' heads. James tensed, waiting to dive at the last second. There was always hope, always a chance of a way out; maybe he could even push George clear and save him, too. He focused on Randolph's mad eyes, trying to read in them the signal that he was about to pull the trigger.

But then he sensed a movement, off to one side, at the very edge of his vision. He was aware of something traveling fast toward them.

Randolph's concentration broke and he turned to see what it was.

It was the piglet.

Hellebore frowned and spat, but then something erupted from the loch with a high-pitched, whining sound, like air escaping from a balloon.

"Algar!"

Algar raced toward his brother, his lips pulled back to reveal his ruined teeth. The pathetic sound escaping from his mouth was the only noise he could make.

"Algar! Stop!" Hellebore cried.

But Algar wasn't going to stop—he was heading straight for Lord Hellebore, his arms outstretched.

"Stop, damn you!" Randolph fired both barrels and the blast took Algar directly in his stomach, but still he didn't stop—he crashed into Randolph, gripping him in his immense arms, and they tumbled into the water with a mighty splash.

It was uncannily still for a moment, as if the two of them had simply disappeared, but then they surfaced, still locked in their awful embrace. Algar was strong, but Randolph was no weakling and his brother was badly injured, so it was a fairly balanced fight. The two of them looked hardly human, though: Algar with his wide, nightmarish face smeared with blood and slime, and Randolph, his hair wet, his eyes crazed, his once-handsome face twisted into a hideous caricature of snarling rage.

The water was stained black with blood from Algar's wound, and it was beginning to boil and froth.

The eels were coming.

Algar put a hand to his brother's face and forced him over backward, his breath wheezing out in a long sigh. They went under again, into the water, which was alive with hungry fish. The next time the men surfaced, Randolph was entangled with wriggling, undulating eels—they were caught in his hair and clothing, and several smaller ones had fixed their teeth on the loose parts of his flesh, where they twisted and turned.

James grabbed George and held his face to his chest so that he wouldn't see the terrible thing that was happening to his father.

Randolph shook his head and roared at the eels, then he slipped back beneath the water with the dying Algar's hands around his throat. A minute later, he came up for the last time, and by now he was covered in the creatures—they were clustered around his limbs, sliding over his face and slipping inside his clothing so that he resembled a writhing figure made of eels. Finally he fell forward and sank, one arm stretched up toward the heavens, so that all that was visible of him was his hand. For a moment the hand pointed upward, as if reaching for something, and then it slowly slipped beneath the water.

The two wretched brothers were gone.

"Come along," said James. "Let's get away from here."

He turned and took a few steps down the driveway. The sun seemed particularly bright, everything around him looked so vivid and alive, the colors intense, and then the colors turned to liquid and bled into one another, like a watercolor painting left in the rain.

"Look at that," he heard himself say, and the voice seemed to come from far, far away.

He felt like he was walking through treacle, as if his legs

were sinking into the ground, and then the light began to close in like a fist. Flickering darkness narrowed his vision, his head felt weightless, as if it were full of bubbles and he was falling forward. He heard a noise like thunder and someone calling: "Look out . . . look out . . . look out . . ." The voice echoed and spun off into the darkness and James spun away after it, shrinking to a tiny speck, and then the tiny speck disappeared.

CHAPTER 28—ON AGAR'S PLOUGH

Du-doo doo du-doo, du-doo doo du-doo . . .

What was that?

It was so familiar. Like a musical instrument. A clarinet or a flute. So familiar.

Du-doo doo du-doo, du-doo doo du-doo . . . over and over again.

No. Not an instrument. An animal. Yes. Of course. A bird. A wood pigeon. A wood pigeon with its distinctive repetitive rhythm—so familiar.

Du-doo doo du-doo, du-doo doo du-doo . . .

James lay for a long time with his eyes closed, listening to the gentle, soothing sound. The bird must be up in a nearby tree somewhere, just sitting there, singing, so peaceful, an easy life, singing in the trees . . .

Then he became aware of other sounds: the wind rustling in the leaves of the treetops, curtains flapping and banging against a window frame, other birds twittering, the river flowing down toward the sea, a dog barking in the distance.

And he was aware of smells as well: the slightly dusty smell of the room he was in, mixed with the sharp, peaty tang from the river and the soft scent of pine resin from the woods, drifting in on the clean, fresh air that was blowing in through an open window and cooling his face, and nearer to hand, the smell of flowers . . .

He opened his eyes and saw a glass vase sitting on the nightstand by his bed—there was a small bunch of wildflowers in it. He was in his little attic room in Uncle Max's cottage, the room that he had gotten to know so well since he had been up in Scotland. There, on the wall opposite, was the little painting of the stag; there, the chest of drawers with a jug of fresh water on it and the oil lamp; there, the shelf of books and the china cat with its chipped ear.

All so familiar. The wallpaper with its pattern of roses, the bright-blue door, the row of shooting prizes . . .

He raised himself on one elbow, but his head swam and his arm felt too weak to support him. He flopped back down onto the bed and took a deep, slow breath. There was a pain in his lungs, like an itch, and his throat was sore.

He lay there for a long while, on his back, staring up at the ceiling, watching two flies chasing each other about and walking upside down. After a while—it could have been a few minutes, it could have been an hour—he heard footsteps on the wooden stairs, and presently his aunt came in.

She looked very pleased to see him.

"James, darling," she said, "you're awake."

"Yes. I still feel dreadfully tired, though. I don't remember coming back here. How long have I been in bed? And how did I get here, and . . . ?"

"Shush." Charmian put a finger to her lips and sat down by the bed. "So many questions."

"But I don't understand . . ."

Charmian stroked his forehead with a cool, dry hand.

"You've been very ill, James. You nearly died. Dr. Walker has hardly left the cottage."

"Ill?"

"A fever, and an infection of the lungs, and complete and utter exhaustion. But you must be a pretty tough old soul, because here you are, as right as rain."

"I don't feel as right as rain."

"Perhaps not a good, strong downpour."

"No." James smiled. "More of a thin drizzle."

Charmian brushed back the unruly lock of black hair that always fell in James's face.

"Compared to how you have been, you are a picture of health, believe you me." A shadow passed over Charmian's face and she look concerned. "We were so worried."

"But I still don't understand, how long has it been?"

"Ten days. I'm afraid you missed Easter altogether."

"Ten days." James couldn't believe it. Ten days lost.

"What about school?" he said anxiously.

"Don't worry about that," said Charmian, shaking her head. "I telephoned them and have sent a letter. There are worse things than missing the start of term. You can go back when you're well enough."

She untaped a bandage from his cheek and cleaned the wound with a cloth and a brown liquid that stung his tender skin.

"But what happened?" said James, looking up into her kind face.

"Your friend Kelly with the red hair came here," she said. "He told us you were in trouble, but couldn't say how. I drove like a madman up to the castle in the Bentley. All hell had broken loose. Part of the castle was on fire, there were police dashing about and the fire brigade, but nobody really seemed to know what was going on. There was no sign of Lord Hellebore—there still is no sign of him apparently, not that I cared, it was you I was looking for. And then I found you, being nursed by Wilder Lawless and George Hellebore. You had collapsed, James. I didn't bother with an ambulance; they were too busy dealing with some men who had been caught up with the fire. I bundled you into the car and got you back here as fast as I could, but you were already feverish, burning up, as if a fire were blazing away inside you. Then, for ten days, you tossed and turned in your bed, pouring with sweat and crying out strange things—you were often half-awake and staring at imagined terrors. You quite put the wind up me. Dr. Walker did all he could. You were too weak to risk taking to the hospital in Kilcraymore. Every night I've sat here till dawn talking to you, urging you to hang on, to fight it. I don't know if you heard me, but at last, yesterday, the fever broke and you slept peacefully for the first time. And now, thank God, here you are and you're all right."

Charmian put a fresh bandage on his wound and poured him a glass of deliciously cold water.

"You've been in the wars, haven't you? The police came a couple of times, asking questions, but I sent them packing. They are still trying to work out exactly what happened up at the castle, and what happened to the laird. George Hellebore is being very helpful, even though the poor lad has no idea what's happened to his father. I spoke to him myself, and he told me how you had gone up to visit him and helped when the place caught fire, but I still don't really know what's been going on."

She stared at James, and James held her gaze. As he looked up into her face, he saw her concern, and realized what she must have been through. He didn't want to hurt her any more.

He closed his eyes. "I'm afraid I don't remember, Aunt Charmian," he lied. "I do remember going up there with Red, but after that . . . it's blank."

"Well," said Charmian, "maybe that's for the best."

Over the next couple of days James stayed in bed and slowly regained his strength. He was ferociously hungry, and Charmian brought him a steady supply of food, starting with soup and broth and porridge, but gradually progressing to more solid food. Kelly came to visit, and Wilder, and they talked of silly, trivial things, never of the castle and the Hellebores. Then, at last, one morning he felt well enough to get up. It was a warm, sunny day, and he pulled his dressing gown on over his pajamas and slipped on a pair of plimsolls.

He tottered down the stairs and out into the daylight. Everything seemed loud and busy and confusing out here: the river roared like a torrent, the trees waved and shivered, a squirrel chattered somewhere like a machine that needed oiling.

He sat down by the river on a big, old log and rested, watching the water as it danced over the rocks and stones. He caught a glimpse of a fish, lurking near a patch of weeds, and wondered if he should fetch his rod.

And then it struck him.

Max.

In all this time, Max hadn't visited him. James had been so preoccupied with his own health he hadn't even thought to ask how he was. He cursed himself. How selfish and rude he had been. He was about to get up and go to find Aunt Charmian when she appeared at his side, carrying a basket of freshly cut flowers.

"Hello," said James.

"You're up." Charmian smiled.

"Yes. I feel a lot better for it. But I was just thinking—"

"About Max?"

"Yes."

Charmian sat down on the log next to James and took his hand.

"A long time ago I had to give you some bad news, James. About my other brother—your father." Charmian stopped and took a deep breath.

"He's dead," said James quietly, "isn't he?"

Charmian nodded, tears in her eyes. She wiped them away.

"It's not fair," said James angrily.

"There's nothing much fair about life," said Charmian, staring into Uncle Max's beloved river. "Good people die as well as bad. You always think you can prepare yourself for it, and it wasn't as if we didn't all know it was going to happen, but when it comes it knocks you for six. Which is why I'm so glad you're back with us, James. I was damned if I was going to lose the both of you."

She hugged James and crushed his head into her neck.

James put his arms around her and hugged her back. The two of them had shared so much, and Charmian was now both a mother and a best friend to him.

"I should have liked to say good-bye to him properly," said James, his voice hoarse. "We were going to go fishing. He was going to show me how to Spey cast, and I . . . I lost his torch, I didn't know how I was going to tell him, and . . ."

"In a way you did say good-bye," said Charmian, "the night before you left to go up onto the moors. I think he knew then . . ." She laughed. "He wasn't the sentimental type. He wouldn't have wanted tears and a lot of fuss and nosense. You know, in a way, your being so ill, it took my mind off things," she said, stroking James's hair. "It's made it easier to cope. We have to remember that life goes on, eh?" She pushed his head back and grinned into his face. "We're going to have to look after each other from now on, you and I."

"Yes," said James. "Don't worry."

They got up and walked back into the house, where May, the housekeeper, was preparing breakfast.

"Mister James, you're up and about," she exclaimed when she saw him. "That's a sight for sore eyes. Will I make you some breakfast?"

"Yes, please," said James, sitting down at the scrubbed, wooden table.

"I was just telling James about Max," said Charmian.

"Oh, aye," said May without turning around from the stove, but James saw from the droop of her shoulders that she was trying to hide her own emotions.

"When did it happen?" he said, fiddling with the spoon in the sugar bowl.

"That first night you were away," said Charmian.

"So soon?"

"We tried to keep from you just how badly sick he was, James." Charmian looked away and took a long slow breath. "I heard him cry out in the night," she said quietly. "And I went up to him, but when I got there, it must have been about four o'clock in the morning, he was lying with his eyes open as if he could see something. And he cried out again, just one word, your name, James, Just that: 'James!' His voice was surprisingly strong, and then his heart gave out and the spirit left him."

James said nothing. He was thinking. Four in the morning, that would have been just about when he was swimming out through the tunnel of eels. He remembered how he had been about to give up, and he had heard a voice in his head, calling his name. He wasn't a superstitious person: he had no belief in ghosts and phantoms and messages from beyond the grave, but a shiver passed through him, and the hairs stood up all over his skin.

Max had been buried quietly two days after he had died. In his coffin were his beloved fishing rod and the little plaster soldier that James had won at the fair.

Now that James was better, Charmian arranged a small memorial service in the local church, which was packed with people from the village and Max's many friends. May was there with her husband, and Dr. Walker and Max's fishing pals, grizzled, red-faced men who looked awkward in their formal suits.

Afterward, as the mourners filed out of the tiny

churchyard, James saw Red Kelly, and he held back to talk to him as the others went on ahead. Kelly had one leg in plaster and was hobbling about with a walking stick.

"I didn't like to come in," he said, nodding toward the church. "It was family and friends and that, and I didn't really know him. I thought I might be, you know . . . in the way."

"That's all right," said James. "It's good to see you."

"I'm off in the morning," said Red with a characteristic sniff. "Back down to London."

"I shall miss you," said James.

"Yeah, same here. Funny, isn't it? Us two being friends. What with you being posh and me being just a common oik. But the first time I saw you, I thought, here's a stand-up bloke. Who'd have known, eh, meeting in King's Cross like that, what was going to happen? And now . . . we'll probably never see each other again."

"We can keep in touch," said James. "I'll write down my address for you, and you can give me yours. If I'm ever in London I could come and visit you."

"I'm not a big writer," said Kelly.

"Nor me," said James, and they laughed.

"Anyways," said Kelly. "I'm not sure you'd like where I live. Might not be what you're used to. It's not exactly a palace. I share a room with three of me brothers. Funny thing is, I miss it. Never did take to the countryside. It's not for me: too much space. I can't sleep without Dan and Freddie and Bill snoring away next to me."

They walked up the lane and onto the road, then along to the dirt track that led to the cottage.

"Everything that happened," said James, "will you keep it secret?"

"Your mate George Hellebore's kept us out of it so far, mate, and I don't see as how we need to change that. Luckily, your aunt got you away from there before the police knew what was going on. Useless sods still don't have a clue."

"You know," said James. "I used to think that George was a coward, a coward and a cheat, but in the end, what he did, standing up to his father, that was the bravest thing in the world."

"Yeah, he come good," said Kelly.

"Even as we were rowing across the lake toward the castle," said James, "I kept wondering if he was leading me into a trap, if he was going to betray me, right up to when he smashed the first rack of serum." James stopped and looked at Kelly. "We did the right thing, didn't we?" he said.

"If it was me," said Kelly, "I'd have killed Lord Hellebore with my bare hands for what he done to Alfie. All right, so I done some bad things in my time: robbed houses, picked pockets, nicked from shops, got into some fights and hurt some people, but nothing like that. What Randolph did, what he was planning to do . . . it was a bloody disgrace. He was a right villain, James. And you stopped him. I'm pleased to know you, mate."

"I couldn't have done it without you, Red. You and George and Wilder."

"Ah, Wilder," said Red, and he raised his eyebrows. "I've been trying my hardest with her, but she seems to prefer her horse."

As if in answer to this they heard a clopping of hooves, and Wilder Lawless came around the corner behind them on Martini. She rode up and dismounted.

"It's the terrible two," she said.

"We'll both be leaving soon," said James.

"It'll be awful quiet around here without you."

"I'm sure I'll be back sometime," said James.

"Well, who says I'll still be here? It's a big world out there, James Bond, and I intend to see some of it. You can't keep me cooped up here forever." She touched the bandage on James's face. "Does that hurt?"

"A little," said James, "but Aunt Charmian said it's healing really well and shouldn't leave a mark."

"That's good," said Wilder, with a smile. "We wouldn't want your handsome face to be spoiled by a nasty old scar now, would we?"

So saying, she gave the two of them a big kiss each, laughed, jumped into the saddle, and thundered away, Martini's hooves kicking up great clods of earth as they went.

James wiped his mouth and looked at Kelly, who was blushing and for once was at a loss for words.

A few days later, having arranged for Max's belongings to be shipped down south, Charmian closed up the cottage. The will had been read and, just as he had promised, Max had left his car to James, though James had no idea what he was going to do with it, as it would be a few years before he could legally drive it on any public roads. The car would be brought down with all the other stuff and would have to stay parked in Aunt Charmian's garage for the immediate future.

They said good-bye to May and Dr. Walker, loaded Charmian's Bentley with their luggage, and climbed aboard.

Soon they were rattling and bumping down the track, and James turned to watch the cottage disappearing into the trees. He was leaving behind his adventures, leaving behind this extraordinary part of his life, and he knew that, despite what he had said to Wilder, he would probably never come back.

The two-day drive down to Kent was gloomy, cold, and dull. The skies remained leaden, and James felt empty and deflated, as if returning to reality from a strange, exciting dream. How drab England was, how safe and solid and dull it all seemed. Dishforth, Leeds, Doncaster, Stevenage, Hatfield . . . a dreary parade of colorless places where nothing ever happened.

Once they got home to Pett Bottom, however, James was plunged into preparations for school, and it was with some excitement that he returned to Eton and caught up with his friends.

They welcomed him back, asking him any number of questions about his illness and the dramatic wound on his cheek. He answered with vague replies and tried to change the subject. They were more than happy to tell him what they'd been up to—the Easter celebrations they had had, the plays they had seen, and all the scrapes they had gotten into.

George Hellebore had not returned to school. There

were all sorts of rumors going around about him and his father, none of them accurate, and James later heard that he had gone back to live with his mother in America.

One morning, James was walking back across Agar's Plough to Codrose's after cricket when he was met by Sedgepole and Pruitt, two of George's old gang. James thought nothing of it, but Sedgepole put a hand on his shoulder to stop him.

"Where do you think you're going, Bond?" he asked, trying to sound menacing.

"I'm going to my house," said James casually. "Not that it's any of your business."

"We'll make it our business if we want to," said Sedgepole, and Pruitt sniggered. "You're becoming a little too big for your boots," Sedgepole added. "And don't think that just because Hellebore has gone, things are going to be any different around here."

James looked from one to the other, of the older boys, right in their eyes, and he realized that they didn't scare him at all. After all he had been through, these two overgrown monkeys meant nothing to him. He had faced up to real terrors and had been in fear for his life. So what were these two to him? In the end, they were just boys. Like himself. A little bigger, perhaps, but just boys, and boys could never scare him again.

He held Sedgepole's gaze, and the larger boy must have seen something there to make him pause, because he slipped his hand off James's shoulder.

"If you ever put your hand on me again," said James

calmly, "I will break it off, and then I will break your arm off, do you understand?"

"Yes," said Sedgepole. "Sorry."

James smiled politely. "That's all right, I just wanted to make sure it was clear."

James turned on his heel and strode away toward College Field, and the two bullies were left standing there, not quite sure what had happened, how this younger boy had so unsettled them; but they had seen in his eyes something cold and frightening. They knew that this was not a boy they should tangle with.

Neither of them ever spoke about the incident.

As for the Hellebore Cup, it was quietly forgotten and never contested again. The trophy sat on Andrew Carlton's mantelpiece, where it was used to hold golf balls.